raptor

Judith Van Gieson Mysteries from the
University of New Mexico Press:

North of the Border

Confidence Woman

Vanishing Point

The Stolen Blue

raptor

A Neil Hamel Mystery

JUDITH VAN GIESON

University of New Mexico Press

Albuquerque

© 1990 by Judith Van Gieson
Published by arrangement with the author
University of New Mexico Press paperback edition 2002
All rights reserved.
Originally published by Harper & Row, Publishers, Inc., 1990
ISBN 0-06-016167-1

Library of Congress Cataloging-in-Publication Data
Van Gieson, Judith, date
Raptor / Judith Van Gieson.
ISBN 0-8263-2974-8 (pbk. : alk. paper)
1. Hamel, Neil (Fictitious character)—Fiction.
2. Women lawyers—Fiction.
3. Gyrfalcon—Fiction.
4. Poachers—Fiction.
5. Montana—Fiction.
[1. Birds of prey—Fiction.]
I. Title.
PS3572.A42224 R3 2002
813'.54—dc21
2002069563

For roads that were taken
And roads that were not
For Jack

I came late to the love of birds. For years I saw them only as a tremor at the edge of vision.

—*The Peregrine*
J. A. Baker

Unencumbered by concepts—such as emptiness,
such as enlightenment—the bird is gone.

—*Nine-Headed Dragon River: Zen Journals 1969–1982*
Peter Matthiessen

Acknowledgments

I'm grateful to Claire and Richard Zieger for keeping me in falcon lore; to attorneys Rosalyn K. Sukenik and Alan M. Uris, who advised me about legal matters; to Michael Ball for sharing his knowledge of the air; to Brad Collier and Pat Johnson, exemplars of Montana hospitality, for checking my facts regarding that beautiful state; to Dominick Abel for his wise advice; and to Eamon Dolan, who never missed the beat in this book.

"Death is a debt to nature due. I have paid it and so must you."

My aunt, Joan Hamel, found that message on a New England tombstone and liked it so much she expropriated it for her own grave two thousand miles distant, six thousand feet higher and light-years in sunshine away. Since her will had made me the executor of her estate, my job was to see that she got her wishes: a tombstone with a perverse warning and disposition of her things to the ever more distant relatives.

On a November day I found myself in her frame and stucco ranch house in Albuquerque (the city where we'd both ended up) deciding who got what, wondering as a person might when faced with a paid debt if anyone would be there when the time came to tidy up after me. Maybe Joan had chosen me as the executor because I had become a lawyer and the only one in the family. Maybe not. If I was the best she had, it wasn't much. Although we were related and lived in the same city, I seldom saw her. She called around holidays; I didn't always answer. I had my life, she had hers. For thirty years she taught high school biology and went on birding expeditions; then she retired. For ten years I'd been a lawyer, the last five with my own office in a building on Lead. Joan had never married, never divorced. I had.

When she died she left no unfinished business that I knew of. There were no dirty dishes in the sink, no underwear at the foot of the bed. Her will was recently prepared and seemed to accurately reflect the state of her mind. I saw a bumper sticker on a 4 × 4 in an Albertson's parking lot the other day: "Are you prepared to meet your maker?" it said. "If you died tonight, would you go to heaven or hell?" A more relevant question for Joan might be: "Would your house be dirty if you died tonight, your nest a mess?"

Joan's house was immaculate—that's how prepared she was. She didn't need me to do her cleaning, only her distributing. The place was delicate, neat, cluttered with knickknacks and polished furniture with spindly legs. The obligatory R. C. Gorman print of a melancholy woman was on the wall. The air was stale and thick with something that made breathing difficult: must, maybe, but there aren't any mold-producing seasons in Albuquerque. It was tempting to walk out of there, close the door behind me, turn the whole place over to an auction house and have them send everyone a check, but I didn't.

I went instead to the desk that was earmarked for Sylvia Hamel, a cousin in Ithaca, New York, opened a drawer and moved on to the next question, not how prepared anyone is to die but whether they had lived. If Joan had lived, I hadn't noticed; I hadn't looked. It's a voyeuristic feeling to be going through somebody else's desk, a guilty thrill like sneaking a peek at a lover's papers after he's gone to work, because there is always the possibility you will come across something you'll wish you hadn't. Along with the receipts of paid bills and little boxes stocked with paper clips, erasers and rubber bands, I found a book with a pink and yellow flowered cover. "The Journal of Joan Hamel, Her Thoughts on Birds and Life" was written neatly on a white label with a fine-tipped pen. Dig deeply enough into someone's closed drawers and you find an aspiring writer. I knew a woman once who went to a workshop in Santa Fe to learn to keep a journal. She was told to appoint someone she trusted to destroy it when she died, so family and friends wouldn't find all the mean things that had been written about them. Apparently Joan hadn't trusted anyone that much; on the other hand maybe she hadn't written anything nasty, or maybe the journal had been programmed to self-destruct at the touch of a slandered family member.

Being a likely candidate I was about to gingerly pick it up when the phone rang once, twice, a loud twang that cut through the stale air, a wrong number or a computer, maybe, reaching out into consumerland to sell a lifetime supply of Kodak film, or to offer a free trip to Florida if I could only identify the tune. Everyone who knew Joan knew she was dead, they'd been at the funeral. The estate shouldn't be paying for a phone that wasn't used; I made a mental note to tell my secretary, Anna, to get it disconnected. Three rings, four. The *National Enquirer* says the dead tap into Mountain Bell, call up sometimes and report from the other side. I picked it up.

"Is Joan home? This is March Augusta calling." It was a friendly voice, Western, masculine, a voice with space and time in it, a voice that sounded like it had something to give, nothing to sell, a new refinement, maybe, in telemarketing. I waited a moment to see if the program would continue.

It didn't, so I spoke to the pause. "Where are you calling from?"

"Fire Pond, Montana. Is Joan out?"

"Uh . . . no."

"Something wrong?" It was a kind, concerned voice,
youngish, though, for Joan.

"You a friend of hers?"

"Yes, I am. I'm an outfitter and a naturalist in Montana.
Joan has been on a number of my field trips. Is she sick?"

"Worse. She's dead. A massive coronary, last week."

"Oh, Jesus, I'm sorry to hear that."

"It was sudden. She didn't suffer," I added stupidly.

"It's hard to believe. Joan had such stamina. She was a
great woman, one of my most knowledgeable birders."

"Joan?"

"You bet. We all have to die sooner or later, but it's a
real shame it happened now. We've got a bird in Montana
this fall that Joan's been wanting to see, an Arctic gyrfalcon. They rarely come this far south and hardly ever so
early in the year, but this one has been hanging around.
It's a rare opportunity because ordinarily you'd have to go
all the way to the Arctic to find one. It's a prime specimen, too, an extremely large and rare white female, a passager on its first migration. Joan was coming up next week.
She'd paid for the trip and everything. I was just calling
to give her some last-minute information. I feel real bad
about this because to see this bird was Joan's dream and
now it won't come true." Apparently they liked to talk in
Montana. Well, it was his dime. "Are you related?"

"I'm her niece."

"Oh, wait a minute, I know. She told me about you.
You're the lawyer, right? And you've got a man's name.
Raymond? Michael?"

"Neil," I said.

"Joan was real proud of you."

"Of me?" That was a surprise, coming as it was from a woman who'd once told me I'd had more than enough men in my life and also that my old friend Cuervo Gold wasn't doing me any good.

"She thought you were a modern woman, brave and independent. She talked about you a lot, like you were the daughter she'd never had. I'd like to make a contribution in her name to the Falcon Fund, it's a cause she believed in."

"Why not? No point in sending flowers."

"A portion of the money she paid for this trip was actually going into the Falcon Fund, but I'd be glad to return all of it, if you think I should, although the plane ticket's probably a discount fare that's nonrefundable."

"If the fund was something Joan cared about they can have the money."

"It seems too bad. Since the trip is going to take place anyway, someone should take advantage of it. Would you like to come?"

"Me? A birding expedition?"

"Why not? You a couch potato?"

There was a time when I used to go on trips at the drop of a telephone and even go hiking, too. "I think I could keep up wherever Joan could. She *was* my aunt, you know, a good thirty years older than I am."

"Geriatrics isn't a requirement to come on a field trip. We take all ages. You got something better to do next week?"

"I do have a law practice." What was on next week? Another real estate closing, divorce negotiations.

"Well, if there's any way you could come, we'd love to have you. Joan thought a lot of you and it would have made her real happy to know you were taking her place. It's a once-in-a-lifetime opportunity."

"Give me your number and I'll think about it," I said.

I picked up the journal and the airline ticket that had been lying underneath it, and I left the house where the air had a taste not of mold but of guilt.

When I got to the frame and stucco building on Lead that I call office it was lunchtime. My partner, Brink, and my secretary, Anna, had gotten Grande Macs to go from McDonald's. The hamburgers, fries and green chile weren't visible in the mound of cartons and paper on Anna's desk, but they were there—I knew it from the deep fat smell. Brink's vanishing belt buckle indicates that he fat- and carbohydrate-loads regularly, but not in preparation for any road race or for attacking the work load on his desk. A messy desk doesn't necessarily mean the person who sits behind it does anything.

Anna carries her junk food well. She likes short skirts and tight pants that show she is no more than a size six. Her hair, however, is size twenty, but today she was wearing it pulled back in some kind of lavender pouf that matched her nail polish. With her long, dagger-shaped nails she picked out a French fry.

"You want one?" she asked.

"No," I replied, having made a lunch stop at Baja Tacos. They were having a burrito sale, but I'd limited myself to one, which I held in a paper bag in my hand. The mingled food odors could make any client who wandered in wonder what kind of junk food palace he or she had stumbled onto, New Mex picante or American grease. Clients didn't wander in, however—Anna told me so daily. You had to go out and find them. I'd been out and what I'd found was a phone that needed to be disconnected.

"Anna, would you call Mountain Bell and tell them to disconnect my aunt Joan's phone?"

"You mean . . . now?" She bit slowly into the Grande Mac.

"After you finish lunch, naturally. Tell them to send the last bill to me."

"You got it."

"How's that matter going?" asked Brink, blinking slowly behind his aquarium-strength glasses.

"Okay. I may have to go to Montana next week."

"Montana? What for?"

"Some unfinished business of Joan's." Brink looked worried, a permanent condition for him. "Don't worry, if I go the estate will pay for it."

"But who will take care of your caseload?"

"You."

"Me?"

"You got something better to do?"

"Well," he sniffed, "I do have clients of my own."

None that I'd noticed lately. Anna finished her lunch, crumpled up the wrappers and threw them away. "You got some messages," she said, handing over the pink slips.

"Thanks."

"Oh, yeah, one more. Your mechanic called and said he'd come by later."

"Car problems . . . again?" asked Brink.

"Maybe," I replied. I went into my office, closed the door, unwrapped and ate the burrito, then flipped through the messages. Nothing there that couldn't wait until later this afternoon or next year. I looked at my desk calendar for the week to come. Judy Bates Larrow was working on her second divorce, which should be a cinch now that she had some experience. Toni Arrowsmith was closing on her condo, a routine matter—even Brink could handle that.

I got out the ticket I'd found in Joan's desk, round trip Albuquerque, New Mexico, to Fire Pond, Montana. An airline ticket is as good as cash, unless it's a discount fare that can only be used from noon Monday to noon Thursday, that must be paid for at least a week in advance, and that—at a savings of several hundred dollars—is nonre-fundable. It's the only way I fly. Anybody who got her hands on one of these tickets couldn't cash it in, but she could use it. Why should the airline get the estate's money for nothing when it could fly me to Montana? I turned the calendar page to Tuesday, November 12, and on it I wrote "Falcon?"

I did some paperwork, took some calls. By the time I left the office at six, Anna and Brink were long gone. The message from the mechanic, a.k.a. the Kid, my lover, my friend, meant he was coming for dinner, a habit he'd fallen into as soon as I started keeping food in the house. I was ready for him with chips in the cupboard and Tecate in the fridge, but I had a stop to make on the way home.

Albuquerque is a logical city with perpendicular streets named after the elements (Silver, Gold, Copper, Lead), the states (Wyoming, Louisiana, New York), the numbers (First, Second, Third). It lies near (but not near enough to be shadowed by) the Sandias, elephantine hulks of gray mountains. I turned my Rabbit down Coal, cut across de-scendingly numbered streets and headed for the drugstore on Central.

What I wanted was behind the cash register, which meant I'd have to ask. The guy manning the register had a Nean-derthal physique: a massively boned forehead, a short thick neck and long arms. The kind of guy who picks up a club when he's hungry, throws on a skin when it's cold, punches you in the shoulder—hard—when he wants you, a cul-de-sac on evolution's highway. Not the person to entrust with your deeper feelings or more subtle thoughts. But it was minimum-wage work, a job that probably paid between $3.60 and $3.80 an hour depending on experience. What could you expect?

"I'll take a box of those," I said, pointing to what I wanted.

"Skin or latex?"

What was the difference? "I don't care."

He sized me up: messy hair, makeup that had gone south, lawyer's clothes. "Latex," he said. "Receptacle end?"

"Why not?"

He laid the box on the counter, the happy couple silhouetted against a pink and aqua sunset. "You're in luck. They're on sale this week for $3.99 a box."

"Two for $10?" I asked, this being the very same drugstore that advertised stick-on digital clocks, one for $1.98 or two for $5.00.

"Just because I have a short neck and sloping forehead doesn't mean I'm stupid," the guy said, taking my money.

"Just because I'm buying condoms doesn't mean I'm smart," I replied.

The Kid sat on my sofa corroding the top of his Tecate can by pouring salt on it and squeezing lime juice on top of that, dipping blue corn chips in the red-hot salsa.

"Kid, I may be going to Montana next week," I said.

"Montana? Why you go there?" Taos was the northern limit of his range. Now that it was November and winter coming on, make that Corrales.

I sat down, cleared a place on the coffee table for my bottle of Cuervo Gold and a glass. I took the salt and rubbed a little on the rim of the glass, splashed some Gold over the ice. "Well, my aunt Joan died—I told you that."

He nodded, sipped at the rotting aluminum.

"A guy in Montana . . ."

"What guy?"

"A friend of Joan's, an outfitter, a nice guy. He was leading a field trip she was going on to look at a rare bird."

"What she do that for?"

"I don't know. Why do people do anything? Some people spend their lives hiking into remote places wearing

9

sneakers and carrying binoculars. They keep a record of all the birds they see and call it a life list. The one who has the most birds, especially rare ones, on his or her life list wins."

The Kid shrugged, made no sense to him.

"Anyway, Joan was planning on going on a field trip next week. She'd already paid for it. It was her dream to see this particular bird, and since it was her dream and she didn't live to do it, and since the guy probably doesn't want to return the money, he asked me if I'd go."

"What's this guy's name?"

"March."

"That's a month, not a name."

"What difference does it make? I'm not going because of him, I'm going because I feel guilty that I never paid any attention to Joan while she was alive and because this trip was her unfulfilled dream and you shouldn't just trash people's dreams when they go."

The Kid mulled that over for a minute, or at least I thought he did, but when he spoke it turned out his mind was on birds, too, and dreams. For small creatures, lighter than air, birds carry a lot of symbolic baggage. They always have.

"I used to keep pigeons, Chiquita, when I was a boy on my rooftop in Mexico."

I never knew that, as the Kid rarely talked to me about his childhood; when he did there was a faraway light in his eyes.

"I had a pigeon once, Blanca. She was bigger than all the birds. She won a lot of races, all the way from Querétaro, one hundred and fifty miles."

I had a vision of Blanca flying over purple mountains, flat mesas, high above the route so treacherous to buses and burros and people. The white pigeon and her black shadow, circling the plaza in colonial Querétaro and returning to her Kid on the edge of the biggest slum in the Western world.

"When I come up here my brother go up on the roof and break their necks—like that." The Kid snapped his black-tipped mechanic's fingers.

I flinched. "That's terrible."

He shrugged, but the faraway light had gone out. "He killed her, too. There was no one to feed them or fly them after I come here. So you going?" He gestured north toward Montana, the bigger sky, the wilder West.

"I guess so." It wouldn't be the first week that we hadn't met. What was bothering the Kid? I took one last sip of my tequila and put the glass down. "Why don't we go to bed," I said.

We were deep in the retrograde eighties and there was a killer virus on the loose aimed at the gay, the addicted, the black, the Hispanic, the alien, the adventurous. Responsibility was the only sane response. No more unsheathed love, no more diaphragm and cream. The sunset box was on the bedside table. "Both you and your partner will be more relaxed knowing you are protected by Trojan brand condoms . . ." it said. Protection from disease, 99.67 percent reliable when used properly, perfect for those who can or will not remain monogamous.

I sat down on the unmade bed. My speech had been prepared, revised, rewritten, revised again. I am a lawyer after all, careful, precise. Here's how it went: "Look, Kid, there's something I've been meaning to talk to you about. We don't see each other all the time. I never ask you about the rest of your life, you don't ask me about mine. I don't want to know. But, maybe, it would be better now if we, um, took precautions, and . . ."

"You mean you want me to use these things?" He picked up the box with the tips of his fingers like it was something slick and dead.

"Well . . ."

"I never." He put the box down.

"Me neither."

Timing is of the essence in law and in life, only there's an inner clock and an outer clock. The outer clock is digital, relentless, flashes red numbers, makes appointments, shows up in court on time. It's the clock that lawyers follow. The inner clock is a pendulum blown off track by every vagrant wind, a lovers' clock, a poet's clock, the clock that Latin America runs by. It tells you when things feel right, when they don't . . . if you're willing to listen. I'd planned this speech and scheduled it for tonight, but it had been blown off course; I hadn't noticed.

"Now you're going to Montana with this April, so you want *me* to start using these things?"

"It has nothing to do with that, I was going to ask you anyway."

"Yeah, I think about it," he said, taking off his clothes, getting under the covers and turning his back to me.

"Kid . . ."

"I'm tired, we talk in the morning."

The Kid has a soft spot on the back of his neck, a downy spot, a place to press a cheek on and dream away. He pulled the covers around his head and covered it up. As far as I could tell *he* went right to sleep, but after a few minutes of staring at a wounded back I said, "Oh, for Christ's sake, you're really being unreasonable." Since he didn't answer, I got up, went into the living room, lit a Marlboro, poured a drink and took out Joan's journal, thinking that would put me to sleep.

It was the record of a biologist's life and her love—birds. Each section was labeled and neatly organized, a scientific treatise, but a romance, too. There was a Personal section and I wondered briefly what could be in there. Joan had never had a lover as far as I knew, few friends and not much of a family either. I skipped it and went to Raptor. By a warm lamp and a cold tequila, I read:

Raptors are the fiercest of birds. They are predators, but most birds are, strictly speaking, even those that eat insects and worms. What distinguishes raptors is that they use their powerful talons to seize or stun their prey and their hooked beaks to tear that prey into bite-sized pieces. Some falcons' talons are so strong they can snap the head off a wooden duck decoy. Raptors have excellent hearing and their eyesight is the best in the animal kingdom.

Hawks are diurnal raptors, most owls are nocturnal. Falcons are members of the hawk family. They hunt during the daytime and their preferred prey are other birds which they like to catch in flight. The female hawk is dominant, the largest and strongest of the pair, which is known as reverse physical dimorphism. As the female peregrine falcon is one third larger than the male, she is called (technically) a falcon, and he is called a tiercel.

The largest and, I think, the most beautiful falcon is the Arctic gyrfalcon, which is native to the polar region, although known occasionally to migrate south into the northern U.S. Once one wintered in the Customs Tower in Boston. Gyrfalcons have a grey morph and a white morph, but even in the white phase they are not pure white—like a snowy owl they have dark streaks on their heads and backs. They will eat mammals, including hare, weasel and mink, but they like ducks and ptarmigan best. It may be ptarmigan shortages that bring them south.

That was the prose. And then there was the poetry. Joan quoted from one of her favorite bird books, *The Peregrine Falcon* by Robert Murphy:

Even in [the falcon's] quietness, sitting relaxed and with his breast feathers loose, he gave an impression of spirit, compactness, strong bone, and hard-muscled power: a rapier quiet in the scabbard.

He was the hunter that men had caught and trained to catch ducks and other birds for them long before gunpowder was used or thought of: for that and for his great style and spectacular powers of flight, which as groundlings bound to the earth they could watch with a lift of the heart.

It is beautiful to see a living creature . . . that is the master of the element in which it moves; beautiful to see the lightning swift co-ordination, the apparent wild reckless abandon that is not abandon but perfect control, and think of the spirit that moves it. . . . it is a spirit of ice and fire, steely hard . . . and marvelously equipped to play with storms and great winds and do the killing that is its function and by which it lives.

And from *The Treatise on Falconry of Albertus Magnus:*

Girofalcon or gyrfalcon means 'whirling falcon', for it is her nature to fiercely pursue her quarry, such as cranes and swans, with a whirling and spinning motion. . . . Other falcons do not fly readily with this species, and even the eagle hesitates to attack her. She likes to be fed delicate meat, so freshly killed that the warmth and natural movements are still present; most of all, she likes the heart and the meat around the heart.

Joan was enraptured with that embodiment of the American West, a cool and efficient killer. Only in her case, instead of a dark gunslinger, it was a white female, one who liked the meat around the heart. Who would have thought it? The falcon was a creature of myth and legend, no ordinary bird. Well, at least I wasn't pissing the Kid off and going into the back of beyond in search of a sparrow.

I got back into my side of the bed. The Kid was gone when I woke up in the morning. He'd left a yellow stick-on note on the door. "Send me a postcard," it said.

2

I knew a man from Montana once, an angry man. He came from someplace in the western part of the state, where high mountains led to higher mountains, where the prevailing winds climbed up and hung a canopy of clouds over his town. The big sky was a big gray sky where he came from. He wandered down to New Mexico to get some sun, because there's one thing you can count on in New Mexico, the sun. It trails you like a faithful dog. Maybe this man didn't get to talk much in Montana, maybe no one was listening; he never shut up when he got here.

I drove up to Santa Fe one night to visit the people who had rented him a room, and I heard his voice as I opened my car door, loud, complaining. New Mexico was corrupt; the Indians sold fake turquoise, bombs were made in Los Alamos and warehoused outside Albuquerque, Santa Fe was overrun by rich Texans, Tiny Annoya was still our governor. He was talking to someone, or was he? When

I opened the door, I could see everyone else had gone to bed, probably with their pillows over their heads. He was alone, with a phone in his hand, screaming into the night. The pebble in his psyche became a boulder as it rolled away.

What was there to get angry about in Montana? I wondered, en route. It was another poor Western state, but there was room and beauty to be poor in, not too many rich people to remind you just how poor you were and not too many minorities competing for a piece of the poverty pie.

Coming into the Fire Pond airport reminded me of Albuquerque, wide open, wider because the mountains are farther away. Fire Pond is on the edge of the Great Plains and the Rockies aren't yet casting their jagged shadows. In the emptiness you can see what's below you, what's beside you, what's coming at you. I saw a lot of blue sky and brown earth and the white letters FP plastered on the side of a hill. There were patches of snow on the mesas and foothills, this being the time of year when the Arctic gyrfalcon sometimes wanders south. South to them, north to me, but I was ready for it in a down parka. I was going into the wilderness chasing one bird, wrapped in another bird's feathers, a naturalist's trip, a little old lady's dream, not mine. Joan's journal was on my lap.

"The DDT devastation began in the late '40s," I read.

The Arctic birds weren't hurt as badly, but the peregrine falcon population was decimated in some areas of the U.S., extirpated in others. There were approximately 600 in the East in 1942, close to zero by 1964, which earned the peregrine the unfortunate distinction of a place on the endangered species list. The use of DDT was an ill-conceived disaster. Once it gets into the food chain, it keeps moving up, becoming more concentrated as it does. Falcons are at the top of the chain and the DDT got into their eggshells and made them so thin they broke before the eggs could hatch.

Falcons are the world's primary feathered dive bombers. They gain altitude by flying upward in ever widening circles. With their spectacular vision they can spot a prey from 8,000 feet away. In pursuit peregrines fold up their wings and dive straight down in a magnificent stoop, which I have had the privilege of observing. The story is often repeated that a peregrine passed a plane diving at close to 200 miles an hour. Falcons stun with a blow from their talons or swoop underneath and gracefully pursue the prey upward in a death dance. The falcon eats often and this dance is repeated over and over again.

As the plane began its descent into Fire Pond, the rancher dozing in the seat next to me woke up. His full belly had popped open the snaps on his plaid shirt. He buttoned up, straightened his string tie, shook his head, rubbed his eyes and grinned.

"Hey, get a looka that," he said, pointing out the window. "A Sparhawk."

"A hawk? Where?" I asked, new to this sport of birding, but already competitive about a sighting. Was this the moment to begin my life list, to reach for my binoculars and field guide?

"Right down there," he said. "The jet."

"Oh," I replied. "A plane." A sleek, elegant little jet, privately owned probably as there didn't seem to be any markings on it, was coming in for a landing. It glistened alone and silvery in the brilliant sun, and its shadow danced down the runway behind it.

"I useta fly when I was in the Air Force," he said, leaning enthusiastically across my armrest. "Wish I had a crack at one of them beauties. That little jet there is top of the line, the razor's edge of the performance envelope."

How sharp can you get?

"A beauty, ain't it? Wish I owned one, but I ain't got one of them ranches that's bigger than a country. I only got a little spread, not big enough that you need a jet to get across it, but if I got in my car in the morning and started driving, I probably wouldn't hit the western boundary by nightfall."

"I've got a car like that," I said. "You want to buy it?"

"Ha, ha," he replied. "And what brings *you* to Montana?"

To see the rare and seldom-sighted gyrfalcon, I told him. Why not?

"Well, like I jus' told you, I'm a rancher," he said. "That pretty bird you're comin' here to look at is a raptor and raptors are killers. An eagle'll take a lamb in its talons and fly away with it. You ever seen a lamb killed by an eagle? It ain't a pretty sight."

"Animals kill each other. That's nature, isn't it?"

"That's the way nature *useta* be. Don't have to be like that no more now that man's got the power. The way I see it those birds are vicious killers. There ain't enough room in Montana for them and ranchers both. Now they want to bring back the wolves. I'll tell you one thing, I see a falcon or a wolf, I'm gonna shoot." He pointed a finger into the air and cocked an imaginary rifle.

In some circles it's sport for humans to kill animals, but cruel and vicious for animals to kill each other. "Some falcons are endangered species," I said. "There are very few left. You kill one, the chances of the species' survival are that much slimmer." Joan would have been proud.

20

"Good," he said, pulling down hard on the trigger finger.

That was one thing to get angry about in Montana.

"Even in November temperatures can drop below zero here," the Falcon Fund brochure read. "Dress warmly." I'd done that. "Bring a day pack and broken-in hiking boots." Those I had, New Balance, fabric uppers, cleat bottoms, used three times in the Jemez, not exactly broken in, but not unworn either. "Bring a good pair of binoculars." I had Joan's, a pair of Zeisses.

"State of the art, can't buy any better than Zeiss," a guy at Harry's told me when I took them to be appraised and found out they were worth more than my car. You can buy better than *that*. "I could see all the way into the Beach with these," the guy said, fondling the Zeisses, then blushing into the roots of his thin blond hair because the Beach he was talking about wasn't in California and I knew it. The Beach was the apartment complex on Tingley Drive.

There was a disclaimer attached to the Falcon Fund brochure (a legal scarecrow), which I signed. "My health is good," it said. "I don't have any medical condition which would endanger the welfare of myself or others on the trip. I am able to hike strenuously. I understand the hazards and responsibilities of wilderness hiking, and I will not hold the Falcon Fund responsible for any injury which results from the hazards of such travel."

The back page of the brochure had a description of our leader, March Augusta, but no picture. "March has a BS degree in biology, specializing in ornithology. He is also a knowledgeable wilderness guide with extensive experience in mountain search and rescue. Before he started his own guide service, he was a ranger at Freezeout National Park for several years." That was unusual because, in my experience, once people get in bed with the federal government they stay there sleeping comfortably until the heavy blanket smothers them.

"Birders will gather under the elk antlers in the waiting room of the Fire Pond Airport at 3 o'clock," the letter that accompanied the brochure said. "You will be met by your guide, March Augusta, who will escort you to your hotel in Fire Pond. Happy birding."

Would I know an elk antler when I saw one? Would it look any different from any other horn? Well, I'd know a birder, I figured, a little old person with silver plumage, running shoes, expensive binoculars dangling from its neck. Was this any place for Neil Hamel? I wondered, walking down the exit ramp. I felt like I was going off to camp with dirty underwear and was more than a little embarrassed. I might have climbed back on the plane except that the next and last stop was two hundred miles west in Bullhorn and that's where the rancher was headed. Damn Joan, I thought, dreams have to be acted on, you can't expect someone else to do it for you.

The not-so-far West is usually a friendly place. When there are fewer people around, they're happier to see you. Montana has half the population of New Mexico with more land, and, except for Bernalillo County, New Mexico isn't even what you would call sparsely populated. There are places where you can drive all day and the one or two vehicles you see are pickup trucks and the drivers wave. There were signs in the Fire Pond Airport, WELCOME TO MONTANA, and a booth that passed out brochures.

Five or six birders were flocked under an impressive set of horns. I introduced myself.

"Neil, isn't that a man's name?" said a little gray wren.

"Not when I'm wearing it," I said. "I'm taking the place of my aunt, Joan Hamel, who died recently. Did any of you know her?"

"Not I," hissed a blue jay.

"I did." It was an owl in deep and sonorous voice. "I met her on a piping plover field trip to Rhode Island. A lovely woman. Very sorry to hear of her death. Very sorry indeed."

He was a small, fine-boned gentleman with snowy hair. His blue eyes were magnified to epic proportions by the thick lenses he wore. All of the expedition members, I noticed, had a certain zinginess about the eyes. The eyes were quick and intense, and, although some of their bodies were beginning to shrivel, none of them were slouches in terms of energy, either, I learned.

"My name is Avery, Avery Wells," the man said.

"Nice to meet you."

"The pleasure is mine."

Avery introduced me to the wren, Muriel, and the blue jay, Bea, and a couple from southern Montana, the Colliers. Marcia, the wife, seemed plump and contented. The husband, Burt, looked like he had spent some hard years in the saddle, but his eyes twinkled and so did his mind. He knew a straight man when he saw one.

"Do you know how to tell a raven from a crow?" he asked me.

"Are you kidding? The only bird I can identify is a robin. I'm here strictly as a gesture to my aunt Joan."

A cluck came from someone, probably Bea.

"It's easy," Burt said. "The wings have notches in them that mark the pinions. A crow's wing has eight and a raven's has nine."

"Got it."

Burt smiled, the crevices in his face deepened, his eyes crinkled up. "So you see, it's a matter of a pinion."

Bea groaned. Marcia laughed although she had probably heard this joke a hundred times before. "I'll remember that," I said.

"I hope so," he replied.

Someone was coming toward us, a man, late thirties I guessed, with a nice Western walk, sort of ambling and purposeful at the same time. He wasn't too tall, but he had a lot of hair and a full beard that made up for the lack of height. His hair was curly and thick, reddish brown with golden highlights. He was wearing jeans, cowboy boots, a denim shirt, a down vest: a worn, comfortable Western look, often imitated, never duplicated. He had warm amber eyes, the kind of eyes that focus sharply on the far away, see clearly in the middle range, get soft and dreamy close up.

"Hi," he said, "I'm March."

Those of us who didn't already know our leader introduced ourselves and he checked us off on his clipboard list, greeting each person kindly, thoughtfully. There was a gentleness to the naturalist.

"Neil," he said when he got to me. "I'm glad you could come."

"My pleasure," I replied.

"We're missing two," he finished up, tapping the pencil against his list. "Cortland James and John King."

"Cortland, Senior or Junior?" asked Avery.

"Junior," said March.

"'Cortland, Junior,' spends his time birding around the world. I understand his life list is full of rare and exotic birds," Avery said.

"With the money in that family," sniffed Bea, "he can afford it."

"That's how he used to spend his time," said March. "His father retired last year as head of the Conservation Committee and appointed Cortland to replace him. This looks like him coming now."

The person approaching came from a place where there

are a lot of people and few of them are friendly—the East. I'd say his native habitat was icy ski slopes, sailboats in the rain, Connecticut. He was about five-foot-six with a slight, boyish build and ready for prep school in khaki pants with a baggy rear end, a striped button-down shirt, beige crew-neck sweater and tweedy jacket. Dressed like a boy, he shuffled like an old man in the deck shoes he wore, Top-Siders with no socks, even though this was Montana in November.

"Cortland James?" asked March.

"Yes," replied the person whose first and last names were mixed up. He sneezed into a white linen handkerchief that probably had his initials embroidered on it somewhere in navy blue letters.

March shook his hand, apparently not worried about the possibility of contagion. "Good to see you. How was your flight?"

"About what you'd expect from Frontier. It's been a long haul from Connecticut today."

March checked his clipboard again. "We're still missing John King. He was due in on Flight 220 from Portland. John is the resident expert from the Raptor Center in Oregon. He is going to give a lecture and a slide show tomorrow in Fire Pond High. John has some outstanding shots of the gyr taken from his trip to Alaska last summer. I'd like to give you a day to get acclimated to Montana before we go out into the field. Avery, would you mind introducing Cortland around while I look for John?"

"Glad to," said Avery. When he had finished the introductions, he turned to the prep. "Congratulations on your appointment. The CC does good work."

"Thanks," said Cortland in a flat voice. Maybe he was tired out from his trip or debilitated from his cold or just plain bored. He looked like he was in his early thirties, which would make him the youngest birder on this field trip, but his elders showed a lot more zip and enthusiasm than he did.

"I guess this will cut back on your birding activities, but I've heard you've already sighted many of the world's rarest birds," Avery continued.

"I've seen a number of them."

"Have you ever seen a quetzal? I went to Guatemala all the way into the Biotopo preserve in the rain forest, but it was so misty I never got to see one," Avery said wistfully. "It's a bird that absolutely cannot live in captivity, and there are so few left, I'm afraid I will never get another opportunity."

"A lot of birders go to great lengths and never get to see a quetzal, but, as a matter of fact, I did see one. The feathers are the most extraordinary color. Are you familiar with the legend of the plumed serpent?" Cortland asked, brushing at the blond bangs that had fallen across his forehead.

Avery nodded. Even I had heard of the plumed serpent, the legendary and contradictory symbol in Central America, half bird, half serpent, sometimes depicted as a bird carrying a snake in its talons.

"Having seen the quetzal in flight, I have a different interpretation of the legend. The quetzal has an extremely long tail with luminous green feathers. I saw it fly down over a mountainside with its tail waving behind it in a serpentine motion so it actually looked like a flying serpent." His hand began to make a slithering motion through the air, but he checked himself. His eyes, however, came alive. They were a pale gray color, but they lit up when he talked about the quetzal. "My personal feeling is *that* is the source of the legend."

"Very interesting," Avery replied.

"Isn't it," said Cortland.

March returned. "John's flight has been held up by a snowstorm and the front is moving our way. This is not the best time to go birding in Montana, but, unfortunately, it's the only time we get to see the gyr," he said. "There's no way of telling when John will get in and no point in all of us waiting here, so why don't I get you folks to your hotel and come back later. I left a message for John with his airline."

We picked up our gear and began moving out.

"Did anyone notice the Sparhawk, the private jet on the runway?" March asked. "It's a beauty. We don't see many of those in Fire Pond."

"I noticed," Cortland replied.

3

I was awakened from the very depths of sleep, the winter solstice of sleep, by a ringing phone, deep into a dream that I was skating on the Irish pond near Ithaca, New York, where I grew up. It was late on a cold day and I was alone etching circles on the black ice. Christmas lights glittered on a tree on an island on the pond. The ice expanded beneath my skates with a loud crack like rippling gunshot. I skated faster and faster. Joan and my father, her brother, stood on the shore, their faces lit by the blinking lights, yelling something, but what? If you're treading on thin ice then you might as well dance?

"Neil, it's March. Sorry to wake you up."

"No problem. I didn't like where the dream was headed anyway."

"John King didn't make it last night. Portland was socked in. The storm is expected to hit here late tomorrow, but in the meantime we've got a beautiful clear day coming up."

Couldn't prove that by me; it looked like midnight from where I sat.

"Instead of hanging around waiting for the front to move in, I'd like to rouse everybody and get out in the field. What do you think?"

Sweet of him to ask. "Okay by me."

"Great. See you in the lobby? Six-thirty?"

"I'll be there."

There are places in America where weather is a factor, where you wait until morning to make your plans for the day, and the skies determine if you go out or stay in, are in a good mood or bad. It gives people a certain flexibility, some might say driftiness, to be ready to change plans at the last minute. Albuquerque isn't like that. People rise and sink in Albuquerque for different reasons; you can't blame it on low pressure.

I sat up, turned on the light and found myself in an efficiency unit at the Aspen Inn in Fire Pond, Montana, sleeping on a plaid sofa that had folded out. There was brown wall-to-wall mottled with yellow spots that were either spilled eggs or an embellishment to the pattern, beige polyester drapes, fake stucco walls, an efficiency kitchen with a refrigerator the size of a Little Playmate cooler. I felt right at home.

A front was coming in, March said. That meant cold and in Montana they know what cold is; I dressed for it.

He was waiting in the lobby at six-thirty next to a table with a coffee urn and some hard, crusted muffins for the road. The other birders were with him, keen-eyed and ready to go. March dressed just as he did yesterday, faded jeans, down vest. Either he was wearing the same clothes or their exact replica.

"If you dress like that in November," he said when he saw me, down parka over my down vest, "what are you going to wear when it gets *cold?*" I laughed and took off the parka.

"Where's Cortland?" I asked, noticing that the prep was not among us.

"Sleeping in. His cold was worse this morning."

"He's going to miss the gyr."

"Maybe not. We may get a few more trips out there before this expedition is finished, if the storm blows over or turns to rain."

It was a two-hour drive to Freezeout and we left in darkness in a gray van. The aggressive jay pushed her way into the front seat next to March. I got elbowed back to second-row aisle. The talk was about birds, birds and more birds. Avery, who sat behind me, tapped me on the shoulder and said, "I hope you will forgive us for being so one-sided."

"I guess most people are one-sided about something," I replied, eyeing the back of March's thick and curly head.

"The gyrfalcon is an exceptional bird."

I turned around to face his incredible, all-seeing eyes. "So I have been reading in Joan's journal."

"Nothing in the air can compare with the speed and power of a falcon, and it is very rare that one gets to see a gyr so far south. The Arctic is their natural habitat. I don't know of any case where such a white gyr has ever been sighted before, particularly such a young one. The young birds ordinarily have black or brown markings but this one is almost pure white. She is extremely unusual and we are very, very fortunate indeed to have her here. In my youth, I would think nothing of traveling to the Arctic to see a rare bird, but at this stage I have to content myself with the lower forty-eight. I love Montana, though. Next to my farm in Kentucky, it's the best place in the world." He had what many wanted, a cozy place to nest in, wilderness in which to roam.

31

"You don't look like you're doing so bad," I said. His eyes were alert to every motion. Even his white hair was alert; it stuck out in an aureole around his head, each strand a quivering receptor.

He leaned close and whispered confidentially, "I'm eighty-two years old. Would you believe it?"

"Not for one minute."

"I don't believe it either." He winked, and a wink from him was like an eclipse of the full moon. "In addition to their speed and beauty, falcons are that rare wild creature that can be tamed. In fact they have been trained for thousands of years. From the Egyptians to the Middle Ages, before the discovery of gunpowder, they were the most efficient means of hunting. Falcons can be trained to hunt, to stun if not to kill, animals as big as a wolf. Gyrfalcons are the biggest of all falcons; the falcons of kings. Even today they are highly prized."

"Falconry still exists? I thought that went out with damsels in distress and chivalry."

"It exists. In fact . . ."

The jay turned around from her enviable position. "Avery," she hissed, fixing him with a cold stare, "you are not going to ruin our day by talking about *that* subject."

"Now, Bea, there might not be any peregrines today—another magnificent falcon"—he said in an aside to me—"if it weren't for falconers. The native peregrine population was decimated by DDT in the fifties and sixties. Birds are indicators, you know. The early Greek soothsayers read their entrails to see the future. Now their deaths tell us when something is going wrong with the environment. It's a tough way to learn. When the Falcon Fund began to reintroduce the peregrine after DDT was finally banned, the breeding stock came from falconers and so did the expertise in raising and releasing them. The peregrine is a high-tech bird, one of the few wild creatures capable of surviving in cities and in close proximity to man. You must admit that its return is one of the rare occasions where man has been able to undo some of the harm he has done; it wouldn't have been possible without falconers."

"I don't approve of imprisoning wild creatures." Bea flapped her wings.

"Did anyone see the full moon last night?" March asked, attempting to change the sore subject. "It was awesome. Katharine said it was the hunter's moon."

Katharine? Who was this Katharine?

Burt Collier, who was either sleeping loudly on his wife's shoulder or pretending to be, snored. "It's a beautiful morning," the wren said. It was, indeed. The sun had just come up and the Rockies were in view on our left, more rugged, jagged and massive than their siblings in New Mexico. Some wispy clouds hovered over the tops of the snow-covered peaks and the sun was working its way up. In New Mexico they call the mountains the Sangre de Cristos, named for the blood of Christ, because that was the color the conquistadors saw as the sun descended the sky; blood was something the conquistadors knew a lot about. But the sun-splashed peaks always looked more like sangria than *sangre* to me, a stain of spilled and spreading wine.

It was magnificent country, Ansel Adams scenery, and the mountains were not nearly as far away as they appeared because half an hour later we were in the park. The high road was already closed by snow but the lower elevations where the gyr was hadn't been frosted yet.

We parked the van at McNamara Campground, got out, stretched a bit and breathed visibly into the frosty morning air, which reminded me of cigarette smoke, something I was trying not to think about in this crowd. Cliffs shimmered in the distance. Georgia O'Keeffe talked about the near far away, and the far far away. I'd put these cliffs in the medium far category.

"That's where we're going," said Avery.

"Great, how do we get there?" I asked.

"We walk."

"It's got to be miles."

"Only three and a half."

Three and a half in, three and a half out. That made seven in my book, seven miles of up-and-down terrain. It was eight-thirty, and it would probably be dark by four-thirty. Allowing a few hours to look at the bird, it didn't leave much time for dawdling.

March was staring intently at the sky. It was deep blue, Montana blue, but he was frowning as if behind the blue he saw something darker.

"You look like you see something lurking," I said. "Can you see bad weather coming?"

"There's always something lurking in nature." He smiled. "You can't really see the weather, but you can feel it. I think it's the change in the barometric pressure when a front comes in. You can subtly feel the drop in pressure. Birds and animals do it all the time. But we lose these senses because we don't use them. You know there are Indians here who can still see Venus? Venus is a bright planet, it should be visible all day, but most of us have lost the ability to see it. Can you see Venus?"

"No, but I know when it's lurking," I said.

"Let's get going, we haven't got all day," snapped the jay, starting off at a brisk pace, a pace which made it hard to keep up a conversation, but didn't stop anybody from trying. I soon learned why. We were walking through a forest that had dropped a carpet of needles and a hundred years of silence beneath our feet.

"What is that delicious smell?" I asked.

"Red cedar," said Bea.

Scattered among the red cedars were trees with dried-out burnt-orange needles that fell silently to the ground. It looked like a fatal virus was creeping through the forest. "Why are so many trees dying?" I asked.

Bea laughed . . . loudly.

"That tree is one of the few conifers that sheds its needles. It happens every fall," said Muriel, the wren. "It's a tamarack."

"Larch," snapped Bea.

"Tamarack, larch." Avery winked at me. "A tree by either name will shed its needles."

Soon we came to the trailhead, where there was an ominous sign. GRIZZLY COUNTRY, it said. PROCEED AT YOUR OWN RISK. BEARS PREFER TO KEEP THEIR DISTANCE BUT THEY HAVE BEEN KNOWN TO ATTACK HUMANS. DO NOT HIKE ALONE. BACKPACKERS LEAVE YOUR ROUTE AT THE RANGER STATION.

"You have grizzlies in this part of the park?" I asked casually.

"Nah, they never come down here," said Burt, "they just say that to scare off the tenderfeet."

"It's very unlikely you'll ever see, much less have contact with, a bear," said March. "There are two million visitors to this park every year. Only seven of them have ever been killed by grizzlies and some of them were asking for it. One got a photographer a few years back. The guy was filming a sow and her cubs through his telephoto lens and didn't realize how close they had come. You do have to exercise a little caution."

"What happened to the bear?" I asked.

"They shot *a* bear. They missed one of her cubs, but they got the other one in the jaw. It was left to fend for itself with a gaping wound. It didn't make it," he said, with more than a touch of bitterness in his mellow voice. He hitched up his pack and his scope and strode ahead.

"You see someone in the wilderness alone with bells on his pack singing to himself, he's not an escapee from a mental hospital, he's just trying to scare the bears away," Burt told me.

"So that's why Montanans talk so much," I said.

"You're catching on," he replied.

"Neil," Avery said. "Wait up. I want to show you something." When everyone had gotten ahead of us he whispered, "March lost his job at Freezeout because he refused to shoot that bear. It's kind of a sore subject."

"I won't mention it again," I replied.

Everybody quieted down as we got further into our hike. You have to concentrate to keep up with a bunch of birders older and fitter than you, and there is something about walking through a forest anyway, putting one foot down, picking it up, that is hypnotic. If you do it long enough, it takes over thought, possibly even caution, but it would take more than a few miles for me to forget there was a grizzly out there who might want me for lunch. It gave an edge to the hike and sharpened the senses. I could imagine the fear and immediacy of being a little brown bird or a little gray woman when the shadow of a raptor passes overhead.

We went on like this for an hour then stopped beside a river and had a snack of nuts and seeds and some cold water from our canteens. The river, which whispered softly as it passed over its rocks, was liquid jade.

Avery took a sip from his canteen. "'You have left your home and birthplace,'" he said. "'You depend on clouds and you depend on water.'"

"Did you make that up, Avery?" asked Bea.

"No. It came from a Buddhist monk, Zen Master Dogen, in thirteenth-century Japan, but it reminds me of the gyrfalcon alone on her first flight south. 'The inconceivable virtue of following the wind.' Dogen said that, too.

Now there's something the gyrfalcon knows all about."

Something invisible sang near the live branches of a red cedar. "What's that?" asked Marcia.

Muriel: "American goldfinch?"

Avery: "Pine siskin."

"How did you know that?" I asked. "You can't even see it."

"Piece of cake. The pine siskin's song is coarser than an American goldfinch's and they are usually heard in flight. Often it's easier to identify a bird by sound than sight. Many birds look alike, some you only get to see at a distance or in flight, some you never get to see at all. Sometimes you just have to rely on jizz."

"Jizz?"

"It's kind of a sixth sense you get when you do a lot of birdwatching, a picking up of subtle or subconscious clues, seeing the whole, maybe, without being able to identify all the parts."

Something chattered loudly from a nearby tree. "What's that one?" I asked.

"Squirrel," said Bea.

As we began to climb again, one foot after the other, I thought of Joan, her enthusiasm and her stamina, her secret life and bliss. Would sighting the falcon have been worth the trek to her? Would it make any difference? Maybe the trek itself was the point: the companionship, the going up, the coming down, one foot and then the other, the falcon only the excuse.

Finally we reached the rocky ledge where the gyr could be sighted in the cliffs across a jewel of a mountain lake. Falcons like water because their victims congregate there, they like cliffs because they can spot the prey. March had been here before and he knew the gyr's habits. He walked to the edge of the ledge next to a cedar and began to set up his scope while the others got out their binoculars.

"I don't see a thing," said Bea.

"Maybe you don't know how to look," replied Avery.

I looked down over the ledge into the lake, which was similar in color to the river, only deeper and bluer, an intense blue-green. The blueness of the sky was reflected in the green of the water. It was a color that you could get lost in, a color that could make you forget all about divorces and partners and an office on Lead.

"See those rocks around the lake?" March said. "A lot of marmots live there. Grizzlies consider them a delicacy; they'll dig all afternoon to catch a marmot while the marmots just sit around and laugh at them. It's possible the gyr has been eating marmots, too, as there don't seem to be that many birds around and something is attracting her to this spot."

While he adjusted the scope, I noticed slashes running up the tree next to him, parallel lines scratched in the bark like someone had been keeping score.

"Are you keeping a record of your sightings here?" I asked.

"Bear," he said, without even looking up. "It climbed that tree."

I moved in a little closer to our leader. He got the aerie in his sights. "Let me focus this a bit," he said. "There it is. Right there, you see, there are three red cedar trees and next to it an opening and if you look very carefully into that opening you can see the gyr sitting still. Look."

I peered into the scope, saw the opening and an ominous shadow, a shadow of death, peering out of the doorway, but what also interested me at this point was the setting: the cedar trees, the opening in the cliff, the way the rocks were arranged around the opening. The pattern itself had significance as it does in dreams or the mind of the Anasazi (the ancient pueblo Indians), in the place that deals with symbols and meaning.

"It reminds me of the cliff dwellings in Canyon de Chelly in Arizona," I said to March, "where the hand- and foot-holds are carved into the cliff leading up to them. It's high, inaccessible, you could see trouble coming from miles away."

"The gyr sees a meal. Trouble comes from on top of her and she can't always see that. Actually, the nest is not as inaccessible as it looks. It would be hard to climb up, but you can climb down from the top of the ridge fairly easily. You see to the right of the opening there are sort of natural steps in the rocks, and the ledge is plenty wide enough for a man to stand on."

"There she goes," Marcia called out. "She's taken off."

The other birders had their binoculars out, rapt with rapture at sighting the raptor. I fumbled with the clasp of my case.

"Look at the spread of the wings," said Avery. "Wow."

"How white she is."

"What a beauty."

"She's rising up. She's spotted something down by the lake."

"Maybe she'll stoop."

I got the binoculars to my eyes, but the best lenses in the world were no good out of focus. All I saw was a blue smear and then, as I lowered the lenses, a gray one. Meanwhile the gyr flew gracefully somewhere, a legendary creature of uncanny speed and beauty, alert and untamed. I heard all about it, but I couldn't find her. I fiddled with the knobs, zeroed in on a section of cliff, a cleft in the stone, and then the three cedars finally came into needle-sharp focus. Binoculars have no peripheral vision. You can see very clearly, but only what you are focused on. Something cut across the lower edge of my lenses with a swift and fierce motion. The gyrfalcon, gone into a stoop, about to pluck the heart from some less fortunate bird? I stuck with the sighting. It was a rapid, rapier-sharp plunge in a straight line, the shortest distance from the cliff to the ground, but there was a certain clumsiness in the fall. It wasn't a bird that was making the dive, it was a man, a man in free fall, wingless but with a jacket flapping around him as he plunged. The thought occurred to me that this was some perverse joke, that my high-powered lenses had their own agenda, like those trick Japanese cameras with naked men leering at you from inside. But it was real, all right. A clothed man in a death spiral crashed broken and bloody onto the rocks at the bottom of the cliff.

Someone screamed. Apparently, it was me.

"It's just a bear looking for a marmot," said March, grabbing my shoulder, noticing where my binoculars were pointing. "It's a long way away."

"It's not a bear," I said. "Look."

I handed over my binoculars and he focused on the spot. What he found to recognize in the bloody pulp I didn't know, but he called it. "Jesus Christ," he said. "Sandy? Sandy Pedersen?"

4

It was murder. That's what the federal prosecutor, Wayne Betts, claimed. He had gotten involved, he said, because the "murder" took place on federal land. The prime suspect sat opposite me the next day in the coffee shop at the Aspen Inn poking his coffee with a dirty spoon.

"A guy falls off a cliff in full view of you and me and five sharp-eyed birders and that's murder?" I asked.

"Yes," replied March Augusta. He and Avery had spent the night guarding the body and escorted it back this morning by helicopter. I'd met them at the airport in the van. By now it was midafternoon and Betts had already talked to everyone who had been on the field trip. The front had moved in and dropped freezing rain on Fire Pond. I'd offered to buy March a cup—he looked like he needed it.

"How do they figure that?" The coffee tasted like it had been suctioned from a dark and stagnant puddle. I pushed mine away, watched March add a packet of sugar to his.

"Someone set a trap on the cliff near the gyrfalcon's aerie. Sandy crawled into it."

"For the sake of argument only, mind you, how did you do *that* when you were birdwatching with the rest of us?"

"That trap could have been set days ago. When I climbed up to the aerie this morning there was nothing to indicate that anyone else had been there recently. The ledge doesn't take any footprints. It was a spooky night, I'll tell you, sitting around with Avery after you all hiked out, waiting for the helicopter to come in and take Sandy's body away. Avery not only sees in the dark, he glows."

"To continue, again just for the sake of argument," I said, "you set a trap and brought us along to see your handiwork?"

"Well, that's one thing in my favor." He opened another packet of sugar, dropped it into the coffee. "I don't think even the Fish and Wildlife Service believes I'm capable of that. But whoever set that trap couldn't necessarily plan when Sandy would be there, or even if it would be Sandy, although that's a pretty good guess given his record. The trap is what is called a wolf-wiper and it's vicious. The animal, or in this case human, crawls into it and detonates .38 caliber cartridges that blast cyanide into its face. There's enough cyanide to kill a man in five seconds just in case blowing his face off doesn't do it. Someone wanted him pretty bad."

"Could the trap have been put there to protect the bird, to trap another predator?" I asked.

"The only predator a gyrfalcon has is man. That trap was built to kill a man and it was placed in the cedars at a point where you have to crawl to get out from under a rock overhang. Unfortunately, I know a lot about trapping and the Fish and Wildlife Service knows a lot about me." He picked up a tin pitcher, added a little milk to the sugar.

"When I was a ranger at Freezeout someone was leaving wolf-wipers around, aiming to kill the same wolves we were trying to reintroduce, the Magic Pack we called them. Wolf hunting is still legal in Canada and the wolves'd come over the border looking for a safer place. I spent one summer pulling the traps out, hoping not to get detonated myself. I've still got a few loaded traps locked up in my shed. I never could figure out how to get rid of the cyanide. I had my suspicions but I couldn't prove who was making or setting the traps. We did scare him out of Freezeout, thank God."

I flagged down the waitress, asked for some hot water and Red Zinger. "What's that?" she asked.

"Never mind," I replied and lit up a Marlboro instead. "Do you mind?" I asked March. He shook his head no, an agreeable person. He probably wouldn't admit minding, even if he did.

"All right, just to continue with this argument for a minute," I said, "you had the means—the trap. You had the opportunity—you'd been out there to see the gyr. But what was your motive?"

"Sandy Pedersen is a sleazy guy. I can't say I really disliked him personally and we had something in common, both being woodsmen. I don't like what he did, but I wouldn't kill for it; anybody who knows me knows that."

I'll admit I'm not always the best judge of men, but I'd go along with that. Having just spent the night in the lonesome with the bare ground to sleep on and only the fire he'd built to keep him warm, the suspect wasn't at his best. There were twigs in his hair and the time had long passed to change his clothes, but he had the eyes of a scout, clear, watchful, amber, sincere.

"Sandy trapped and sold animals, endangered species, he didn't care, whatever people would pay for. He'd get bighorn sheep as trophies for rich Texans, elk antlers for the Asian aphrodisiacs market, falcons for falconers. He was busted for dealing in elk horns a few years ago and did time, but he was paroled after six months. The penalty for poaching is supposed to be a two-hundred-fifty-thousand-dollar fine and five years in jail. But basically, they let him out with just a slap on the wrist." He sipped at the sludge. "Makes you wonder about the government's priorities. It didn't make much of an impression, apparently, because ever since he's been bragging all over Montana about the birds he could get. He was in there to get the gyr. Somebody wanted it out of there, somebody wanted Sandy out of the way."

"What *is* the market for these birds, anyway?"

"I've heard it's big in this country, big in Europe, biggest of all in Saudi Arabia, where the sport has a long history and where you're not going to find any native gyrfalcons. The birds falconers like best are passagers, falcons that are on their first migration, young enough to have spirit, not too old to be trained. That bird you saw is a prime specimen, young, big, healthy. Best of all, a white female—and nobody has to go into the Arctic to get her."

A white female. Having been one all my life, I'd say the mystique of *that* was overrated. But maybe there was a thrill to owning one that didn't come from being one.

"It's probably an exaggeration, but I've heard that people will pay up to one hundred thousand for one of those birds," said March.

"It's a lot of money for a bird, but enough to murder for?"

"Why not? In New York City they'll do it for a pair of sunglasses."

He put down his spoon and stared morosely into his coffee, which by now was as thick and muddy as the Rio Grande in springtime. "I'm in deep, deep trouble, Neil. The feds would love to pin this on me."

"Why you?"

"Because I beat them, that's why. I was fired without a proper hearing from my job at Freezeout. It was a case of wrongful discharge. I sued for damages and I won. I might as well tell you the whole story, everybody else knows it. Remember the photographer I told you about who was killed photographing the sow and her cubs?"

I nodded.

"The order came down immediately afterwards to kill that bear. There was no way of telling which bear it was until she was dead and the contents of her stomach examined, so basically the order was to kill any female bear with cubs that happened to be in the area. But if you shoot the mother, you might as well kill the cubs, too, because they're too young to survive on their own. I refused to do it."

I'd already heard the bare bones of this story from Avery, but I wanted to get his perspective.

"They were within their rights to fire me, but they didn't follow the proper procedures, so I sued and won enough to start up my guide service. It didn't make me happy. I've often wished I had never done it, but my lawyer saw an opportunity and Katharine felt strongly about it."

That Katharine again. "It sounds like you have an effective lawyer anyway."

"When he works. He used to be a county attorney, and he's had some experience prosecuting accused murderers. This would give him a chance to defend one, but he's not here at the moment. Right now he's sailing in Baja, fishing and looking at whales. He's supposed to be back in two weeks, but I'll believe it when I see it."

"Maybe I could help out, if it turns out you need help."

"That's right, you're a lawyer, aren't you? The best in the West, your aunt said." He managed a smile.

Apparently when Joan was in Montana, she did as the

Montanans did—talked. About me. Who would have thought there was so much to say? "Since it's a federal crime, I can be admitted to practice in the district if I'm sponsored by local counsel. If it gets to that, does the sailing lawyer have any kind of staff who could assist me?"

"His name is Tom Mitchell and he's got Marie, a crackerjack secretary. She'll help. As far as I'm concerned you're hired. Every other lawyer I know is in bed with the federal government. I'll call Marie and tell her you'll represent me. Don't worry about money, by the way—I'll pay your going rate. I haven't used up my judgment dough yet. Not much to spend it on here. There's nothing that you have to get back for?"

Only the usual condo closings and divorces. Brink could handle it—he'd have to. "My partner can handle the work load," I said. But what about the Kid? Who would handle *that?* How long could it take anyway, a few weeks till the sailing lawyer got back? I'd have to send a *very* carefully worded postcard to the Kid. It was an opportunity I couldn't refuse—a murder case, the top of the line in my business. Every group has its risk takers, its dancers on thin ice. In their field, they are the ones with the finely honed skills, those who dare the most, accomplish the most, fly the highest, have the furthest to fall: the high-wire act in the circus, the pitcher in baseball, novelists among writers, litigators among lawyers, gyrfalcons among birds. It was a challenge I couldn't resist, but there was one question that needed to be asked.

"I'm afraid I have to ask you something . . ."

"Shoot." He feigned like my arm was loaded and he was ready to dive under the table.

"How did you know it was Sandy Pedersen?"

"Jizz?" He smiled slightly. "I guess it was his long sandy hair; there wasn't much else identifiable."

I could accept it, but I had to wonder if anyone else

would. I'd hate to see it discussed in a court; I hoped it would never get that far. The evidence against March looked bad. His reputation and character looked good, but that might not be enough. If I couldn't prove he didn't do it, I might have to find out who did. I don't believe in perfect crimes. It's dangerous for human beings to be too good at anything, even crime. Perfection takes more courage than most people possess; it brings down wrath and possible annihilation at the hands of your siblings, your peers, your God, your mother. Some Indians put an error in their weavings, a black line that leads out of the blanket, so as not to anger the gods by appearing to emulate them. A human had committed the crime, a human had left the way out. I intended to find it.

We happened to be sitting in the window of the coffee shop in plain view of the street. The door burst open and a tumbleweed blew in, caught a gust, spun around in a crazy wind-driven dance, and landed at our booth. It turned out to be the aforementioned Katharine, poetry in motion, motion in motion. Her black hippie hair was probably halfway down her back when it hung down, but I bet that didn't happen often. Right now it spun out wildly around her head. She had fine features, a creamy complexion, sparkling black eyes, a face that might have been ethereally beautiful if it weren't lividly angry. It was the face of a younger Elizabeth Taylor and she had the figure that went along with it: short legs, wide hips, and breasts that were unrestrainable. She made the most of it in a long denim skirt and cowboy boots. This was not a lanky, long-legged, blue-jean woman. Superficially, she had that romantic, hippie look that had also become endangered, but she was an angry, angry woman, a woman maybe who preferred the meat around the heart. It's hard to tell what glue binds any two people together. She was angry, March wasn't. Was that enough? But they were a couple, I could see that—March's eyes turned soft and unfocused as she moved up close.

"Those assholes," were her first words. She moved fast and she talked fast, too. "Assholes, assholes, assholes." It was at least one too many. "Sandy Pedersen got what he deserved, all right. It couldn't have happened to a better poacher, and whoever did it deserves a medal. But Betts is accusing you? You? What kind of an asshole would think *you* did it? God, it makes me sick." She pounded the table, sending the Rio Grande over its banks onto the saucer. There is an abandon that *is* abandon.

"Katharine, simmer down a minute. This is Neil Hamel; she is going to be my lawyer."

She cast a look in my direction, noticing for the first time that another human sat there. "You?"

And then there is the perfect control. "Me," I said. "No one has officially been accused of anything yet."

"Oh, yeah? Then why is Greg Porter waiting in the lobby with handcuffs in his lap?"

"He's not waiting any longer," said March.

Porter ambled over and hovered beside our table in his law enforcement suit, staring with embarrassment at his feet. He shuffled a bit, looked up. "I don't like this any more than you, old buddy, but I've got to read you your rights."

"Go ahead," said March.

Katharine brought her anger under control, at least she didn't swear at Porter or punch him out. But the hot fury in her eyes gave fair warning of what was to come.

5

Wayne Betts, the prosecutor, had filed an arrest warrant and had twenty-four hours to bring March before a magistrate. I took the same twenty-four to prepare and file a motion to admit me to the bar of the district court for this case. Time was of the essence.

March had called Marie; she was waiting for me in Mitchell's office. There seemed to be plains people and mountain people in Montana. Marie was of the plains, calm and competent, focused on the middle distance. She wore polyester pants and had a sensible haircut. Her kids had been raised and she was ready for the next challenge. As Montana doesn't have suburbs, the women missed out on being stuck there with the kids, the television and the washer-dryer, with not enough to do and no respect for not doing it, the phase when modern appliances took the status and dignity from their work, when women were considered amusing toys and adapted their behavior accordingly. But being cute has no value on a ranch. My impression was that Montana valued humor in men, competence in women. Marie was competent and she wasn't ambivalent about it either. She just did what needed to be done, quickly.

"You can count on me to help March," she said.

She had already tracked down Tom Mitchell by phone before he went out sailing in Baja. "I told him March wants you to represent him at the bail hearing. He doesn't see any problems with bail, but he'll call back in a few days to see how it's going. He can't believe anyone—even Wayne Betts—would charge March with murder. Neither can I." She shook her head. "I checked with the court and they said you can file the motion without local counsel accompanying you."

"Thanks, Marie."

"No problem. I'm glad to have something to do."

She knew more about preparing the document than I did; between us we were ready in time. Since I had the degree and had passed the bar exam, I was the one who went to court. I would have preferred to see the prosecutor before the bail hearing, but there wasn't time.

Fire Pond, located at the juncture of the Rockies and the plains, handled the affairs of both: the legal issues involving poaching and wildlife manipulation in the mountains, the commerce of the plains. It was a calm town of about fifty thousand people with big trees, Victorian houses, wide avenues. Even though the front had blown on and the big blue had reappeared, the traffic moved slowly and no one was on the street. The courthouse had been built in the days when the West was won, when they were good at erecting buildings and eliminating Indians. It was a massive stone building with pillars and a cupola that brought the bright Montana sunshine into the depths of the stone. There were tufted black leather sofas in the lobby and large potted plants in brass pots on the patterned tile floor. A curved staircase with a railing of polished wood ascended to the second floor, where the courts waited.

I climbed the stairs and found a guard sitting on the landing. "Afternoon, ma'am."

"Afternoon."

"I'm afraid I have to go through your purse," he said politely. It was a formality that had to be endured these days when no one trusted anyone, especially a lawyer. The federal government wanted to be sure I wasn't bringing a Magnum into district court to waste a judge or jury if the verdict didn't turn out right. The guard felt through my purse, squeezed a pack of Marlboros, picked up my wallet and the change fell out.

"I used to charge people to get in," he winked, putting the change back, "but they won't let me do that no more."

I filed the motion with no problems. At the bail hearing I could see that March's incarceration was already beginning to tell on him. His eyes were not nearly so clear as they had been yesterday. It's not natural for a naturalist to be in captivity. He needed sleep, but even more he needed his freedom; I intended to get it. For the moment it seemed it was just a matter of posting bail.

I gave him my reassuring, don't-worry-I'll-have-you-out-of-here-on-bail-in-no-time attorney's smile, but it was a sham because Betts held the cards and he played them all. My client, he said, posed a clear and present danger to the community, there was a likelihood he would kill other people, the offense was extremely serious, the prosecution had a strong case. March had the means—his fingerprints had been found on the trap that killed Pedersen. Betts had already obtained a search warrant and found four more wolf-wipers in March's shed. He had the motive—he was known to be hostile to poachers. He had the opportunity—he had openly admitted visiting the site. Therefore, there would be no bail. I argued. I lost.

March was right, someone wanted very badly to pin this on him. I'd say this for Betts, he moved fast. I'd also say he overreacted.

I made the point that a former ranger accused of killing a poacher would not be safe among the general prison population, many of whom probably were poachers. It was agreed that March would be given his very own cell in the county jail where he could be kept for thirty days before he'd have to be indicted by a grand jury, in other words, before someone other than Wayne Betts would think he was guilty. A very dejected March was led back to prison. I was glad Katharine hadn't shown up and pulled her madwoman act. March's depression was enough for me to cope with. "Don't worry," I said before he was led off. "I'll have this out with Betts and be by in the morning."

Wayne Betts had naturally fair skin that had been unnaturally mottled by too much exposure to the big sky, a perfect candidate for Retin-A. I thought about suggesting it while he gave me the reasons it was necessary to incarcerate my client, March Augusta—the big three: means, motive, opportunity. The accused admitted publicly that he'd been to the aerie, his fingerprints were found on the wolf-wiper that killed Pedersen, wolf-wipers were found in his shed. That and his identification of the body at a great distance were all solid evidence to Wayne Betts.

"He did have an excellent pair of binoculars," I said.

Betts widened his wide blue eyes until the irises fluttered and darted like moths in a jar. They were the sort of technicolor that some people admire, but I find unnatural.

"What about character?" I asked.

"Character?" His butterfly eyes didn't have the sharpness of the mountains or the calm of the plains either. They came from someplace else.

"Are you from Texas?"

He cracked his knuckles, a sound that sent a lizard racing down my spine. "How did you know that?"

We know about a few things in my state: sun, low riders, chile, Texans. "I'm from New Mexico," I said. "A neighbor."

He smiled but there was no joy in it or in my presence either. The man was not at ease.

Nevertheless, at ease or not, it was time to get down to business. "You can't seriously believe that my client is capable of murder. He's a gentle person, a fine, upstanding citizen, a naturalist who cares deeply with every fiber of his being about preservation, not killing." It was hyperbole, but what could you expect in a federal prosecutor's office?

"This wouldn't be the first time someone in Montana killed over an environmental issue." He opened his eyes even wider, implying perhaps that a Montana lawyer would know that.

"We have environmentally related crimes in New Mexico, too," I said, and continued my line of reasoning. "My client has never been in jail, has never even been accused of a crime. It is highly irregular to hold a person of such good reputation and moral character without bail. Montana is my client's life. His business is here. It is obvious that he is not going to flee the state."

He cracked his knuckles again, sending the lizard back up.

"It's not obvious to me," he said slowly. "Incidentally, it's not the first time your client has been in trouble with the federal government."

"For what? Refusing to kill a bear?"

"For refusing to obey orders. He was an employee and an employee has obligations to his employer."

So that was why I worked for myself. Maybe Betts was

overzealous or badly in need of a conviction. Maybe it was a personal vendetta, but who could dislike March? If it was a reaction to March's lawsuit, it was an overreaction. The government could certainly afford whatever it had lost. My overriding impression was that in the cave behind the butterflies, something was lurking.

"I don't need to remind you that there are rules of discovery. If you know something about my client's guilt or innocence that I don't, I am entitled to that information. I can always file a motion if need be."

"I am not concealing anything about your client," he spoke very slowly, enunciated very clearly and cracked his knuckles again.

"I wish you wouldn't do that."

He laid his hands on the table. "Any further questions?"

"Not for you," I replied.

I went back to the Aspen Inn, where Avery and the birders were waiting for news of their incarcerated leader. Spending a night in the wilderness hadn't done Avery any harm. In fact, he looked ten years younger than he had the day before yesterday, when he'd already looked fifteen years younger than he was. His eyes were electric and there was a little dance in his step. "What a night that was," he said, "what a night. I haven't spent a night in the wilderness in several years. How magical it is. Where's March? Has he been released?"

It's a rare pleasure, a good mood. I hated to be the one to destroy it. "March is still in jail and being held without bail."

"What for?"

"Murder."

There were quacks and croaks and expressions of outrage.

"That's ridiculous," said Avery. "I've known March for ten years—he didn't murder anybody. He ruined his career as a ranger because he couldn't bring himself to kill a bear."

"Unfortunately, Betts, the federal prosecutor, doesn't see it that way."

"What are you going to do?"

"Get him out. What are you all going to do?" Now that the expedition had become a bummer, I thought they would probably turn tail and go home. But people who fly thousands of miles and hike another seven to see one bird dive-bomb another are not likely to be intimidated by a mere murder; exhilarated was a better word.

"Stay," said Muriel the wren.

The jay: "We'll lose our discount fare, if we go home early."

Burt Collier: "Got nothing to do at home anyway at this time of year."

Marcia: "Maybe we can help March out."

Cortland James, however, hadn't said anything at all. "How's your cold?" I asked.

"Much better, thank you. The day's rest was beneficial."

"I'm John King" came from the remaining birder, the one I hadn't met yet. It was easy to see how he'd been attracted to ornithology—he had a beak to equal any in the bird kingdom. From one point of view he was an extremely homely man. His nose was grotesque, his legs were too short, his hair was mouse gray and falling out, but he had a kind and melodious voice. After talking to him for a few minutes, it was all you'd notice.

"You look tired," he said.

"It has been a trying day."

"Why don't we all get some dinner and let Neil rest up."

I guess I looked like I needed it. "Thanks."

"Tomorrow I'm going to give my lecture and show my slides of the Arctic."

There was a noticeable lack of enthusiasm. They wanted to get back out in the field and see some more prey get zapped. Slides seemed pretty tame now. John King took charge, however, and led them away. "You relax and get a good night's rest," he told me.

I had the use of March's van—he wouldn't be needing it where he was—and I went down the road to an Albertson's that was the size of a large airplane hangar. I stocked up on Red Zinger and Lean Cuisines.

I went back to my motel efficiency, turned on the oven, took out my bottle of Cuervo Gold. I put some ice in a glass, poured the Gold over the ice, put a vegetable pasta in the oven, sat down and picked up the telephone book. It's one way to rest up. I looked at the Hamels first: there was Rebecca Hamel, Edward Hamel, Michael Hamel and the Louise and Bill Hamel family with a separate phone for the teenagers. Next I tried the yellow pages. Under "lawyers" there was a three-quarter-page ad that emphasized serious injury and wrongful death—vehicular, machinery, pharmaceuticals, railroad, power line, aircraft. No wolf-wipers. Tom Mitchell was listed only as an attorney at law, no specialty for him, no credit for Marie. I went through the rest of the names—nobody I knew from law school or anyplace else. At the moment, I was on my own in Fire Pond up against the infinite resources of the federal government with a falsely accused murderer to represent and as yet only a dim notion of how to do it. The yellow pages were sprinkled with little boxes containing helpful hints and words of wisdom. "Obstacles should be regarded merely as obstacles, not as stopping-places—Frederick William Nichol." I turned the page. "Life is the art of drawing without an eraser." Or swinging without a net, dancing on thin ice. I turned once more: "REMOVING GUM FROM HAIR—Rub in a dab of peanut butter. Massage the gum and peanut butter between your fingers until the gum is loosened. Remove with facial tissue."

I thought about writing the Kid, but what would I say? Miss you, be back when I solve a murder? Wish you were here? I decided to wait a few days and see how the cards fell. No one was expecting me till next week anyway.

I picked up Joan's journal, skipped Personal and turned to Falconry, the art of training hawks to hunt that has been practiced someplace in the world in every age from the unwritten past to the overwritten present.

Records show that falconry was in China 2,000 years B.C. Bas-reliefs from the Middle East dating back to 1700 B.C. show falconers carrying hawks on their wrists. In all that time there has never been a total lapse in the practice of the art. The Crusaders brought the sport back with them to Britain and Western Europe around A.D. 860, where the species were allotted according to rank: Eagles were flown by emperors, gyrfalcons by kings, peregrines by earls, goshawks by yeomen, sparrow hawks by priests, while commoners got the kestrels.

Female has always been the falconer's favorite sex. White gyrs the rarest and most prized bird. Philip the Bold ransomed his son for twelve white gyrfalcons that probably came from Greenland, known then as the land of the white falcon. It took two years to round them up.

Birds are bred in captivity or taken from the nest as fledglings, but the highly prized falcons, the ones with the most spirit and best hunters, are the passager birds taken from the wild after they have learned to fly and hunt. A significant effort goes into teaching them to unlearn their native cunning and fear of man. Among the wildest and shyest of creatures, they must be taught against their better instincts to trust the falconer.

Once the bird is trapped, a soft leather hood is placed over its head and tied on. Jesses (leather thongs) are attached to its legs as a way to control it. A leash may be attached to the jesses. A furious and frightened bird will resist by bating (wildly beating its wings), hissing and cakking. Keeping the hood on and the bird in darkness helps to calm it.

The captive is "manned" (trained to endure the presence of its captor) by being carried on a gloved hand, spoken to and softly stroked. This process works best when the bird and the trainer stay awake together until a bond is formed in mutual exhaustion and the captive learns to accept the captor. The purpose is to control the bird's anger and put it to use, not to break her spirit. A portion of her life thereon is spent in the darkness of the hood, and then there are the exhilarating moments when she is released to be flown at prey.

The falcon is kept hungry and fed only from a lure, a padded weight with pigeon or other food attached, which it becomes accustomed to returning to. Albertus Magnus said: "In order to be sure that your falcon will be fond of you and never leave you, grind together equal quantities of ache, black mint, and parsley and give this to the falcon on warm meat."

Eventually, a falconer can trust his bird to go out and hunt for game yet return to him and the lure to be fed. Although there is always the possibility that she will fly higher in her gyre until she spots some far distant quarry and never comes back. Falconry is romance, not science.

The Lean Cuisine was done. There were no dishes in my efficiency, so I ate my zucchini lasagna from the metal tray, pulled open the plaid sofa and closed my eyes. I imagined being kept hooded in darkness and in hunger, being held and stroked and forced to tolerate a dreaded enemy's voice and leather-gloved touch. I imagined bating and waiting and then finally being released on a hunting expedition, circling higher and higher and higher.

6

The next morning there was a note for me at the Aspen Inn desk typed on plain white paper. It had been dropped off by an anonymous person at dawn. "I must talk to you about your client, March Augusta," it said, not bothering to mention who "I" was. "Be in Ampersand 10 o'clock tomorrow Sunday morning alone."

"Why Ampersand?" I asked March as he pointed it out to me on the road map, a dot on the plain, about three hundred miles from where we sat in the visiting room of the Fire Pond County Jail. As jails go, it was top of the line, a massive stone building from the same Indian-slaughtering era as the courthouse. They thought so well of their prisoners in Fire Pond that they had built a residential neighborhood around them. There were condominiums for sale across the street.

"Did you know," March said, "that there are no straight lines in nature?"

"Or in conversation."

He laughed, a sound that was good to hear. "There are no straight wounds, either. If you find one on a man or an animal, you can be sure it was not come by naturally. But look at this. Highway 510 in and out of Ampersand, and put there by the Highway Department, is absolutely straight for eighty miles. If anyone's following you out there, you'll know. The country is so open and empty, you'd notice if a plane flew overhead. Except for that, I can't think of any reason why anyone would want to meet in Ampersand. It's another prairie town, some people work for the highway department, most are ranchers. Nothing special going on."

"Did Sandy Pedersen hang out there?"

"I doubt it—there's only one saloon." He looked down, embarrassed by what he had to ask. "Are you going to go?"

Was I? Into the Great Plains on behalf of an imprisoned client who was afraid to meet my eyes because I might see him beg? "Yup."

He began picking at a tear in his jeans. "It could be dangerous."

"It could."

He looked up quickly, looked down again.

"But it's highly unlikely," I said. "You're the accused. What good's it going to do anyone to harm me?"

"I don't know, but be careful."

"Just don't tell anyone that I'm going."

"I won't," he replied.

"Can you think of anything you've forgotten to tell me?" I asked, picking mentally at my own jeans. "Any reason why Betts is so overzealous?"

He shrugged. "No. As far as I know, he doesn't even dislike me."

"Your wife seems to feel strongly about him."

"Katharine's not my wife. We live together but we're not married. She's been through some bad times, she tends to get emotional about things. She'll be here any minute, by the way, if you want to talk to her."

Reason enough for me to be on my way. "Maybe later. Let's see what's waiting in Ampersand first. You doing okay in here? Sorry I wasn't able to get you a phone and a color TV in your private room."

"I'm surviving. They took away my belt and shoelaces just in case I got the urge to hang myself. If I'm here long enough I'll make you some beaded earrings—that's what the prisoners do to keep busy. Thanks for getting me my own cell by the way. Some of the guys in here aren't too crazy about rangers, even ex-rangers."

"I'll get you out, don't worry. If I can't prove you didn't do it, I'll find out who did." I stood up.

"Be careful, Neil, and . . . thanks."

If I had left one second sooner, I would have been struck down in the doorway by a heat-seeking missile. The guards here were pretty casual about visiting hours, particularly when it came to Katharine. She burst into the room with her black hair flying. At least I knew she hadn't been eavesdropping—she couldn't sit still long enough. I wondered what fuel she was running on, high octane, low lead?

"You got anything yet?" she asked me.

"Working on it."

She looked at me quickly, with all the attention of someone who glances at the face of their watch and two minutes later can't remember the time.

"March's life is in danger here."

"I'll get it solved by Thursday—I don't want to lose my discount fare. See you soon," I said to March.

"Good luck," he replied.

*　　*　　*

63

Three hundred miles. There are probably people who go that far for lunch in Montana or a drink, but I wouldn't do it for breakfast, so I left Fire Pond early Saturday afternoon. I checked the AAA guide in March's glove compartment for a place to stay. Ampersand, caught in a time warp, still had one of those dwindling bits of rural Americana, a hyphenated motel known as the Y-Go-By. I didn't think reservations would be required.

Avery and Cortland James, who happened to be sitting together in the coffee shop discussing their life lists perhaps, spotted me on my way out of the Aspen Inn. I'd have to talk to John King; he wasn't keeping his birders busy enough.

"Neil, wait up," called Avery. "Where you off to?"

"The plains," I said.

"East?" Cortland perked up, that being his preferred direction. He'd taken to wearing socks with his Top-Siders, I noticed. At least his feet were warm.

"How far?" asked Avery, his white mane sending feelers in my direction.

"I can't say, Avery, I'm following a lead."

"Somewhere east of Fire Pond," Avery punched that into his memory bank to see what came up. As he went into receptor mode, his antennae quivered. "Ah, if you are going east of Fire Pond you will be entering the Crazy Woman Mountains. There was a wagon train that passed through that area back in the days before the West was won. It was attacked by Indians and everyone was killed but one woman. It was a superhuman feat, but she managed to survive alone in those wild mountains for years, attacking and killing Indians. They had a lot of respect for her."

"No doubt."

"They named the mountains after her, the Crazy Womans. They say her spirit haunts the place to this day and Indians still don't like to go there."

"Avery is quite a historian," Cortland said.

Maybe these two had struck up a friendship based, like some marriages, on similar interests, different personas: the visionary and the prep; the youthful old man, the aging boy. One of those relationships where the participants are attracted one day, repelled the next.

"It's interesting talking to you two, but I have to get going." I looked at my wrist. There was no time written there for me to forget because I don't wear a watch, but I can fake it. In their own way, each of these men wanted to come with me. They didn't say so, but I could see it expressed in one's eyes, repressed in the other's. Avery would follow like an owl seeing all, hearing all. Cortland would come with a tape recorder in his hand, seeing nothing but recording it anyway.

Avery accepted the inevitable. "It's good to be alone sometimes," he said. "It sharpens the perceptions."

Compared to the Rockies the Crazy Womans were gentle hills, but still no place a woman or anyone else would want to winter alone. Highway 510 passed through the foothills and entered the plains. Straight as a line, it cut through space like a knife through water, in nature but not natural. There was space in front of me, space around me, space inside me. Space is no stranger in New Mexico, either, but at home I knew what to expect. There I could be alone between destinations, alone with my thoughts, alone in a crowd. Here I was alone in the alone and rapidly putting the mountains behind me. March's side-view mirror had a blind spot big enough to hide a semi in, but beyond that I could see the Crazy Womans. Mountains are something you should be driving toward or beside, not away from.

In New Mexico even when they are behind you they are in front of you or beside you, too. March was right about no one sneaking up on me on Highway 510. If anyone was, I would have seen them coming for miles. Once the Crazy Womans disappeared from the mirror, the view from the rear and the front became exactly the same: gray road, yellow line, blue sky, except for the dips in the middle distance that were filled with the illusion of water. When the sun caught the chrome on a rare approaching car it sparkled like a diamond as it entered the water: the fire, the pond. As I passed through an Indian reservation square white crosses began to appear beside the highway. Sometimes there were several crosses attached to each other like paper doll cutouts, always at a point where the road was absolutely straight with no curves to throw a driver off. Something else was causing these cars to wander off the road and flip the drivers into oblivion.

If nature doesn't understand a straight line, it abhors a vacuum. In the emptiness, other dimensions stumble in; I began to think about the crazy women who haunt our nation's highways. In New Mexico we have La Llorona, the weeper. She has many manifestations, appears on many different roads, always has something to cry about. We also have the hitchhiker, a young girl in a summer dress thumbing a ride. You pick her up. It's cold and she's shivering, so you lend her a coat. She lives on a bumpy dirt road and, as you take her home, you can see a light shining in the distance. The next morning you realize the girl still has your coat. You drive back up the road, the light is still burning, the girl's mother comes to the door. You ask to see her daughter, tell her you need the coat. "That's impossible," the mother replies. "My daughter's car crashed on the highway. She died there last summer."

*　　*　　*

In the distance sometimes, I saw someone beside the highway, a woman, not weeping, but angry or crazy, shaking a fist, but when I got closer it became a tree or a fence post. Could it be Katharine waiting for me in Ampersand? But why there and why would she have sent a note?

About one hundred miles from my destination a sunset began and it wouldn't stop. I'm no stranger to sunsets, but this one was a phenomenon. I'd never seen the sun drop off such a flat horizon and it took a long time doing it. At first the colors were subdued, green tea, teal blue, soft rose. A smoky gray cloud slipped over the sun and then suddenly it burst open like a trap door to the beyond and the sun's radiance beamed through. It was a radiance you could get lost in, so I stopped the van, got out and leaned against the door, the better to appreciate the performance. The wind picked up, tumbleweeds flew across the road, birds chattered in the dead weeds. It had been a dry year in Montana and the dust that hung in the air refracted the sun's light and added to the brilliance. With no mountains to frame it, the sky was enormous and the sunset filled most of it. Where it wasn't setting directly it was bouncing off clouds. I noticed something circling high above me, looping circles around the straight line that was the road, a predator, maybe, in a playful mood, not hungry enough for a kill, toying with the prey. I became conscious of a drone, saw a flash of silver. The sun dropped out from under the cloud, shot its rays upward and turned the airplane into a dazzling gold enticement that would have sent the conquistadors off to conquer and brutalize the skies, had they only known. The gold leapt higher into the clouds, bouncing off peaks of cumulonimbus. The plane turned and went back whence it had come. The sky shifted to mauve and apricot and peach and still showed no signs of quitting. I was out of the mood, though, so I got in the van. "If anyone is following you out there, you'll know."

It was dark by the time I reached Ampersand but my headlights picked out the welcome sign that said BOYS STATE BASKETBALL FINALISTS, 1969, and found the Y-Go-By, which offered quality, service and honesty at its best. I wouldn't want it any other way. The owner, Henry, a thin, gawky fellow, was very glad to see me, his first customer of the evening, if not the year. He took my name, license number, checked me in.

And then he leaned over the counter and whispered, "You believe in the debil?"

"You mean the . . . 'devil'?"

"That's him."

Ghosts, sure, but the devil? Well, it was his place, I was his guest for the evening.

"I saw the debil once, out in the prairie alone at night. I saw a red glow, but there weren't no fire there. It was the debil. I saw him as clear as I'm seein' you now."

I took a look at my hands, my dusty running shoes, my dirty jeans. How clear was that?

"The debil tempted me. 'Here,' he says, handing me the bottle, 'jus' take one little drink.' "

"Oh, you mean that little guy in the sombrero."

"He weren't wearing no sombrero. He had horns and a long tail. 'Jus' one,' he says. 'Jus' one little drink.' "

Henry's wife was probably watching but not listening to Vanna White in the next room. I could hear a TV blasting, and it sounded like a game show. I lowered my voice. "Did you do it?"

"Yes," he said.

"Oh, God."

"I saw him, too. He rescued me from the debil."

"What did *he* look like?"

"A light, a yellow light. The debil was red."

"Was that your last drink?"

"Nope, but close to it. I'll tell you a secret. You got to

68

get empty, real empty, to leave room for God to come in."

"Suppose the devil gets there first?"

"Then you ain't empty enough. God is faster than the debil."

I was pretty empty. "Thanks, Henry. I'll think about what you said, but in the meantime, do you know where I could get something to eat?"

"The Ampersand Cafe right down the street. We're having a service tomorrow, Sunday, at the Baptist Church, you want to come?"

"Can't. Have an appointment."

"Watch out. Debil makes appointments, too."

The Ampersand Cafe was a bright light on the dark plain, with plastic flowers on every table and a mimeographed menu in a gravy-stained wrapper. It looked like the same gang of cowboys, highwaymen and welfare recipients ate there every night. It was clear to them that I didn't fit into any of the above categories.

They were into the two major food groups at the Ampersand Cafe: fat and sugar. No one was worried about too much cholesterol or too little fiber here. There wasn't a sprout or a whole grain to be had, just plain, unwholesome American food. Meat with potatoes and gravy, balloon bread with butter, iceberg lettuce, three bean salad and Jell-O. There have been days when I've whipped up a batch of black-cherry Jell-O and, the minute it stuck together, eaten the whole thing, but I wouldn't let anyone see me doing it.

I ordered the meat, mashed potatoes, gravy. The remains arrived gray and desolate on a white plate—road kill. The highway was the top of the food chain in Ampersand. Take away the varmint, I wanted to say, take away the gravy, take away the plate, but that would have been rude, so I cut it up and pushed it around and tried to make it look like I had taken a bite.

When I got back to the Y-Go-By, starved, I said "please" before the devil even had to ask. The next morning Ampersand sparkled in the sun, or at least the cars in the parking lot of the Baptist Church did, which is where everybody seemed to be. I was feeling removed from my body, a sensation caused, perhaps, by trafficking with the devil and an absence of food.

Under the big sky and crystalline air the town had a hallucinatory quality, like a mirage or a movie set where the buildings were wooden fronts, six inches thick, propped up from behind. The only building that had substance was the bar—Lucy's Wildlife Sanctuary. That looked like a place you could step right into, put your foot up on the rail and challenge everybody to a drink. I began walking down Main Street, the lone gunslinger, but the gun had no bullets. Exactly where this encounter was to take place I didn't know, but I figured that when the prey gets conspicuous, the predator appears.

I had walked past the general store, the hardware store, the garage and that was it, so I turned around and started back. A car appeared at the far end of town, sparkling like a red diamond before it got covered up by its own dust. The car stopped and the dust settled to reveal a red Mercedes-Benz. I watched warily while the door opened, and something white flapped and fluttered out. An Indian in ceremonial feathers, a bating bird, the ghost of a crazed woman, the devil in disguise? This was beginning to go beyond your run-of-the-mill hallucination to the place where devils danced and weepers wept. As the apparition walked toward me, the flapping white wings settled down, draped and turned out to be robes. Just how empty had I become?

The robes were inhabited by a man, or maybe a boy— he was pretty enough with velvety, dark eyes and an aquiline nose.

"Prince Sahid," he said, offering an elegant manicured hand.

"You know who I am."

"Indeed and it is my pleasure, Ms. Hamel." He spoke beautiful English, the kind of English you don't learn in the U.S. of A. "Perhaps we could go somewhere and talk."

"Lucy's?" That's something I would like to have seen, the prince in his white robes entering a cowboy bar at ten in the morning.

"I don't drink. I have another suggestion. We shall sit in the car. It's quite comfortable and I will send Heinz for coffee."

Some suggestion; a plan would be more like it. "Who is Heinz?"

"My driver, but more than that. He is also, you might say, my agent. But this is a conversation he needn't participate in."

How many times must one be told not to get into cars with strange men, even (or especially) biblical figures in white robes? But with the driver gone, in the middle of Main Street in a devil-fearing community, how dangerous could it be? Heinz was dressed in polyester and had a clipped haircut. He was the prince's foil, coarse where the prince was smooth, short where the prince was tall, obsequious where the prince was in command, polyester where the prince was cotton. He hadn't learned his English in the same place either. He agreed to get the coffee and leave us alone, not necessarily willingly, but obediently. There appeared to be a lot to gain from dancing to Sahid's tune. Before he left, Heinz opened the back door and let me into the Mercedes, where I sat gripping the door handle.

It was soft as velvet in that automobile, snug as down, dark as tinted glass could make it and silent, too. The temperature could be heated or cooled with a flick of a wrist. It sped faster, probably, than you'd ever want to go. I was wrapped in money, or what money could bring, ease and comfort. Once you got accustomed to it, it was a lure that could turn you aside from whatever goals you once had. The cars would get shinier, the houses bigger, and you'd have to fly higher and higher to reach the point where you couldn't see them anymore. I pulled myself up to the edge of the seat, pushed a button to roll down the window and let some dust in.

"Forgive me," the prince said, watching from across the plush with a certain rapacious intensity, "for asking you to drive so far, but privacy is of the utmost importance and I did not want anyone in Fire Pond to see me talking to you. It is a beautiful drive, though, is it not? The great sky reminds me of my own country."

"And what country is that?"

He spread his long, elegant fingers as though he were balancing a transparent ball. He didn't really want to tell me where he was from, but his exquisite manners demanded it. "Saudi Arabia."

"Do you dress like that at home?" I asked.

"For important matters, ceremonial occasions. For me this is an important occasion."

"Perhaps if you had told me, I might have dressed, too."

He smiled, tossed the invisible ball. "Of course, you want to know why I am here. I have a proposition for your client, March Augusta, and I would like you to present it to him since it is impossible to contact him directly. You are his attorney, correct? I had a business arrangement with Sandy Pedersen. He promised me a bird that I want very much, a very rare and beautiful passager bird, young enough to train." His eyes glowed as he talked about the gyr, envisioning the beautiful, spirited, white female who will fly far, but only as far as he wanted her to go. His manners were impeccable, his goals despicable.

"The white female," I said, noting that what came naturally to me he had to dress up to achieve.

"Precisely," he replied. "I am willing to pay very well for that bird, but, unfortunately, your client . . ." He struggled for a polite way to put this. What was the euphemism for murder, anyway? Terminated? Put to sleep? He balanced the ball in one hand, waved with the other. I knew what he meant.

"But my client didn't . . ." I had a hand of my own to wave.

"Of course," he said, but it was only another layer of politeness on an edifice whose foundation had been laid on sand countless centuries before. "That has yet to be proven or disproven. Nevertheless, putting aside all matters of your client's guilt or innocence, I believe your client can help me and I am willing to pay him very well."

"Just how could my client help you?"

"He and the deceased were experienced woodsmen. Pedersen told Heinz of the respect he had for your client. He even mentioned that if anyone could stop him from taking the bird, it would be Mr. Augusta."

I grimaced. How many people had Pedersen told *that* to? "I'm sure Pedersen wasn't talking about murder when he made that statement."

The prince smiled graciously. "Well, we don't know, and Mr. Pedersen is dead, isn't he? But that does not change the fact that I must have that bird and that Mr. Augusta knows where it is and that he is the only one who can get it for me."

Heinz had come out of the Ampersand Cafe and was standing across the street holding styrofoam cups of coffee, waiting for a nod from the prince, but Prince Sahid's attention, all of it, was focused on me.

"Just for the sake of argument, how could my client help

you when he is in prison and guarded twenty-four hours a day?"

A mere formality to a prince. "I'm sure Heinz could arrange it. How many guards are there at a time? One? Two? March Augusta could leave at dawn, be back at noon, if he chose to return. Go anywhere he wanted to, if he didn't. It is by no means impossible."

"I suppose you've got the means to fly him anywhere he wants to go?"

"Of course."

"And you were following me in it yesterday."

"We took the Sparhawk out for a ride not to follow you but to see if anyone else was."

"Why on earth would my client want to help you trap a rare bird and take it from the wild when doing that is the thing he most despises?"

Why indeed? The prince smiled a smile that had a billion dollars behind it, a million oil wells behind that. "I can pay him very well."

"If you know so much about my client, you would know that he can't be bought. In the first place he finds what you are doing not only illegal, but despicable. That's the difference between March and your Sandy Pedersen. Pedersen used his knowledge to exploit the wilderness, March preserves it. In the second place my client doesn't care about money. There's nothing he would even want to spend it on."

"But there is." It was the beginning of a delicate little maneuver. The ball balanced on the tip of a finger and began to spin. "Money would set up a new life."

"He wouldn't leave Montana. He'd rather be a prisoner here than a free man anyplace else."

"His choice, of course, but if he stays in Montana, he has a murder charge facing him. I could help him buy the very *best* legal representation." Thousands of years of politeness couldn't disguise the insult of *that*. "Please don't take offense, I'm sure you have your areas of legal expertise."

Judy Bates's divorces, the Kid's speeding ticket.

"But have you ever handled a murder trial?"

"What difference does that make? My client is innocent."

He was not deterred. "I have spoken to Attorney Dwight Stillman."

Dwight Stillman, known all over the West for his six feet six and six inches of Stetson on top of that, also for having won the Mary Hanover case and . . .

"He is very interested, but he is expensive. I think it would be in your client's best interests to consider my offer."

"I'm a lawyer and asking me to advise a client to break the law is a little like asking a trained falcon to refuse the lure and fly away. It's done—I'm not saying it isn't—and maybe it's even natural, but it's not what I'm trained for. I will, however, tell him about this conversation."

The prince opened his window and called to Heinz. "Please, the coffee has gotten cold. Would you get another? Do you care for one?" he asked me.

"No."

"I am staying at the Freezeout East Hotel. Please call as soon as you have spoken to Mr. Augusta. Time is of the essence."

"And if I don't, I suppose you will call me?"

"Precisely," the prince said.

7

The next day in the Fire Pond County Jail I told March about the prince and he was, just as I had said he would be, appalled.

"Jesus, that's who is after the gyr?"

"He may look like Jesus, but they don't have much else in common."

"Maybe that's the guy I heard about who's willing to pay a hundred thousand for the right passager bird."

"No figure was discussed."

"What's the difference to a Saudi prince anyway? Saudi money probably has the same relationship to the dollar that the dollar has to the peso. We're the Third World to the Saudis; a hundred thousand would be chicken feed to them. What chance does any rare or endangered species have against that kind of exchange? What he could afford to pay would be a fortune to a poor trapper, even to Sandy Pedersen. Poachers took a bull elk from Bison Reservation last week and someone probably paid them a bundle for it. They took the whole head, left the rest of the animal there. I guess that means a rich guy is looking for a trophy and the horns won't be turned into powder for an Asian aphrodisiac. Trophy hunters are the worst of all in my opinion. I suppose there's some justification for taking an animal if you're starving, or if you think it's going to increase your potency, or because you believe it's killing your livestock."

"What are they going to do with the head? Put it on their wall?"

"Probably. It was a magnificent set of antlers. Taxidermists are required to turn in game taken illegally, but you could find someone to do it if you paid enough. People will do anything for money, which is why conservationists are fighting a losing battle. The return of the peregrine falcon is the rare success story in nature so far. Supposedly there is someone out there who is making a collection of rare and endangered birds—kind of a disturbed modern-day Audubon—and they say he'll pay whatever it takes to get one. He wants to have them stuffed in his living room when all the live ones are gone. It's an investment, I guess, and he's banking on the destruction of the environment and the extirpation of species. Each time he takes one he hastens the day. Then we've got the Saudis leaking their oil all over the world, destroying habitats and paying huge sums of money to smuggle the birds that are left in the wild out of it. Why does this prince want the gyr so badly anyway?"

"It's white, it's female. Those are primo in Saudi Arabia where they keep their own women hidden in black veils. There's something else I must tell you. Not that I am suggesting you break the law or do something you despise, but the prince suggested that he would buy your way out of here if you would get him the bird. He offered to set you up in a new life someplace else, or, if you chose to stay in Montana, to get you, as he put it, 'the very best legal representation,' someone with experience in trying murder cases. He suggested Dwight Stillman."

"Dwight Stillman? He's a hired gun."

"He got Mary Hanover off for killing her cowboy husband and that wasn't easy."

"Mary Hanover was probably guilty. I'm not. Besides, why would I want Dwight Stillman when I've got something rare and primo—a white female."

"Thanks."

"Don't mention it. Neil, I think there is someone else you ought to see," March said. "His name is Leo Wolfe and he lives around forty miles west of here. He's a falconer with a kestrel that he's devoted to; he also knew Sandy Pedersen. If you should run into Katharine, by the way, don't mention you're going. She hates Leo."

"With the exception of you and Marie, I don't mention anything I do on this case to anyone and neither should you." I hoped I was making myself clear. The last thing I wanted was him discussing what I was doing with Katharine.

"Of course not, I won't."

"Just for the record, why does Katharine hate Leo Wolfe?" A rhetorical question, perhaps, since Katharine seemed to hate everybody.

"Partially, it's a personality conflict, but also because he's a falconer. Katharine is an animal rights advocate. She thinks it's cruel to keep wild animals."

"What do you think?"

"In principle I'm not crazy about it, but I know Leo takes good care of his bird."

Leo Wolfe lived on the L&W Ranch, a small place by Montana standards, probably only five thousand acres. It was accessed through an arch with a wrought-iron lion

79

forged on the left side of it, a wolf on the right: the L, the W. It had been a long time since the dirt road to the ranch house had seen rain. Montana had had a big dry summer, the kind of summer where the top layer of the state ends up in Pennsylvania and the national parks end up in smoke. I rolled up the windows, held my breath and plowed through the dust thinking that I wouldn't want to do it more than once a year. The house itself was freshly painted and well cared for, a place where a woman's touch had civilized the prairie. There were some cottonwoods and, in season, probably flowers and grass. But the outbuildings, a series of ramshackle, unpainted barns and sheds, looked like whoever took care of them had his eyes on the sky. A beat-up brown truck with a license plate that said TALL was parked at the end of the road. I pulled up next to it.

Leo met me at the door to the house. He was a large, expansive man around fifty, but a young fifty, one of those people who make it seem like the beginning of a decade rather than the end of a life. He wore jeans, boots, a Levi's jacket. His hair was black with only a little gray around the edges. I introduced myself and told him that March had sent me.

"Ma'am, I am pleased to meet you," he said shaking my hand in his large paw. "Anyone who works for March Augusta is a friend of mine."

"I don't exactly work *for* March, I represent him. I'm his lawyer."

"A lawyer? Is that right? Come on inside for a minute, have some coffee, meet the little woman." He hung his cowboy hat on a peg beside the door, sucked in his gut and squeezed himself into the house.

Fay, his wife, was little all right, a tiny gray bird of a woman. If she was at the beginning of anything it was probably old age, retirement, Social Security, senior citizen's discounts. He was a person who expanded as he got older, she contracted, which had probably exaggerated all those little differences that make up a relationship, but it looked like they had settled them by a division of territory. Her domain was obviously the inside of the house; his ended at the peg where he had hung his hat.

"Where are you from?" she asked me.

"Albuquerque, New Mexico."

"Mexico!" she said, fluttering around bringing coffee and cookies that I didn't want. "Goodness, that's another country." One of our fifty was missing again.

Leo settled into the one spot in the room that seemed to belong to him, a faded brown leather armchair with an ottoman. His large hands moved restlessly in his lap. The rest of the room was filled with knickknacks and fragile furniture. I wouldn't want to sneeze suddenly in this room.

"Leo and I took a trip around the country once in the Winnebago, didn't we, dear?" Fay asked, as if the trip would be voided from her memory if he said no. He nodded. "We went across the border into Mexico, and we stopped and I bought salt and pepper shakers." She took the trouble to show them to me, little ceramic imitations of adobe houses; the chimneys were where the salt and pepper came through.

"Actually I'm from *New* Mexico," I said. "It's a state, and we have salt and pepper shakers there, too."

"Oh. We'll have to go there the next time."

Leo listened to this from the depths of his chair maybe to prove that he knew how. "Now, Fay, this lady didn't come all the way out here to talk about salt and pepper shakers. She wants to talk to me about birds. Ain't that right?"

"That and Sandy Pedersen."

"Oh, my goodness, don't get him started on that," Fay twitted. It was a delicate balance, a lion and a wolf in a china shop and already getting restive.

"I'll tell you what, Fay, since Ms. Hamel here is interested in falcons, why don't we just go on outside and take a look at Mimi?"

"I think that's a good idea," said Fay.

I followed Leo across the dusty yard to one of the sheds. It was time for Mimi's lunch—dead mice. Leo opened up a small refrigerator and pulled out a tray on which the mice were laid out like cookie dough, lumps of white fur with pink feet where the chocolate chips belonged. Leo selected one and picked it up by its tail. While he affixed it to Mimi's lure, I took a look around and noted a trap hanging from the wall, a vicious-looking metal instrument caked with dried blood.

"You a trapper?" I asked.

"I do a little predator harvesting now and then. Just my way of cutting back the excess, protecting the habitat. I never caught a human being, but I did get a wily coyote the other day. You want to see him?" He pointed to a pelt hanging on a stretcher in the corner. It was a beautiful coat, thick, luxurious, desert sand, black tipped. I wanted to sink my hand deep into it. It was a treat to see so close, but a large pain for the coyote for such a small pleasure for me.

"Where's Mimi?" I asked.

"Out back."

We went behind the shed to Mimi's chicken-wire enclosure. I was expecting a fierce, angry, elegant bird, a Black Shade, a Shadow of Death or an Avenger, but Mimi was smaller and browner than I had expected. She was about ten inches tall with reddish-brown wings and a white breast that was streaked with cinnamon. She had enormous dark eyes and black sideburns on her white face. She sat on a post with jesses dangling from her legs and cakked once when she saw us.

"She has incredible eyes," I said.

"Hawks see a hell of a lot clearer and farther than any other animal and they see in color. A peregrine falcon's eyes are larger and heavier than a man's. Hawks have big mouths, too, just like some people I know. You always feed 'em from the lure." He threw the lure with the dead mouse attached to it toward Mimi.

She flapped her wings and fluttered down from her perch. I expected her to rip rapaciously into the meat around the heart of the mouse, but she sheared off the head first, tore out some guts, then ate delicately with careful, precise bites. As she ate she wrapped her wings around her like a cape.

"That's called mantling," said Leo. "It's her way of keeping her food to herself."

Mimi was fascinating, but she was not the falcon of myth and legend for which people are willing to kill and pay a lot of money. Even Leo seemed disappointed. "There are no good hawks and bad hawks," he said. "You can say that about people, but not about hawks, hawks just do what they do, but my Mimi is well trained. I trained her myself. She's loyal, too. She's not gonna fly away from me on some winter wind."

But there's a price for loyalty. Mimi wouldn't stun wolves and dive at speeds of two hundred miles an hour. She was a female, but she wasn't big and she wasn't white either. She was a kestrel, the falcon of commoners, not of kings.

We left her to her mouse, went back out front and sat on a split-rail fence. "I'm gonna be real sorry if they send March away," Leo said. "Real sorry. March is a good guy and all heart from the belt up. His life wouldn't be worth a damn in a federal prison. There are too many people inside already who are there because of him. Anyone knows him knows he didn't kill Pedersen, or anybody else either.

Betts knows it, too. He's got some other reason for locking March up."

"That thought occurred to me, but I don't know what the reason is, do you?"

"Guess you'd have to ask Betts that."

"I did. I didn't get an answer."

"He can be a tight-lipped son of a bitch when he wants to be. I don't suppose he told you what Pedersen's been up to either."

"Only the obvious."

"Pedersen was pretty obvious, all right, and so's that damn government. Well, here's the way I see it." He hitched himself up higher on the fence, settling in for a good yarn with himself exactly where he wanted to be—the center of attention. "Sandy was a fool. He got himself arrested for dealing in elk horns a few years back and you got to try real hard to get arrested by the federal government for anything, especially that. He was sent up for three years, out in six months—parole. No sooner does he get out of the pen than he's driving a new Buick, visiting every bar in Montana, talking about the raptors he's got to sell. He's got peregrines, he's got gyrs, he's even got bald eagles for the Indians, and he's looking for buyers. Pretty soon he starts calling up falconers all over the West and then before you know it, he's snooping around here telling me about this gyrfalcon, largest, whitest falcon in the sky. Can stun a wolf, did you know that?"

"Yes, in the Middle Ages they were used to hunt wolves." If he'd heard me, he didn't let it show.

"It's a passager bird, he says, just the right age, the most beautiful bird he's ever seen and he wants to sell it to me. There's no way you could come by a bird like that legally." He shook his head, took the cowboy hat off, put it back on.

What would that do to a man with a Fay and a Mimi?

"It was like bringing Marilyn Monroe around and asking if she could spend the night," he said wistfully.

"What did you say?"

"I said I'd think about it, but it's illegal to buy and sell raptors and the price he was asking was a whole lot more than I could afford anyway. So what's it sound like to you?"

"It sounds like . . ."

"A sting operation. Damn right and Pedersen was about as subtle as a buffalo. Could hear him coming a mile away with your blinders on. The second time he comes out here to talk to me a cherry picker is right behind him. It sets up out there like it's playing with the phone lines, but there was nothing wrong with my phone. I called the phone company just to make sure that it wasn't their truck. It was the feds trying to tape my conversation with Pedersen. They didn't get nothing from me but a suggestion of what else they could do with their money."

The fence railing was digging a channel into my butt. I stood up. "Betts lied to me."

"No he didn't. You think about it for a minute. I know Betts pretty well. Maybe he didn't tell you the whole truth, but he didn't lie to you either."

What had Betts said? "I am not concealing anything about your client."

"Just last Friday Pedersen calls me up again and tells me he's got an offer for a hundred thousand dollars and he's giving me one last chance to up it and get the gyr. That's a whole lot of money for a bird, but I guess there was someone around ready to pay it because I stop hearing from Pedersen and the next thing you know he's dead. The government's trying to entrap someone, but whoever it is didn't kill him."

"Why not?" He heard what he wanted to. He looked down from his railing, at me, at the ground. He was the almighty man, I was the little woman. The egos of middle-aged men never cease to amaze me.

"Because they didn't get the bird." He spoke slowly like he was teaching me the language.

"So?"

"So, if they didn't get the bird, the government hasn't got anything on 'em, and there's no reason to kill Pedersen. Anyway anyone who really wanted that gyr would get it first and kill Pedersen later, don't you think?"

"Not necessarily. Maybe the killer knows how to trap the gyr, or can find someone else to do it. In the eyes of the law anyone who negotiated with Pedersen would be guilty whether that person actually purchased the bird or not. It could be a falconer who found out Pedersen had set him up and wanted to get rid of the source of the evidence."

"It wasn't a falconer, I'm tellin' you. There are plenty of other people around who hated Pedersen's guts. That man had it comin' and goin'." He climbed down from the fence. "You give my best to March. Goodness is a rough trail, especially where he is. And don't forget to say hello to that girlfriend of his, Kate." He grinned. "Now there's a woman with spirit. She can park her boots under my bed anytime she wants to. I like the way she moves, like she's carrying an armful of puppies, and I like the way she drives tearing up the highway like a bat out of Carlsbad."

"I hear she speaks well of you, too."

"I bet she does, but I'll tell you something. She hated Pedersen's guts and she's got a lot more traps in *her* shed than I got here."

8

So our government was out
trawling for poachers. When they spread the net they would
pull in a dolphin (the prince) along with the tuna (Heinz).
That could explain why Betts wanted so badly to get
someone in jail for the murder. Pedersen had been a government operative and the government does not take kindly
to the murder of one of its own.

A mile or so beyond the iron archway of the L&W I
pulled off the highway and picked through the tapes in
March's glove compartment until I found a map. Freezeout East, where the prince was staying, was only fifty miles
north. Hadn't he asked me to call as soon as I spoke to
March? Betts acted fast; it might be our last chance to talk
before he pulled in the net. I couldn't imagine the prince
in jail, even a minimum security country club where he
could bring his own servants and perfect his golf game,
but Heinz was the kind of operator who could make himself at home in prisons all over the globe and probably

already had. Maybe that was where he'd learned his English.

I headed north, alone with my sharpened perceptions, through the wide open spaces of the Blackfeet Indian Reservation, the purple mountains' majesty on my left. The Blackfeet are a plains tribe famous for a dance in which they rip the flesh from their chests. How different they are, I thought, from the peaceful Pueblo tribes of the Southwest. The Plains Indians were the warriors, the Pueblos were the farmers; the hawks, the sparrows; the predators, the prey. Maybe there was something about the wide openness of the plains that brought out predatory instincts. More likely it was the other way around. The narrow valleys around the Rio Grande, with their temperate weather and soft cliffs that face south to provide sun in the winter and shade in the summer, brought out latent cultivating instincts. After all, man was a hunter for hundreds of thousands of years before he planted his first kernel of corn.

I don't live far from the Rio Grande but it hasn't brought out any desire to garden in me. I have a cactus that has forgotten whatever it knew about water and a Kid who doesn't require a lot of tending either. Does that make me a hunter? When you think about it, the hunter has an interesting relationship to the natural world. She waits and watches and enters the mind of the prey. Her senses are sharpened but she's not really alone because she is always relating to her intended victim. There is a mythological dimension to the hunter, the sense that she has a special wisdom, but what does she know except her victims? It's the hunter with her knowledge of the interconnectedness of species who wants to preserve them, if only so they'll be around in sufficient quantity to kill. The hunter understands that nature has a carefully worked-out system of checks and balances, or did before man came along. Predators keep the herd healthy by killing the old and weak. They also keep any one species from destructively multiplying. To cultivators, however, predators are pests to be gotten rid of.

The Freezeout East Hotel stood at the edge of the Rockies, one of those places built by the railroads in their heyday to lure tourists from East to West. It was a massive building supported by uncut logs about six feet in diameter, an Adirondack camp magnified a few hundred times. It wasn't the peak season and the only vehicles in the parking lot were the prince's red Mercedes and a couple of pickup trucks. I was hoping to have a few words alone with Heinz, but didn't know how I'd manage it.

I parked the van, walked up to the porch and let myself in. The place was as big and empty as the hotel in *The Shining*. Down some back corridor I expected to find a crazed Jack Nicholson sitting alone at his desk typing maniacally, "All work and no play makes Jack a dull boy." There was no one to be seen at the front desk or anyplace else.

If I were the predator and Heinz the prey, how would I track him? I tried to enter the mind of a polyester fellow who negotiated in the international black market. Where would he be at dusk of a November day? In the bar, of course, but this bar was closed. I tried again. My prey would be frustrated, angry, in need of escape. That would place him in his room with a good detective novel or bad TV. Stalking the prince was easier. At sundown he'd naturally be in his room, prostrating himself toward Mecca and praying to Allah.

I walked up the stairway, down a long carpeted hall, silent as my running shoes could be. There was nothing but more silence behind the first ten pine doors, but then my efforts were rewarded, and I head a guttural, mystical mumbling. The prince at prayer. I didn't think Heinz was servile enough to sleep on the carpet outside the master's door, but I didn't think he would be far away either. I stopped at the next doorway and eavesdropped on the relentlessly cheerful, international language of a TV commercial. I knocked.

Heinz came to the door holding a glass with something dark brown and unappetizing inside. He was wearing polyester pants and a shiny shirt. His face had a mashed-in, flattened look as if he had just walked into the door. He had pale skin, clipped hair and flat reptilian eyes, a man who'd be at home wherever snakes meet. "Ms. Hamel," he said, attempting a smile.

"I'd like to talk to you," I said. "Do you think we could go downstairs? I wouldn't want to disturb the prince while he is saying his prayers."

"Of course." The smile didn't make it; the flattened-out bones were working against the lips. His eyes brightened, though, with the obsequious glow of an operator about to make a deal. He thought I had come to tell him that March wanted nothing better than to hasten the extinction of another species and possibly replace present counsel with Dwight Stillman.

Heinz followed me down the hallway and the stairs, obviously accustomed to stepping lightly. If I hadn't turned around occasionally I never would have guessed he was there.

We arranged ourselves on a sofa in the lobby where some invisible person had turned on the lights, illuminating the massive beams crisscrossing the peaks of the cathedral ceiling.

"Nice place you've got here," I said.

"The prince likes to be comfortable." The lips persisted, the bones yielded, and he managed a stiff grin. "So your client has decided to accept our offer." He didn't bother to make it a question.

"Not exactly. He wants to know a little more about the prince before he makes up his mind." Maybe the words weren't March's, or the thoughts either, but the goal was. "If he is going to take a great personal risk by escaping from jail to get the prince his bird, he'd like to know exactly why the prince wants it."

"Prince Sahid is the second son." He stopped as if that explained something.

"So?"

"His father, the king, is dying. Cancer. But nobody knows this, only the sons. The king loves falcons and he wants more than anything in the world to have a white female. There will be a big party for him next month. The prince wants to give him his dream—the bird—before he dies."

"And he probably also wants to get his fair share of the inheritance, too," I thought out loud.

"It's not like that. In Saudi Arabia people respect their parents. The prince is very good to his father."

Good to his father, bad to the gyr. The prince was thinking locally but not acting globally. "Have you been working for the royal family long?"

"This is the first time." There was a slight twitch at the corner of a hooded lid. It was a big-time career move, naturally he was eager to succeed.

Heinz waved his hand, a gesture he had probably picked up from his boss, only he lacked the prince's natural grace and long fingers. Heinz's own fingers were short and stubby and his nails bitten down. "Money is no problem, you know."

"But my client's health could be. After all, the last person who tried to remove that bird from its nest took a high dive into an empty pool and that was after he'd had his face blown away."

Did he believe March had committed the crime? Did he

not? I was curious to see his reaction, but there wasn't one. "I assume that the day Pedersen died he had gone to the aerie to get you the bird," I continued.

"That was our agreement."

"You trusted him?"

"Not exactly. Pedersen was playing with us, trying to get the price up. We made him an offer and he said he had to think about it. Then he came back and said he had a better bid. The prince went to school in England. He never learned to bargain like the old man. Everybody says bargaining is natural to the Arabs but they have to be taught like everybody else, and the prince was never taught. Every time Pedersen comes back, the prince offers more. He is an impatient boy and he doesn't care how much he spends, but it's bad for my reputation to pay too much." His reptilian eyes got a few degrees colder. "I did not like Pedersen. He was a liar. I prefer to deal with someone I trust. Your client is honest, right?"

"As honest as can be." Pedersen provoked interesting reactions in those who knew him, a fool to some, a knave to others, like the Koshares at Pueblo ceremonials who paint themselves in black and white stripes and weave among the dancers, acting like clowns while they draw the heat from the crowd. Heinz was telling me too much. Maybe it was the confidence my professional manner inspired, maybe it was the poorly developed ingratiating skill of a naturally uningratiating man. "But you did trust Pedersen to bring you the bird?" I asked.

"In the black market once an agreement is made it is an agreement. We don't have lawyers or courts. You give your word, you keep it. If you don't . . ."

You get your face blown off and fall from a great height. He didn't need to elaborate. "Do you think Pedersen was betraying another bidder by promising the gyr to you and that's why he got killed?"

"You want to know what I think?" It didn't sound like he was asked very often. "I don't think there was anybody else. I think Pedersen was making another buyer up. Who else would pay a hundred thousand for a bird? I think the person who killed him was a conservationist. They care about animals, but they don't care about people. If it was your client, I would say congratulations to him except that he has kept us so far from getting the bird."

"So you were going to meet Pedersen Wednesday night and get the gyr?"

"Yes." He was beginning to get suspicious of my direct examination. The hoods over his eyes lowered.

But I only had one question more. "How were you going to get her out of the country?"

He shrugged. "No problem. The prince had diplomatic immunity. He can take out anything he wants in his diplomatic pouch. Customs will not bother the prince."

Betts's eyes would flutter when he found *that* out.

"Good evening." Those words were spoken regally by His Majesty, who leaned over the rustic balcony and smiled at me from the second story. "So your client has decided to work with us."

"We've been discussing it. Why don't you come down so we can talk."

The prince walked down the stairway. With his slender boyish figure, he had a natural elegance even without the robes. This time he wore a white shirt of the finest cotton, a number of gold chains, and Ralph Lauren jeans.

"Ms. Hamel and I have been having an interesting discussion," Heinz said.

"I'm certain you have," said the prince. "Have you agreed on terms?"

It's tough to have a job where you represent someone as an agent, a lawyer or a black marketeer. When you get right down to it, the person you are representing almost always thinks he can do it better himself. The prince already seemed eager to get rid of Heinz.

"Not exactly," I said. "My client's first concern is for the welfare of the bird. Before he will even consider your offer, he must know how the gyr will be treated."

"Excellently," said the prince. "My father has the best falconers in Arabia. Their families and ours have been intertwined for generations. If the welfare of the gyrfalcon is his only concern there is no problem. She will be treated like a princess—even better, she will be treated like a prince." He threw his transparent ball way up into the beams and clapped his hands. "So, if we have an agreement we must have some coffee to celebrate. Heinz, would you see if you can find some?"

Heinz stood up. Before I had a chance to disavow this so-called agreement, the front door opened. Two men stepped into the lobby wearing Stetsons, guns and law enforcement suits. One was Greg Porter, who had not so long ago put March in jail, the other was his deputy. Betts hadn't slowed his pace any.

"Prince Sahid?" Porter said. "Heinz Hoffman? I have warrants for your arrests. Conspiring to buy and sell wild birds is a felony."

The prince smiled, opened his palms and let the ball fall in. "Bird feathers," he said.

Heinz uttered a short word in an ugly language and then he said in English, "We have done nothing wrong. We have taken no birds anywhere."

"You ought to read them their rights," I told Porter.

Heinz's lids dropped another millimeter as his flat eyes focused on me. "Did you have anything to do with this?" he asked at the same time Porter said, "Haven't I seen you someplace before?"

"No," I answered and, "Yes."

Porter read the suspects their rights and then he and his deputy handcuffed them and escorted them to the back of his car for the drive to Fire Pond. I presumed the jailer would find suitable accommodations for their stay, and they'd find out for themselves how easy the county jail was to break out of. If that didn't work, they could always afford to hire the very best legal representation.

I let them get a head start as I didn't want to be tailgating the law all the way down the highway. I hung around the lobby for a few minutes enjoying the peaceful atmosphere of Freezeout East out of season and looking through a rack of postcards: the park in spring, summer, winter, fall, the lakes, the snow-covered peaks, the bears, mountain goats, elk and birds. A young man with blond hair and a Mormon smile appeared in a doorway—the missing hotel staff.

"What was that all about?" he asked.

"Your guests were arrested."

"No shit. What for?"

"Trafficking in wild birds. It's a felony."

He shook his head. "Wow!"

"You said it."

"If you're looking for a room we don't have any. But there's a motel in Barton that stays open all year." This kid's megawatt smile was out of season, too. He should have taken it back to Utah with him when the summer was over.

I thought fondly of my wall-to-wall efficiency at the Aspen Inn. "I've got a room," I replied. "But it looks like you're open to me. Weren't the prince and Heinz staying here before their accommodations in the Fire Pond County Jail opened up?"

"Are you kidding? They rented the whole place just for them."

Was there no respect for the value of the declining dollar?

I picked out some postcards and paid $1.25. Then I drove back to Fire Pond under the big stars and a lopsided moon, keeping my attention focused on the road past all those white crosses that indicated others before me had not.

"Time is of the essence" is one
of those colorful phrases that show there's romance in the
language, if not the spirit, of the law. My outer clock said
it was Monday evening, the return trip ticket was for
Thursday, and unless I solved the murder in forty-eight
hours and got March out of jail, I wasn't going to make it.
I'd have to cancel the discount ticket and pay the full fare.
Was the difference in fare a legitimate legal expense? Yes.
Was I going to bill it to March? Maybe. There were issues
to consider: Could he afford it? Would he think I was a
greedy attorney? Was he a sweet person, a gentle person,
a person who might not refuse to use a condom if you
asked him, who might even offer? A naturalist with a re-
markable lack of ego unlike certain members of my profession? Was I getting soft on a client, losing the beat of this
case and my fine edge as well?

I decided to call my partner, Brink—that always sharpened me up. It was now eight o'clock in the evening and

I sat on the plaid sofa bed at the Aspen Inn. Brink would either be at home or at Bailey's mooning over Sally, a former bartender who'd moved to California, probably to get away from him. The chances of his being in the office were minute. I found him at home watching TV.

"You're going to stay in Montana?" he asked me.

"Just for a while, anyway. It's a great opportunity. It's been a long time since I've defended a murder case—law school to be exact." It might have been interesting to argue the various legal points with my partner. Did Betts have legitimate grounds for holding March? What were the ramifications of the sting operation? What would I do when Tom Mitchell got back? But Brink likes to limit his arguments to the mundane, matters of concern to self.

"That means I have to go on handling your cases."

"What cases?" I'd only been away a week, but I was already having trouble remembering. It seemed to me there was a divorce in there, a real estate closing, possibly a DWI.

"Well, the Larrows are arguing about health insurance, Toni Arrowsmith didn't get her mortgage and, let's see, what else? I'm not in the office, you know, I don't have all your information at my fingertips."

It wasn't the first time I'd wondered what rotten thing I had done in a past life to deserve him. "Brink, you can cope. I know you can. I'm taking on the federal government here. Just think of all the new business that will bring in when I win."

"Well," he sniffed.

"I have to go. There's someone at the door. I'll call in a few days."

No one was at the door, but it seemed counterproductive to pay long distance to argue with Brink. Now that business affairs had been taken care of, there was the inner clock where timing was of the essence—the Kid. If I mailed the postcard tomorrow, he probably wouldn't get it by Thursday when I was due back, not unless I sent it Express Mail. We're the ones who keep Express Mail and Fed Ex in business anyway—procrastinating lawyers. I could call, but he probably wouldn't be home and whoever answered the phone might not speak English. Besides, some things are best said on paper. With the written word you can say precisely what you wish, no one will interrupt you, no one will answer back, and you can revise until you get it right. That's what lawyers are good at—revision.

I took out my first postcard, a picture of a mama grizzly and her young sampling the flowers in an alpine meadow. "Kid, I'm going to be later than I expected. Something has come up, an important case that I am working on. Miss you. See you soon. Love, Neil."

It wasn't exactly right. I picked up the next one, two mountain goats balancing on a tightrope-size alpine ledge. "I won't be back on Thursday. I'm working on an important case here. Hopefully, it won't be too long. I'll be in touch. Best wishes, Neil."

That wasn't it either. I took a blue-green, crystal-clear mountain lake surrounded by snowy peaks. "Kid, the opportunity has come along to work on a really important murder case, so I won't be back Thursday. Shouldn't take too long. See you soon. Neil."

I was beginning to wish I had a word processor. There was one more mountain goat card. I liked the symbolic significance of that and tried again: "Kid, I won't be back on Thursday as the opportunity has come along to work on an important case. It shouldn't be too long. Montana is beautiful. See you soon. Love, Neil."

To put love in or not, that was the tough question. It

was a lot easier to use words of endearment in Spanish. If I sent it in an Express Mail envelope at least it wouldn't be read by his partner at the shop.

That accomplished and with a postcard to spare I turned on the oven, got out the Cuervo Gold, went to the refrigerator where there was a plastic ice tray that someone had forgotten to fill. The ice machine was located in an alcove in the stairwell but it was tough getting there because the hallway was squished full of plump-armed women in pastel evening gowns. The Rebekahs, I figured, as I'd seen them welcomed with the movable letters on the sign outside the Aspen Inn along with their counterparts, the International Order of Odd Fellows, known to some as the 100 Fs. The ladies wore polyester pink, aqua and lavender gowns with one bare shoulder or a modest slice of cleavage. Their hair was curly white or blue-gray. Most of them wore glasses, talked and smiled a lot. As I squeezed my way through, I wondered if it was necessary to have an Odd Fellow to be a Rebekah. It could be a species that mated and nested for life.

I got to the ice machine under the stairs, dipped in the dipper. A woman stood next to me playing the keno machine that appears in out-of-the-way niches in this state. She had a thin, weathered face that could be described with an *h* word: hawk, hatchet, hard. A cigarette dangled from her lip and she wore skin-tight jeans with high-heeled boots. A woman maybe who had traveled hard, lived in other people's abandoned nests and mated only for the season.

"Jesus Christ," she said, "can't win for losing no more. You play these shit fuckers?"

"Not yet."

She sized me up, wondering maybe if it was too late to start or too early. "Name's Gloria," she said.

"Neil."

She didn't even suggest my name belonged on a man. I liked her already for that. "You got time yet." She plugged in her quarter.

"It's of the essence," I said.

The Rebekahs had gone into a conference room and shut the door behind them. The hallway was empty, but the air seemed disturbed. There was an echo of coos, the smell of cheap perfume. I walked through it and stopped in the bar to see if I could pick up a few limes for my drink.

Cortland James happened to be sitting in a booth nursing a beer. "Good evening," he said.

"Hi," I replied. As I had a few minutes to kill while the bartender got my limes together, I joined him.

"How's the criminal investigation going?" he asked me.

"Coming along."

"I'll buy you a drink if you'd like. I'd be interested in hearing your theories."

"Some other time, maybe, I'm pretty tired right now." The bartender hadn't come back yet, so to make conversation I said, "You like that beer?" He was drinking some bland American brand.

"It's cheap," he replied. "In my family that's enough to recommend it."

Being bland probably didn't hurt either. He brushed his bangs back from his forehead, a boyish gesture that might be considered endearing by some. It made me wonder what his nickname had been: Corie, Cortie, Cortlie?

"I didn't think anybody drank American beer anymore. Even in Montana they probably sell Dos Equis, if they don't have Tecate," I said.

"Tecate. That's the one they drink with the lime and salt, right?"

"Yup."

"You have interesting drinking habits. Did you pick them up in Mexico?"

"Sort of. Did you get into aguardiente when you were in Guatemala? You can't get drunk much cheaper than aguardiente. That ought to appeal to your family." Aguardiente was rotgut that some people drank out of a plastic bag with a straw, clear as gin unless it was tinted pink or blue or gold. You could probably get blind drunk on it for less than a quarter.

Cortland was amused. "I skipped the aguardiente, but I did drink Tecate in Mexico. They always said that they put the lime and salt on the can to disguise the rotten taste."

He waited for me to ask him what he was doing in Mexico, but I didn't, so he told me anyway. "I was in Nuevo León looking for the aplomado falcon. It's a lovely bird, very rare in the United States, but they still exist in Mexico. I was fortunate enough to find one."

The golden lights that came on in his pale eyes when he talked about the falcon were a rogue element in his bored face. He leaned forward enthusiastically, pulling back the sleeves of his Shetland sweater and revealing the frayed cuff of an Oxford cloth shirt. The collar, I happened to notice, was frayed, too. Maybe Cortland, like the Great Gatsby, had a cabinet full of shirts, only his collection was valued not for its beauty or silky fabrics but for the signs of wear and tear. Instead of picking the most elegant shirt for a particular occasion, he'd pick the shabbiest. Is this an occasion for a ripped sleeve or a frayed cuff? As the Kid asked me once, why do people in this country dress like they're poor?

"Your shirt is torn," I said.

"Really," he looked down at the cuff. "That puts me in good company; so, I might add, are your jeans."

He had me on that one. My Levi's were a little tattered around the edges. They'd been to Mexico, too, but at least real people wore Levi's, or they used to before the price went up to thirty dollars a pair. The bartender showed up with my limes.

"You're positive I can't interest you in a drink?" Cortland said.

"Some other time, maybe." I picked up the limes and prepared to go back to my room. That's the kind of drinker I'd become.

"I hope so." He smiled. His expression had something other than birders' camaraderie in it, but I couldn't say what. If it was a pass, it was pretty half-hearted, but, except for exotic birds, half-hearted seemed to be Cortland James's style. Maybe it went with the territory. There's a mixture of arrogance and self-loathing that seems to be endemic at certain Eastern schools. Guys like that can't even make a pass with conviction.

"Good-bye," I said.

I went back to my room, fixed my drink and just as I was getting comfortable with it there was a knock at the door. "Yeah," I opened it up. Avery was standing in the hallway, his eyes aglow as if he'd spent another night in the wilderness. He executed a happy little two-step when he saw me. "What a day we had," he said, "what a day."

Now that I was set up for entertaining, I invited him in and offered him a drink which he declined—he had a natural high. "Did you go back to Freezeout?" I asked.

"Sure did and we got a great look at the gyr. She's a beauty. We saw her take a duck. She flies—zoom—fast and straight like that." He made a dive-bombing motion with his hand. "I'd love to take you back there. I bet you never even got to see her the first time."

"You're right about that."

"Let's go before you leave. When *are* you leaving?"

"Not till I get March out of jail I hope. I'm canceling my return discount fare. I called my office to tell them they can manage without me. How about you?"

"Discount fares don't mean a thing at my age. I might as well waste what's left before my children do. Besides, I wouldn't want to leave while March was still in prison. Have there been any breakthroughs?" He sat down lightly on the arm of the sofa bed.

"There's been a development. I don't know whether I'd call it a breakthrough."

"Anything you can talk about?" He jumped back up.

I thought about it. Betts's sting operation would probably be all over the news tomorrow, so what difference would it make if I told Avery tonight? It would give me a bit of an edge with Betts to keep my silence, though, if only in my own mind. "You'll hear about it soon enough. What have *you* come up with? Anything?"

"Only that Pedersen was sleazy and dishonest and that nobody seemed to care whether he lived or died."

"Did you happen to hike up to the aerie while you were out there?" I asked, thinking about the black line that leads out of the rug.

"John King wanted to, but Cortland talked him out of it."

"He would."

"Cortland comes from a very prominent family. Did you know that? His grandfather was a U.S. senator. His father is one of the most respected conservationists in the world, a tall, distinguished-looking gentleman. It's a family that has quite a standard to maintain. I guess it's made Cortland a bit of a stuffed shirt."

Prick might be more accurate.

"Cortland used to be a ne'er-do-well. No one ever thought he would amount to much, traveling all over the world looking at birds as if he hadn't quite found his niche in life."

One of those hobbies that the rich and bland went in

for. "He can afford it and it seems to be something he cares about. Isn't that enough?" I asked.

"For most people it would be more than enough, but in a family like that one is expected to do good works so his father made him the head of the Conservation Committee."

"Nice of Daddy to start him at the top."

"He was right about the aerie. You shouldn't walk up to a bird's nest because one predator will smell and follow another predator's tracks. If the first predator doesn't succeed, the next one probably will."

"There's something I'm curious about, Avery. You've worked with falconers. What do you think of them?"

"It's a desire to connect with another species, with wild bloods, with nature. A songbird can be bought with a handful of sunflower seed, but even a trained hawk will always retain its fascinatingly remote essence. They are alien and they are stubborn. For myself I'm happy just to watch. When the Falcon Fund first reintroduced peregrines in Kentucky we had a pair that nested on Rolling Rock. Peregrines had always nested there before the DDT tragedy; it's a perfect site, a high cliff with a lake below. Both of these falcons had been released elsewhere, but came there to nest. They had two young; unfortunately, before the young had fully fledged, the female was injured. She was found about ten miles from the nest with a damaged wing, and a farmer brought her in to us. We were able to heal the wing, but it took six weeks. In the meantime the male was making a valiant effort to feed the hungry young but then another female flew in. She wasn't banded and we have no idea where she came from or how she found the male, except that the vegetation is lusher around the aeries, because it has been nitrogen-enriched by the excrement. She was very large and powerful so we named her Diana, the huntress. Di drove the fledglings from the nest and she wouldn't let the male feed them anymore either. Although she didn't attack them directly, they probably weren't mature enough to survive on their own. We lost track of them, anyway."

"What happened to the first female?"

"We released her when she was healed, but she disappeared, too. Diana stayed and she and the male came back the following year and nested again."

"It's a good story." And the essence of wildlife's appeal: to do so naturally all the things humans try to repress.

"Isn't it? You see why I am content to observe. But falconers seek more intimate contact. It's not enough for them to watch. They want to control the wild spirit. They're the ultimate romantics."

But not the only ones. There was Avery himself, who bid me good-night then and would have bent over and kissed my hand if I'd offered it. A nocturnal being, his eyes widened as the night deepened, and he probably went out and scanned the hallways until he found someone else to watch and talk to. Avery seemed to be peaking at his present age of eighty-two, but he'd probably excelled at every age he'd been through.

I picked up Joan's journal and thought about the role models that were available to me. I didn't know any eighty-year-old women lawyers. I didn't even know any forty-five-year-old women lawyers and very few my own age either. Close at hand there were the Rebekahs, ladies who'd taken one great big risk in their lives—gotten married. And then there was Gloria, who probably risked what little she had daily on the keno machine. A woman could grow old soft and protected or hard and on the edge, a plump hen, a hungry hawk. Or like Joan, soft and malleable on the surface, but with a secret, flinty dream. Single older women were in an interesting position these days. They were becoming the risk takers, maybe because they had nothing left to lose.

I was getting near the end of the Raptor section, close to the Personal. I read:

The Falcon Fund is making a major effort to reintroduce peregrines into the wild and should be commended for it; they are doing an excellent job. They breed the birds in captivity and raise them until they are about four weeks old when they are placed in a box at a cliff site. Until they are ready to fly and hunt for themselves, they are fed by the staff who are very capable and careful not to let the birds see them. They call this hacking. Even with no adult role model, the young peregrines instinctively know how to fly. Flying comes easily to them, but landing is hard.

Like athletes or knights, falcons perfect their skills by lengthy practice. But even when they are mature and skilled flyers they reenact their adolescence every day by repeating the steps they went through when they first learned to fly. Like knights or sportsmen there is a code they follow. Those who adapt to the code survive, those who break it don't.

The older birds, the haggards, are glad to be free of the young once they are raised. They like their solitude.

Falconry has always been a male sport, that is, the falconers have been male, the preferred falcons female. Men seem to be fascinated by wild, passionate, abandoned females; they want to control them. Falconry gives them that opportunity. Traditionally when women abandoned themselves to their own passions, they were considered to have broken the code.

In *The Peregrine Falcon* Robert Murphy wrote about the capture of a female: "The wide sky and its safety net were gone, the men were staring at her. In her world a stare was preliminary to an attack, and for a moment she was prepared to withstand it; her feathers stood out, her eyes burned with fury, and she hissed at them."

"Hawks are psychic," T. H. White wrote in *The Goshawk*. They sense the mood of those around them, and "rage is contagious between unconscious hearts."

Falconers become very fond of their birds, a deep rapport develops. Some have kept and flown a peregrine for as long as thirty years. Some people think falconry is a master-slave relationship, but in my experience with falconers, the master becomes the slave.

It's an obsession I can understand. Once you start observing falcons, it is impossible to see enough. The best passage I've read on that subject is from *The Peregrine* by J. A. Baker: "To be recognized and accepted by a peregrine you must wear the same clothes, travel by the same way, perform actions in the same order. Like all birds, it fears the unpredictable. . . . Hood the glare of the eyes, hide the white tremor of the hands, shade the stark reflecting face, assume the stillness of a tree. A peregrine fears nothing he can see clearly and far off. Approach him across open ground with a steady unfaltering movement. Let your shape grow in size but do not alter its outline. . . . Be alone. Shun the furtive oddity of man, cringe from the hostile eyes of farms. Learn to fear. To share fear is the greatest bond of all. The hunter must become the thing he hunts. What is, is now, must have the quivering intensity of an arrow thudding into a tree. Yesterday is dim and monochrome. A week ago you were not born. Persist, endure, follow, watch."

10

The next morning the Rebekahs, still in their pastel evening gowns, were having breakfast in the coffee shop, noisy and irritating as songbirds that sit in a tree outside your window and warble until you're forced to throw something at them or get up. Either they put their evening gowns back on in the morning, or they'd been up all night.

"Good morning," the hostess said, but I knew my morning would be a whole lot better without a roomful of Rebekahs.

"Do they always dress like that?" I asked her. "It seems kind of impractical."

"They had an initiation ceremony, so they stayed up all night. Care for a table or a booth?"

"Neither, thanks."

I left the coffee shop, drove down the road to McDonald's and had an Egg McMuffin. You could count on two things at McDonald's, the food was full of cholesterol and no one was cheerful. It was a little after nine when I finished. Time for Betts to be in his office so I called from a pay phone in the parking lot.

"I can see you only if you come by immediately," he said. "I've got the press coming at ten and a full day after that."

"I'm on my way," I replied. It didn't leave me any time to get to the post office and mail the Kid's postcard Express Mail, but as long as I got it in by late afternoon I'd be all right. Betts sat at his desk with a big smile on his sun-dappled face. He was pleased with himself and why shouldn't he be? The federal government had just spent millions of dollars to stop a few-hundred-thousand-dollar trade in raptors, a cost-effective operation from their point of view. His name would soon be in the papers and some nameless superior in D.C. was no doubt pleased with his performance. He was a lot calmer, his eyes darted more slowly, he cracked his knuckles less. His success had put him in a talkative mood.

"We had one hundred agents in twelve states over the weekend. I've pulled in thirty falconers, all of whom were negotiating illegally for birds of prey. There's a large international trade in these birds." He smiled and his butterfly eyes had a new luster, as if a storm had blown up and washed off a layer of prairie dust.

"I suppose a lot of your evidence came from Pedersen," I said.

"He was instrumental."

"I can see why you were so upset by his untimely death."

"We missed a few falconers that we hadn't collected enough evidence on yet, but we got the major offenders, including Heinz Hoffman, an international dealer. You may be sure he won't be getting out on bail."

"What happened to the prince?"

He blinked. "We had to let him go."

"Why's that?" I asked just to see his eyeballs flutter.

"He has diplomatic immunity," Betts said.

"Too bad. Wasn't he your biggest purchaser, the one who kept the prices up?"

Betts slowly cracked the knuckles on his left hand, then the right. The lizard ran up, down and spun around in the middle of my back. "I am aware that you were in touch with the prince and Hoffman. I wish you had left the investigation to us."

"Actually, it was the prince who got in touch with me. It would have helped if you had told me what Pedersen was up to. As I said before, there are rules of discovery."

"I was about to close down the sting operation. I couldn't jeopardize the government's position."

"It wasn't exactly the world's best-kept secret."

He let that one go by.

"We lost the prince but we still have thirty other falconers to prosecute. The government feels very strongly about raptors," he said. "After all, the bald eagle is our national symbol."

"It does seem a little unfair to use one felon to lure in some more."

"What's unfair about it? They committed a crime, they ought to pay. I've learned something about falconers from this operation. I've learned how they think and how they feel and I'll tell you something. Most of them have gone off the deep end. They become obsessed with these birds; it's all they think about and care about. We pulled in a state biologist in Wyoming who risked his career to buy a peregrine." He shook his head, a careerist himself, certainly not a romantic.

"Most passions are absurd when you stand outside them, aren't they?" I said. "Besides, the criminal is probably no more obsessed with what he does than the cop who's obsessed with catching him. If you think like them, what's so different from being them?"

He didn't answer me, just laid his swollen-knuckled hands on the table. My back tensed, the lizard approached the starting gate, but Betts picked up a pencil instead.

"I gather you are relying on evidence you received from Pedersen to prosecute your case against the falconers," I continued.

"I've got what I need."

"You must know that he didn't have the best reputation around town—not only was he considered a crook, he was considered an incompetent as well. A knave *and* a fool."

"Maybe, but he was ours."

"You've pulled in thirty falconers, you said."

"Right."

"You know, any one of them could have figured out he was being entrapped and had more of a motive to kill Pedersen than my client did, and probably the means and opportunity besides. I've been told that Pedersen was about as subtle as a buffalo. Don't you think it's time to let up on March?"

"Aren't you forgetting some very important pieces of evidence? March Augusta had wolf-wipers in his shed; his prints were on the trap that killed Pedersen. Now if you will excuse me, I have reporters waiting outside." He began to arrange his hair and straighten his tie in preparation for the media event.

"You're excused," I said.

I went next to the stone fortress in downtown Fire Pond where my client was incarcerated, a building created in the pioneer spirit to withstand the vicissitudes of time. For a prisoner under Betts's control, March was in a rare good mood. He knew as much about the sting as anybody— news traveled fast in the Fire Pond County Jail.

"My status has gone up a lot here," he said, "now that I am suspected of killing a government operative rather than just another poacher. A sting operation. Who would have believed it? You know what the Fish and Wildlife Service was doing? They were taking endangered species from the wild to use them to entrap people. Does that make any sense? And they were letting Pedersen take an extremely rare bird to use as bait for some poacher. I hate to say this, but the birds are probably in better hands with the falconers than with the feds. At least falconers know how to care for their birds. You can count on the government to screw things up. They probably killed more birds than they sold. Well, at least the prince won't get the gyr. She won't be living out her life in a hostile habitat—the Saudi desert."

"Maybe they would have air-conditioned the desert to keep her comfortable. The prince could probably afford to. I went up to Freezeout East yesterday to visit him. He'd rented the whole place just for himself and his buddy, Heinz, who told me a touching story about how the prince wanted the gyr as a gift for his dying father," I said.

"I bet. How did you make out with Leo, by the way?"

"Okay. He had some nice things to say about you and he showed me Mimi, his falcon. Pedersen had been to see him and offered him the gyr. Leo says that he guessed what Pedersen was up to and he didn't bite."

"Leo's pretty cagey."

"Do you think he would have bought the gyr if he'd thought he could get away with it?"

"I don't think he'd keep an illegal bird." It seemed to be March's nature to believe the best of people. "I've met Heinz Hoffman in here, by the way. He's a piece of work—he still thinks if he throws enough money around he'll get us both out of here and end up with the gyr."

"No doubt he'll have the very best legal representation.

The prince was released. He has diplomatic immunity, you know."

"I heard. With all those falconers out there being set up and Pedersen being the incompetent he was, any number of them could have guessed what was going on. Do you think Betts will lighten up on me now? Seems like any falconer the feds were trying to entrap had a lot better motive than I did."

"I made that point with Betts, but it didn't get me anywhere. Your fingerprints were on the trap that killed Pedersen."

"It was concealed by brush, and I touched it accidentally when I crawled through the cedars."

"So far you're the only one with wolf-wipers in your shed."

March looked down at his hands, hands that would soon be beading earrings if I didn't get him out of here, hands with cuticles that had been bitten raw. "I wish I'd detonated or buried the damn things."

"How many did you have anyway?"

"Four."

"Betts got one. Would you mind if I went out there and took a look at the others?"

"Please, go right ahead. Katharine will be there this afternoon, she'll be glad to show you around."

I had my doubts about that, but when it comes to evidence there's nothing like examining it firsthand.

"Thanks. I'll be by tomorrow."

"I'll be looking forward to it," he said.

11

What kind of a place would March and Katharine live in? I wondered on my way out there. I'd seen the tip, but what would the submerged iceberg of their life be like? Katharine was probably a craftsperson, March a photographer. There might be a loom in the living room, or a potter's wheel in the barn. Or maybe she was a painter. If Katharine painted she'd paint oversized canvases with swirls of red pierced by black lines. Nature photographs that March had taken might be hanging on the walls, but the walls themselves would be unfinished. The whole place would be unfinished: an old house where layers of wallpaper peeled like onion skin to reveal more old paper, or a new house where the walls shimmered like tinfoil because no one had gotten around to covering the insulation with Sheetrock. A visit to someone's house could be seen as a peek into his or her secret heart, but then if you lived in a motel-modern apartment with gold shag carpeting and fake stucco walls what did that say? You had no heart?

Their house was about ten miles out of town on the mountain side and, fortunately, on a dust-free paved road. It was a place where the directions had to do with landmarks instead of numbers and signs. March was good at directions and I found it on my first go-by. It turned out to be a log home nestled in a clump of evergreens, a miniature Freezeout East. The house was two stories with a peaked roof; it had a sun deck on the upper level. In the yard a scarecrow watched over the dead stalks and dry remnants of a large, unkempt vegetable garden. There was a shed where the rakes and hoes were probably kept along with wolf-wipers and other instruments of destruction. The Toyota pickup that was parked in the driveway wore bumper stickers that read DON'T BUY EXXON and SAY YES TO WILDERNESS. I was driving his vehicle, that one must be hers.

I parked the van, walked up to the door on the lower level and knocked. No one answered so I pulled the clapper on a nearby bell. Katharine leaned over the railing above my head and yelled, "Come on up."

The lower level was a mess. There were signs that it had been used as a darkroom, an artist's studio, a workroom, a trash barrel. I followed the path through the clutter. Was this the jewel in the heart of their iceberg? The foul mess where dreams start? I climbed the spiral staircase, already wishing I were back in my motel room. When you have nothing, you've got nothing to mess up. But entering the living room was like stepping from the dark, messy subconscious into daylight. It was spacious and well lit under a beamed ceiling. A glass wall looked into the trees and the blue sky beyond. It was done naturally, log walls, pine floors, beautiful rustic furniture with white cushions and pillows made from scraps of Indian rugs, a cast-iron wood stove. There were, as I expected, a few exquisite nature photographs on the walls. There were, as I had not expected, no potted plants or cats, although the anticipated crystal hanging in the window bounced rainbows around the room. The effect was warm, serene—not entirely finished, but close to it. Someone had carved a woman's face on a post at the top of the stairs, Katharine in a calm and contemplative mood. It was a loved and tended nest, a carefully crafted lure, and if you had created it, you might never want—or need—to fly any higher or farther.

Even Katharine seemed content in this room. Her mass of hair curled around her head. She wore a long denim skirt and a lavender sweater, and a chunk of crystal on a velvet rope hung from her neck.

"You have a beautiful place," I told her.

"We've put a lot of work into it."

"The furniture is great."

"March made it. Can I get you a cup of tea?"

"What do you have?"

"Orange Zinger, chamomile, mint, maybe some Almond Sunrise."

"Orange Zinger."

"Honey?"

"Why not?"

It was a house with no visible ashtrays and a "no smoking" aura; besides, I hate to have to ask. I left my Marlboros where they were in my purse and followed Katharine into the kitchen, past the bedroom where a white bedspread was sliding off a four-poster log bed that had probably been handmade, too. What would it be like, I wondered, to be living in Montana with someone who could make you a four-poster bed? And what would it be like to be sleeping with that someone in the bed he had made? To look up and see his amber eyes and feel his soft beard?

An unworthy thought and unprofessional besides so I banished it, but not before I'd wondered if there were any condoms in the nightstand beside the bed.

"Have you lived here long?" I asked.

"Five years," Katharine said. "March built the place before I met him, but I helped him finish it up."

I sat down at a counter in the kitchen under a bunch of dried something and watched while Katharine put the water on. What were we going to talk about while it simmered? Gardening? Crystals?

"You like being a lawyer?" she asked me.

"There are things I like about it. I like having my own office. I'd like getting March out of jail."

"I bet," she said, fondling the rock in the rope around her neck, getting in touch with the crystal energy. "March's life is in danger while he sits in that hole. I want him home, here in bed with me, and soon. If you ask me all the law does is put the wrong people in jail, set criminals free and take forever to do it."

The wheels of justice grind slowly; I'd be the first to admit it. But how did *she* propose to get him out—crystal power?

"It must be miserable work spending all day dealing with people's greed and pain," she continued. Or their yearnings to be compensated for something they had done or released for something they hadn't. "It's a rotten job if you ask me."

There was the question of what she did for a living— nothing, that I'd noticed so far—but I was charging for my time, why waste it? "Maybe, but someone has to do it," I said and changed the subject. "I understand you didn't like Pedersen."

Her face changed, the beauty slipping out as the anger slipped in. She let go of the crystal, took the teapot off the stove. "Let's go outside. I want to show you something."

I noticed, as I followed her down the spiral staircase, that another face had been started on the backside of the post, but had been left unfinished. The scowling face, maybe, that Katharine presented to the world. "Pedersen was a poacher," she said when we got outside under the overhang of the sun deck. "A scum." Too foul, apparently, to even talk about in her living room.

"Come here, Pookie," she called and a thin, yellow, devoted dog limped up. "I found this dog beside the highway with a broken leg. Someone had hit him, driven off and just left him there to die." Pookie gratefully accepted a pat on the head and followed us behind the house where an aviary was hidden from view. It was a series of wire cages housing birds that had been injured and nursed back to health by Katharine. "If they are capable of going back into the wild, I release them, but if they are not I keep them here. You have to be very careful with an injured wild creature so it doesn't become too attached to you, it doesn't lose its native distrust, it doesn't identify you with food, because if that happens there's no point in releasing them, no matter how whole they are. Animals have to fear man to live in the wild. That is the first order of survival. Most of my birds were found on the road, victims of highway accidents. People know what I do and they bring them to me to be healed." She showed me a red-tailed hawk, a white snowy owl of unearthly feathered beauty and a tiny saw-whet owl; a wounded claw, a blind eye, a broken wing.

"This crystal is rose quartz. It has healing properties for winged creatures." She waved it over the saw-whet's cage and then took him out to show me. "Ollie, say hello to Neil, March's lawyer." Ollie blinked his luminous indifferent eyes. My profession didn't impress him either.

She also had a shiny black bird in her aviary that cawed loudly when it saw us. "Is that a raven or a crow?" I asked.

"Raven," she replied.

"I guess that's a matter of a pinion."

She didn't laugh. If Katharine had any sense of humor I had yet to see it. She shifted abruptly from childlike gentleness to extravagant outrage, grinding the gears as she went. Some humor might have greased the transition.

She stroked the tiny owl, who seemed blissfully happy in her hands, then gently put him back in his cage and waved the crystal again. Not so gently she turned toward me. "I am furious when someone hurts an animal or removes it unnecessarily from the wild. Can you understand that? It is the worst sin in the world. Because man has the power to destroy everything in his path he has the responsibility not to. Wild birds should be free, free as the day they were born. This smuggling ring with Saudi princes and black marketeers is disgusting. So you still want to know what I think of Pedersen?" Her porcelain skin wrinkled in anger, her black eyes sparked. The transition was complete. Katharine the gentle bird tamer had become Katharine the Untamable again. "He was a poacher and like all poachers, a vile, evil man. He deserved what he got."

If there were a crystal to eliminate poachers from the face of the earth she probably would have used it. As far as I could see Pedersen was just another rotten human who'd fucked up, but then I was used to dealing with human greed and misery; I did it every day. She had made him into a devil and was crediting him with too much power. The only advantage to investing your opponent with superhuman qualities is that you make yourself even more powerful when you strike him down. It was myth making, the same mistake some feminists make, but men are only human, too. Nothing was to be gained from exaggerating anyone's abilities, and Pedersen's were suspect to begin with.

"I'd like to see the wolf-wipers," I said.

"That's why you came, isn't it?"

I agreed it was and we walked down to the shed, the front of which was filled with the normal implements of gardening and maintaining a place: shovels, axes, hoes, rakes. The back half looked like an inquisition chamber. There were the leg-hold traps that March had removed from the wilderness, shiny metal instruments that would hold a coyote's leg in bondage until he got so desperate and crazed with fear and pain that he chewed it off. And then there were the wolf-wipers, three of them.

"Betts has the fourth. Greg Porter came by with a warrant and took it. I guess you know that," Katharine said. "You want to see how they work?"

I nodded.

"If it's a wolf you're after, you put the bait back here, see—the wolf pulls on it and sets off the cyanide. Or it can also be detonated by putting weight against this piece. A man on his hands and knees like this would be just about the height of a wolf. March said that the trap was set at a place where you'd have to crawl to get under the overhang. It was concealed by the red cedars. Pedersen put his hand into it like this." She knelt down and placed her hand on the trap. I stepped back quickly.

"Afraid I'm going to set it off? You've got to lean on it harder than that to detonate it. When you do, the cyanide blasts out right about here, into your face."

"Charming. Did they ever get any wolves in Freezeout?"

"A couple, but that was half the population."

"March said he never did find out who was setting them."

She stood up and brushed the dirt from her palms and knees. "That's bullshit."

"Excuse me?"

"It's bullshit. Everybody knew who was doing it, March just didn't want to believe it."

"Why not?"

123

"He knows the guy. March never wants to believe anything bad about anybody, especially someone he knows, so he convinced himself it wasn't him. But he's a trapper and he makes traps that will kill anything. If he doesn't use them himself, he sells them to someone who will."

"Does this guy have a name?"

"Jimmy Brannen."

"Where does he live?"

"Warren, a few miles down the road."

"Maybe I should see him."

"You wouldn't want to." Her eyes narrowed.

"Why not?"

"He's a scum."

"I'm used to dealing with rotten people. It's my profession. Brannen might have some information that could help March."

She thought it over. "He might," she replied, then gave me directions to Brannen's place. I never did get my Orange Zinger, and if Katharine was sorry to see me leave she didn't let it show, but Pookie followed me to the van. He wagged his skimpy tail, which set his rear end in motion and got his scrawny ribs shaking and then his whole self vibrating until I leaned over and patted him on the head.

The Kid's postcard, carefully addressed to 9 Callejon del Viento, little street of the wind, was still on the passenger's seat. I'd have to go like the wind to get to Jimmy Brannen's and back to Fire Pond in time to mail it today. It was already 3:15 by the clock in March's van. Although it might not be correct about the minute, it probably was right about the hour. If I got the card in the mail tomorrow, he'd get it Thursday morning a few hours before I was due back anyway. "Sorry, Kid," I thought. "It's a lead—I have to check it out."

March's directions had been simple and clear, as directions should be. Go five miles, turn left, go another mile and a half, turn right. Katharine's directions were neither simple nor clear. There were too many inconsequential landmarks and too few measured distances. It made me wonder how badly she wanted me to get there. "A few miles down the road" turned out to be thirty. "After the town of Warren," she'd said, "you go a little way and you'll see a Texaco station on the left" (it wasn't Texaco, it was Mobil). "When you see that, keep going. Then a little further down the road on the right is the Constant place where Jim and Mary used to live. After that there's a road on the left that leads to the Forked River Ranch. Take the second left. Jimmy's place is down that road on the right. You'll see a sign." I found the Forked River Ranch Road all right, but did she mean the second left down that road or the second left after that road? I tried both and began to think, as they say in New England, you couldn't get there from here. It shouldn't be that hard; there weren't many roads in this area to begin with and even fewer houses. The first road I tried came to an abrupt end, no "places," no sign for Jimmy Brannen. The second one went on and on. Neither had seen rain in recent history and, even with the windows rolled up, I was eating dust.

I knew better than to go out in the West without a lot of gas and a container of drinking water. After five miles down the second "second left" I stopped, drank some water and let the dust settle. This expedition was beginning to resemble a nowhere love affair, when you've invested too much to quit but don't see anything promising coming up either. Or those exits that you come across on unfamiliar interstates late at night. The sign says gas, you need it, so you get off. The gas station isn't there, it's somewhere down the road; you drive and drive and it doesn't appear and you wonder if you've reached the point of no return, as pilots call it, when you've used up the better half of your tank. There's not enough to get back, but there may not be enough to go forward either. It's one of life's hardest decisions—when to cut your losses—but five miles of road dust (ten counting the return trip) was enough for me. Besides, it got dark early at this time of year—November, the month when Montana is bare and brown and more lonesome than lonesome. It's a time of brooding and introspection, a time to hide your nuts and prepare for the darker days to come. We don't have November where I come from. We have summer and winter, which is similar to summer only colder, but we don't have any dark brooding months.

As the sun slipped out of the clouds and neared the horizon, long shadows formed wherever there was anything to make a shadow. I didn't want to be driving around lost after nightfall, so I got back on the highway and stopped at the Mobil station for gas and help. The mechanic, with a Sam Shepard kind of snaggle-toothed smile and a certain clarity of expression, told me that the second left was the second left past the gas station and Jimmy Brannen was a mile down the road. Why hadn't she just said so?

JAMES EARL BRANNEN, read the letters burned onto a slab of wood, TRAPPER. The place was bare and brown as the season, a series of ramshackle, unpainted and unkempt buildings. There were no vehicles visible and it didn't look like anyone was at home, if there was a home in this stack of weathered wood. I slammed the door loudly as I got out of the van just in case. "Hello?" I called. No response. "Anybody home?" I tried again. "I'm looking for Jimmy Brannen." If anyone heard me, they didn't let it show.

Since I'd gone to this much trouble to find the place, I decided to peek around and see what I could before darkness settled in. There was the hum of a motor running somewhere at Jimmy Brannen's, but otherwise it was quiet as Montana at dusk. I walked up a slight incline toward the buildings, hoping a snarling dog wasn't going to leap out at me. None did and I made it to the first shed unmauled. The door was padlocked shut. I walked around it with my hand trailing along the rough planked siding. There weren't any windows in this building, just a few chinks in the wood. I looked through one and couldn't see anything but specks of dust in the waning light. I circled this shed and went on to the next, which was large enough to be called a barn. The door was wide open, so I went in. The glass that was left in the windows was filthy, but, as most of them had been smashed out, there was enough light to see a row of stalls—for horses I guessed—but it didn't look like any horses had been there recently. There was still some hay in the stalls and a feathering of hay dust hung in the air and made me sneeze. I went on to the next building, another shed larger than the first, also pad-locked, but with a heavier lock, a bigger bolt. The hum-ming motor was in this building and when I put my hand to the wall I could feel a steady vibration like a mechanical heart. There were windows here, but high up. Even on tiptoe I couldn't see in. I worked my way around the place looking for something to stand on and came across a large rock, which I rolled and pushed back to a window. I bal-anced on it, pressed my fingertips against the windowsill and peered in. I saw metal hooks and springs and chains. I couldn't see what the motor was, but it was a place that hummed with pain and mutilation and death to come, with fear and paws and blood. It was a rotten way to make a living. I shuddered and climbed down, being careful not to twist my ankle as I stepped from the rock. I began kick-ing at it—no point in alarming Mr. Brannen by leaving it under the window—and was pushing it around the corner of the building when I looked up and found myself staring down the dark end of a rifle.

"You looking for something?" a voice said. The man holding it, I noticed once I was able to disengage my eyes from the darkness that lurked in the depths of the barrel, was medium sized and skinny. He was wearing pants that resembled tree bark, a camouflage hat with a peak, like a feed-store giveaway, and a matching vest with lots of flaps and pockets and places to put ammunition. He'd camou-flaged himself so good I hadn't even known he was there.

"I'm looking for Jimmy Brannen," I said.

"You found him."

"I couldn't figure out which building was your office."

"Ain't got one."

"While I was looking, I tripped over this rock and I thought I'd kick it out of the way before somebody sprained an ankle or something." It sounded like bullshit, even to me.

"That right?"

"Would you mind putting down that gun? It's hard to talk with a rifle staring at you. I'm not armed." The barrel had a hypnotic pull like deep, dark, still water. I didn't want to ever look into it again.

He sized me up and could see that there was no place to hide a weapon in my well-worn Levi's and sweater. He pointed the gun toward the ground, but kept his eyes on me.

"So what are you looking for me for?"

"I want to talk to you about traps."

"What kind of traps?"

"Wolf-wipers."

"Wolf-wipers. Why? You got some varmint bothering you?"

"Not exactly."

He inclined his head toward the road. "We can talk down there."

I led the way, wondering all the while which part of me the gun was pointed at. When we got to the van and his pickup he said, "Stop right here." He leaned against his truck, I leaned against the van. This I guessed was his living room, the truck his couch. "Ain't that March's van?" he asked and spat in the dust.

"Yeah."

"You taking Katharine's place?"

"No."

"Then why you drivin' it?"

I told him—why not? The best way to tell a lie is to put a little truth in, the best way to tell the truth is to put in everything you've got. "March is taking the rap for someone else, you know. He could spend the rest of his life in jail because of a trap he didn't set," I finished up.

"Katharine told you how to get here?" was his comment.

"More or less."

He spat a brown goober into the dust at his feet, just missing a combat boot, a soldier of fortune in spirit if not profession. "Did March tell you to come here, too?"

"No."

"I didn't think so. There's a lot of loose talk around but March ain't the kind of guy to accuse anybody unless he's sure." He relaxed a little and lay the gun down on the back of his truck—the coffee table. "He's been pussy-whipped, but March ain't a bad guy. He's always been straight with me so I'll tell you what I know about wolf-wipers. They'll kill a predator like a wolf or a coyote pretty fast. They'll also kill a human being." The Velcro made a sucking sound as he ripped open one of the flaps on his vest. He pulled out a hunk of something brown and bit off a wad. "That's all I know."

It was getting dark. Brannen had a lean and sinuous body, a body that could slide easily into tunnels and burrows, and he had the sharp little face that went along with it, a face with crevices for shadows to settle into. They spread beneath his eyes and alongside his nose and were about to swallow the face up. It was time to shine some light on his outdoor living room.

"Oh, yeah, there's one more thing. The kind of person who'd buy a trap like that wouldn't worry too much about killin'. That answer your questions?"

Some of them it answered, some of them it didn't. "I have one more."

"Yeah."

"What's that motor I heard running in the shed?"

"My washing machine," he said. "Now why don't you just get yourself on out of here?" He spat again.

"You got it." I climbed into the van and turned on the headlights. Trapped momentarily in the flash of the beams his eyes glowed red and feral like the eyes of a predator slinking across the highway.

The van bumped along the dusty road in the dark. If March hadn't needed new shocks before this trip, he would now. I'd forgotten about the cattle guard, a series of metal corrugations that connected Brannen's road to the highway, and I hit it too fast, jarred the van and set it rattling. Something had been knocked loose, a tailpipe, maybe, or worse. I couldn't drive all the way back to Fire Pond with the bottom falling out, so I stopped at the friendly Mobil station. There was already a car up on the lift and the lone mechanic was working on it.

"Be with you in a minute," he said.

"No hurry."

I sat on a hard metal chair in the office and waited. The radio was playing "Take It to the Limit," an old Eagles song about spending your love and time and hitting the road. I was hungry so I got some cheese crackers with peanut butter from the vending machine for dinner and peanut M&M's for dessert. They'd put the red ones back in. I ate those first, and then the yellow and the green. "Care for an M&M?" I said to the mechanic, but there was nothing left but two shades of brown and who would choose them?

"Thanks anyway, I got dinner waiting when I get home."

What would it be? I wondered. Steak? A three bean

salad? That seemed to be the only vegetable they ate in Montana. It probably wouldn't be a Lean Cuisine or even two, although he was skinny enough and tall besides with appealingly crinkled blue eyes, all the bluer in contrast to the dirt on his face.

He smiled. I smiled back. His teeth were crooked but they were nice and white. "I hope I'm not keeping you too late," I said.

"Well, I promised this one for first thing tomorrow morning, but I'm about done. I'll put the van up there next and take a look."

He guided while I drove onto the lift. I got out, watched him lift the van up and move around gracefully underneath. There's an appeal to a man who eats light and can fix things. There's an appeal to hard-working, dirty fingers. I have a weakness for mechanics, I'll admit it.

"Just knocked the tailpipe loose," he said. "Won't take but a minute to fix."

"No hurry."

He tightened it up and lowered the van back down to the ground, a cumbersome elephant of a vehicle, designed for leaf picking, not road running.

"Well, what do I owe you?" I said. It was good and dark by now, we were miles from the nearest dwelling, it might be hours before anybody else needed gas. Just the mechanic and I alone here in the night. There's a kind of electric charge you get when you're home alone during the day and an attractive guy shows up to deliver a package or repair the plumbing. Suddenly you're alone with a man in your space and that space is filled with erotic innuendo. I wondered if it was like that for him being with me in the garage.

"Oh, I don't know, how's ten dollars sound?" He smiled again.

"Is that enough?" It was tax deductible, what the heck.

"It'll do."

"Well, thanks a lot."

"Come back again next time you're out this way."

"I'd be glad to."

He began slowly closing up the place, watching me carefully while he did. Desire and risk hung in the air, but so did condoms and grease. The sexual revolution had ended, like a lot of revolutions, in tyranny (in this case the tyranny of disease) but maybe it wasn't all bad. There was a time when it seemed like an obligation to explore every opportunity, take every risk, but there comes a point when you're ready to settle for what's implied.

I said good-bye and turned the lumbering elephant onto the highway. The clock said 6:15, but it felt like midnight to me. It had been a long day—too much talking, too much investigating. I was ready to go back to the Aspen Inn, run a hot bath and curl up with the phone book—or Joan's journal, but then that would require thought and I knew what the thoughts would be: Had *she* ever flirted with a mechanic or busboy? Had she ever kept condoms in the nightstand beside her bed? Had she ever even had a lover? When she was at her sexual prime it was the fifties and peaking sexually in the fifties was probably like the peaks of egg whites that hadn't been beaten long enough and just fell over. By the time you were sixty-eight what did it matter anyway? Could memories ever compare to the now, to the quivering intensity of the moment? Joan's moments had apparently been filled with intense stalking, fearful flight. There's only one feeling more intense than desire and that's fear. I knew a little about fear, a lot about desire; hardly anything about the two of them mixed together.

At least by leaving so late I'd missed the evening rush. There was a long stretch of lonesome highway between Warren and Fire Pond and there weren't many of us on it. It was too dark to wave or be friendly, although you could always flash a high beam just to say we're all in this alone. A truck or van approached from the opposite direction. I couldn't say which, except that the double headlights seemed to be too high up for a car, and too bright to be on the road, even in New Mexico where they have no inspection. "Turn 'em down," I said and, when that didn't work, flashed my own high beams and, when that didn't work, flashed them again. It kept right on shining those piercing lights, nearly blinding me. "Asshole," I said. I looked away while the vehicle passed, thinking of the white crosses, those straight-as-an-arrow places where drivers go off the road. This place was as straight as any and, once the taillights had disappeared from my rearview mirror, there was nothing to see but yellow line and the arcs the van's lights made, not even a coyote slinking off into the darkness, its red eyes burning holes in the night.

I was getting sleepy. I pulled a tape out of the glove compartment, any tape, I didn't care, and plunked it in. There was a whirr and then a gnashing sound as the tape deck ate it up. I'd have to talk to March. He couldn't expect me to drive all over the state with no music to listen to. I began singing lonesome highway songs just to keep myself awake. There was "Take It to the Limit," of course; James Taylor's "Sweet Baby James"; Janis Joplin, "Me and Bobby McGee"; "Born to Run," Bruce Springsteen. Songs from the sixties, seventies and eighties, the decades blend in the lonesome night. Songs come up out of the melt, stab you with memories and sink back in. There's always a station your car radio pulls in late at night from hundreds of miles away, one of those stations that believes in yesterday, someplace like Harlingen, Texas, or Topeka, Kansas, or Roswell, New Mexico, that's playing songs aimed right at your heart. March didn't have a working radio, so I had to do it myself. I went way back to Judy Collins's song about the man who loved the rodeo, but that was entering another category—man who got away songs, or a subcategory, man who got away down the lonesome highway songs.

The highway had gotten a little less lonesome while I sang, as a vehicle was coming up behind me. I'd been so wrapped up in my musical reverie I hadn't noticed. It was gaining on me very fast—and I was doing seventy-five myself. It pulled up close and instead of dimming the high beams, the driver turned them on. "If anyone is following you out there, you'll know." It was a new twist to an annoying trick. Another asshole, maybe even the same asshole, the lights were double and bright enough, piercingly bright lights, lights that spotlighted me to whoever was watching, but when they hit the rearview mirror they blinded me to them. March's van didn't have one of those mirrors you could flick down to block the assholes out. I ducked my head and blinked rapidly, trying to get my vision back. In that split second while I looked away, I was rear-ended. "What the fuck?" I said. It was happening very fast and very bright in the glare of the lights, but there was time enough for the rush to the extremities of fear and the chilling at the bone. Whoever was stalking me rammed again. The van was not exactly road steady. It was square and unwieldy and hard to control. There was one more thud and then a sickeningly out-of-balance lurch and I drifted into the slow-motion time of car wrecks as the van left the road, skidded across the shoulder, hit a ditch, lifted into the air, turned over, came down ever so slowly and heavily, crunched the roof and rolled over again. There was all the time in the world to observe it but no time at all to prevent it. On the last roll I saw the brake lights of the offending vehicle come on and then, as the van landed on the driver's side, my head snapped forward and hit something hard and unyielding; the lights went out.

13

I came to bathed in light. "It's
going to be a bitch getting her out of there," I heard someone say, but somehow they pulled me out through the
passenger side. Emergency medical technicians got me into
an ambulance with a wailing siren, even though there was
nothing on the road to wail at. The bright lights and the
siren didn't help the pain in my head any. Neither did the
noise in the overly bright hospital in Fire Pond where I
ended up. Since I was barely conscious when they found
me, I wasn't asked to take a Breathalyzer test, which turned
out to be unfortunate for me because, when it came time
to fill out an accident report, no one believed that I had
been run, cold sober, off the road. They did believe my
head hurt and they gave me something for it. I wasn't
showing any signs of concussion, fracture, whiplash or any
lawsuit-provoking injury, but they asked me to stick around
overnight for observation and to rest up.

Fire Pond Hospital was the noisiest place I'd ever tried

to rest up. It would be quieter at the junction of I-25 and I-40 in Albuquerque with the windows wide open in the middle of summer, but I guess I needed the rest because I did finally fall asleep. Late in the morning I had a dream that someone was standing at the foot of my bed. He was tall and skinny as a street dog but he did have shoulders and black curly hair—the Kid. It was a wonderful dream and I wanted to snuggle down into it. But then there was a loud crash as a bedpan hit the floor. I fought to stay in the dream, but when it didn't go away, I began to believe I was already awake.

"Kid?" I asked.

"Chiquita." He walked around the bed. It was the Kid all right—he was carrying his well-worn copy of *Cien Años de Soledad*, a.k.a. *One Hundred Years of Solitude*, in one hand. The Kid had already read that book five times and probably once more on his way here. With his free hand he touched my cheek. His hand was dark and callused; it never felt rougher or better. "Are you okay?" he asked.

"I think so. I have a bit of a headache, but I'm all right. They wanted to keep me around for a while just to be sure I didn't have a concussion or something. I am still in Montana, aren't I?"

"Yup."

"Well, uh, what are you doing here?"

"The police call me, Chiquita, last night. They find my address on a postcard in your car."

Did that make the Kid my nearest and dearest, the one to come if I lived through a wreck, tidy up after me if I didn't? Well, he was young enough to outlive me anyway. My purse and the address book, which should have been in it, were not in the car—the police had told me that—but they hadn't told me they found the Kid's postcard or called him. Maybe they didn't want to be blamed if he didn't show up. "You're a sweetheart for coming," I said.

"I leave right away when they call, get the midnight flight to Denver, then I get a plane here early this morning. I was worried. What happen to you anyway? Were you . . . ?" He looked around him to see if anyone was watching and tipped an imaginary bottle to his lips.

"Of course not," I said, wondering what to leave in this soon-to-be-edited version of the episode, what to leave out. "I . . . I guess I just fell asleep. I wasn't drinking."

"You just fell asleep?" asked the naturally skeptical Kid. "Yeah."

"If the doctor says you are okay to leave, maybe we can get on the same plane tomorrow."

"I can't go back tomorrow, Kid. I'm working on an important case, a murder. I told you all about it in the postcard." But I told him more about it in person. I told him about seeing Pedersen dive off the cliff and March ending up in prison and the prince and the sting operation. I told him about all the people in Montana who had an interest, criminal or otherwise, in the gyr, but I didn't tell him that one of them had tried to kill me. I didn't tell him that like 99 percent of the animal kingdom, I had become a prey, a little brown bird stalked by a predator, not necessarily larger or faster but more willing to kill. He'd worry.

"People kill for a bird?" he said.

"Apparently."

"And that guy March is in prison?"

"Yes, but he didn't murder anybody."

The Kid shrugged. He has a certain Mediterranean quality to his shrugs. I'd always suspected there was Italian blood in him somewhere, probably from his mother's side, the Argentine side. In New Mexico he blended right in; in Montana he didn't. Dark-skinned, but too curly-headed and lighthearted to pass for an Indian—he'd never looked better to me. "So you've been driving all over Montana looking for a murderer and then you . . . drive off the road?" he said.

The police hadn't believed me when I filled out the accident report and told them I'd been forced off the road. The Kid didn't believe me when I said I hadn't been. No credibility when I told the truth, none when I lied either.

"I can't leave, Kid, until I find out who did it." He didn't ask what. "How long can you stay?"

"I have to leave tomorrow night," he said. "I play the accordion at El Lobo Friday."

It wouldn't be like him to ask me to come home with him again. It wouldn't be like me to ask him to stay longer either. He didn't. Neither did I.

"The birders are having their farewell dinner tonight. You want to go with me?"

"Sure, why not?"

The Kid was a closet birder himself, something I had only recently found out, but there were a lot of things about the Kid I didn't know and one reason was that I only saw him at my place or his shop. We didn't exactly have a social life or a network of friends. But when he heard I was in trouble he jumped on the first flight. Wasn't that enough?

The Kid went down the hallway to get himself a Coke. While he was gone, I called March to tell him about the accident. But the news had already made its way into the Fire Pond County Jail.

"Are you all right?" he asked.

"Yeah, I'm okay."

"What happened?"

"Someone rear-ended me and pushed me off the road."

"Jesus. Who would do that?"

"Someone, I guess, who thinks I am closer to finding the murderer than I am. Someone in a four-wheel-drive or a pickup."

"That's ninety percent of Montana."

"You haven't heard any rumors there, have you?"

"No. Only that you had the accident and also, actually, I did hear that your boyfriend was in town. I hope he's watching out for you."

"He's helping. The van is a wreck."

"I know. It was totaled, but don't worry about that—it's insured. You're lucky you're all right. That's the important thing. Were you going very fast?"

"Fast enough."

"It's pretty risky to rear-end someone at high speed—to both parties. I'd say whoever did it was a very careful driver."

"Very careful . . . or very crazy," I said.

"The police called here, by the way, when they saw the car was registered to me. I gave them the name of your law firm in Albuquerque and they called but it was late and no one was there, so they tracked down your boyfriend instead. How long is he staying?"

"He's going back tomorrow."

There was a pause while March probably looked down at the tear in his jeans and picked at a loose thread. "Be careful, Neil."

"Don't worry," I said.

The Kid was coming down the hallway with his Coke in his hand. "I'll come by tomorrow," I told March and hung up the phone.

At the farewell dinner, the Kid and Avery hit it off right away. A young eccentric and an old one, they had a lot in common, enough to set Avery's hair in motion: a shared interest in pigeons (Avery had kept pigeons in his youth, too) and a shared disbelief that I had driven off the road.

"That's a very straight stretch of highway," said Avery, who knew everything there was to know about Montana.

"You see white crosses beside those straight stretches all the time."

"There's a reason for that." Avery raised his hand to his lips in a similar gesture to the Kid's, only Avery indicated a glass rather than a bottle.

"Everyone assumes every accident involves drinking," I said. "Isn't it possible that people just fall asleep or their minds wander?"

"It's possible," said Avery. "If you think of the mind as a series of flickering images like a movie, a dotted line rather than a straight line, it is possible for something to slip in between the dashes, so to speak."

"Or slip out," I said. "I'm going to see what's at the buffet." I left them talking about pigeons and dotted lines and wandered over to the buffet table. For reasons known only to management, the Sheraton was holding our dinner next to the pool room and the food smelled, naturally, of chlorine since someone had opened the sliding glass door. The water that lapped at the edges of the pool was just about the same artificial and uninviting blue as Wayne Betts's eyes.

The dining quarters had a crimson carpet, thick enough to soak up the food scraps, hideous enough so stains were an improvement. The fluorescent lighting made the food look like it was being X-rayed for disease. There was a slab of roast beef, a pink and gelatinous ham with a slice of pineapple and a maraschino cherry on top, a whole pineapple with toothpicks spiked with wedges of cheese sticking out of it, chicken in a gloppy creamed sauce that looked suspiciously like cream of mushroom soup, a tri-colored Jell-O mold, the ubiquitous three bean salad, a carrot and raisin mess, a bowl of creamed cottage cheese. Was it the food that made me queasy or was I suffering from a car rollover hangover? Just to be safe I ordered a ginger ale and put only a dinner roll and a pat of butter on my plate.

The same fluorescent lighting that zapped the food aged the birders badly. Marcia and Burt were helping themselves to slices from the end of the beef. Under the glare of the lights I noticed something that I hadn't before—Marcia was older than Burt. Burt looked weathered and sallow, although twinkly eyed, but Marcia looked even worse. She was overweight enough to plump out the skin's fine fissures, but she had a double chin and crepe beneath her eyes.

"That your old man?" asked Burt, nodding at the Kid.

"You could say that."

"He's cute," said Marcia, and then she leaned over and whispered confidentially, "You know something? I'm ten years older than Burt."

"Would you believe it?" asked Burt.

Seven or eight maybe, but ten? "Never."

"We've been married for twenty years and we get along great," said Marcia. "We always have."

"Never even had a cross word," said Burt. He smiled, she smiled back.

I followed them over to a circular table and sat down with Bea, Muriel and John King. Avery and the Kid were still engrossed in their pigeon conversation. Avery's hands made swooping motions through the air, while the Kid nodded. *"Claro, claro."* Cortland James hadn't shown up yet.

"We'll be watching the newspapers but I'm also going to give you our address so you can let us know what happens to March," Marcia said. "We know you'll get him off soon."

"I hope you're right. I guess you've heard all about the sting," I said to John King, who had tried to pick a vegetarian path through the buffet. There was a lump of cottage cheese on his plate, some corn relish, a few carrot sticks, barely enough to feed a bird.

"It's hard to believe our government would have set up such a clumsy, stupid operation," John replied. "Or maybe it isn't. You know they took forty birds out of the wild to use as bait to trap the poachers? Some of those were endangered species that will be hard put to recover from the loss. Pedersen was a pro compared to the rest of the guys who were involved in the operation. Many of the birds were hurt, eggs were taken from the nests and broken. Falcons are vulnerable to predation and have a fifty to seventy-five percent mortality in the wild in the best of times even without the government's interference." He shook his head sadly and looked down into his food, which probably didn't help his mood any. "I don't like poachers, but taking birds from the wild to entrap them isn't the answer. As you may have noticed I have a strong commitment to raptors. Some might say it borders on insanity. It breaks my heart to lose even one bird. All the condors had to be pulled in from the wild to save them; if the falcons go, the eagles will be next. When that happens, as Chief Seattle said, it will mark the end of living and the beginning of survival. Well, you can be sure the Falcon Fund is going to have something to say about this."

"I hope so," I replied. "Well, in spite of everything, has it been a good trip?"

"Yes," said Bea.

"I'll never forget it," Muriel agreed.

"We've kept busy," said John King, "and seen a lot of birds. We went back to Freezeout and saw the gyr again. She really is spectacular, one in a million."

"So Avery told me."

"We spent a couple of days at The Pipes Sanctuary. One day I gave a lecture and showed slides of the Arctic."

"What did you all do last night?"

"Last night was free time. Some of us went to the movies, some of us stayed in and went to bed early."

Cortland James had just come through the sliding glass door from the pool and was heading our way. His shape grew in size as he approached, but his outline remained the same. He wouldn't cause alarm by being unpredictable in his baggy khakis and faded Shetland sweater, the look of old money pretending to be no money, but not hard enough to fool anybody. He'd made a concession to Montana and the season, however, by replacing his Top-Siders with a pair of hiking boots that he'd probably ordered from the L. L. Bean catalog.

The Kid and Avery had moved on to the buffet table. Avery had the appetite of an eighty-two-year-old man. A couple of nuts and seeds were all right with him, but the Kid, who was only twenty-five years old, had taken a giant helping of just about everything on the table. His plate overflowed with gravy, meat and cheese and anything else that clogged your veins. I cleared a spot at the table for him next to me.

"I guess you didn't like the airline's food," I said.

"No, it was great," he replied. "They had eggs and sausages and . . ."

"Good evening, everyone," said Cortland.

"Good evening," everyone replied.

"Are you going to introduce me to your young man, Neil?" he asked with a smile that might be called amused, might be called condescending, might even be called friendly where he came from.

My "young man" stood up and shook Cortland's hand. "This is the Kid," I said. "Kid, Cortland James."

"The *Kid?*" asked Cortland raising an eyebrow, implying perhaps that was an unsuitable name for a "young man."

"Mauricio Babilonia," said the Kid. *"El gusto es mio."*

"My pleasure," said Cortland. If he'd learned Spanish in his peregrinations, he wasn't doing anyone the favor of using it.

Mauricio Babilonia was the garage mechanic in *Cien Años* with the dreamy air and the stupefying odor of grease, the man who loved Meme Buendía, was followed by yellow butterflies and was shot (unfairly and maliciously) for being a chicken thief. The Kid's favorite character. Mine, too.

"Did you hear about the New Mexican fireman who had twins?" asked Burt Collier, inspired by the Kid's grandiose Hispanic alias. "He named the first one José, the second hose B."

"I hear you got the night off last night," I said to Cortland, while the Kid sliced into his roast beef and some people laughed at the joke.

"I did. I spent it reading and turned in early. How's the roast?" Cortland asked the Kid.

"Good," replied the Kid, taking another bite.

"At least they're giving us some meat for our money. On most birding trips you're lucky to get chicken. I guess we should be grateful for that, although that roast is a little on the gray side."

The Kid took another bite. Gray, pink, red—made no difference to him.

"Sorry to hear about your accident," Cortland said to me, leaning forward and brushing his bangs from his forehead.

"Just a little bump on the head. It won't slow me down any."

"Are you sticking around or leaving tomorrow?"

"I'm sticking it out," I answered. "And you?"

"Leaving tomorrow. I've got no reason to stay on here."

"Won't you lose your discount fare?" Muriel asked me.

"Yes, but I wouldn't consider leaving without solving the case."

"She's stubborn," said the Kid.

"Really?" said Cortland.

"You're going back to Connecticut?" I asked him.

"Yes."

To the house he grew up in? I wondered. Or had he moved out and bought himself a condo by now? The family homestead probably had twenty or thirty rooms and was filled with sloppy dogs and dull antiques, a house where the grand piano was covered with pictures of extinct ancestors, where they hung the past on the wall and sat on it as well, where they had the best of everything old and boring.

"What exactly does the Conservation Committee do?" I asked him.

"My father has access to a number of conservation-minded individuals. . ."

Wealthy conservation-minded individuals, of course.

". . . who are willing and able to buy up land to keep it out of the hands of developers. Our particular mission is to preserve and protect wildlife habitat. The world is being destroyed at an alarming rate. Seventy-four thousand acres of rain forest vanish every day. The Conservation Committee tries to save what it can." For a man with a mission there was a lack of enthusiasm or conviction in his voice.

"Is the committee successful?" I asked.

"They try." He shrugged.

The birders began talking about what time their planes were leaving and what airlines they were flying, and making plans to get to the airport.

"I'm on American Three-oh-Four. I leave at eleven-ten," said Cortland when Bea asked him. He was leaving on

American, but he'd arrived on Frontier, I remembered, which meant no discount fare for him. He didn't seem like the kind of guy to pay full fare just because he could afford to.

"Didn't you come in on Frontier?" I asked him.

"Yes, I guess I did."

"Two different airlines. You won't get a discount fare."

"Really? I'll have to mention that to my travel agent."

We finished up with a selection of gummy pies and dry cakes for dessert. My head was hurting again so the Kid and I decided to turn in early. We bid the birders adieu and wished them good birding. "It's been a pleasure meeting you," I said and in most cases I meant it.

"You get March out of jail soon," said Bea.

Marcia: "And let us know how you make out."

Burt: "Don't forget all you learned about field identification."

John King: "Raptors deserve their place on the planet, too, and not just because they are fast and beautiful and we enjoy watching them, or even because they serve a valuable role in nature's system of checks and balances, but simply because they are here and they have been for millions of years. That's reason enough. Spread the word."

Cortland James: "Good-bye."

The Kid felt right at home in the Aspen Inn. I made us some tequilas and he pulled out a package of smoked almonds he'd saved from the plane. We opened up the plaid fold-out couch and sat on it.

"That Avery is fantastic," the Kid said. "I want to be like him when I get old." I could see it; he was already showing signs of eccentricity that aged well, but he'd have to change his eating habits.

"Would you ever keep pigeons again?" I asked him.

"Not now. I am a man, I was a boy then."

"Do you miss them?"

"Sure." He shrugged, Third World and sentimental as always.

"Mauricio. That was great but why didn't you give Cortland your real name?"

"Why did he have to ask?"

There was a brief silence and then I said, "Kid, I'm really glad to see you, but we may have to improvise because I lost my purse in the accident."

"You mean you don't have your 'friend'?" That's what he called it. I called it a derby. Some would say diaphragm.

"Yup."

"Don't worry, Chiquita." He stood up to get into the pocket of his jeans and pulled out a three-pack of condoms.

It was the beginning of sheathed love and responsibility and, while there was certainly much to recommend it, it wasn't the same.

I slept with my cheek pressed against the soft spot on the back of the Kid's neck and dreamt soft, silky dreams. The first time I woke in the morning I kissed his shoulder and whispered, "You awake, Mauricio?"

The next time I woke he wasn't there, but he'd left a note: "Gone for coffee, Chiquita."

I showered, dressed, walked down the hallway. Gloria was under the stairway playing the keno machine. My Odd Fellow, the Kid, watched as a few hard-won quarters tumbled out.

"All right," he said.

"You speak English?" she asked.

"Sure, why not?" he replied.

She shook her head. "I was in Mexico for a while, but I didn't learn much Spanish."

"You must have learned something," I said.

"Yeah, but I wouldn't want to repeat it here."

"Hasta luego," said the Kid.

"See you later," she replied, recycling her quarters.

We were on our way to the scene of the accident in the gray, no-frills Pontiac the Kid had gotten from Rent A Wreck. "Couldn't you have gone to Avis or Hertz?" I asked.

"What's wrong with this car?" He thumped the dash. "Runs good."

"I don't like the name." It didn't have a radio either. Montana was big silence country. Nobody blasted a boom box under your window at midnight, or left their windows open at red lights to share their favorite song. You didn't have to listen to other people's music in Montana or look at their trash either. You didn't even have to look at them.

"I never see such an empty place," said the Kid, once we were out of the Fire Pond city limits. "That's why they care about animals so much; they don't have people."

The roadsides were devoid of the signs of passing motorists—beer cans, plastic bags, soda bottles. The shoulders were spotless and the trails I saw at Freezeout had been, too. In the Sangre de Cristos you can backpack ten miles in and still come across beer cans beside the trail. It makes you wonder at the trouble people go to lugging their trash all the way into the wilderness just to leave their mark, but they do it on horseback; you can cover a lot more ground that way.

The Kid covered the distance in about the same time as the ambulance, and we were at the site of the wreck all too soon. It was a blight on the clean landscape, and reminded me of the place behind La Vista Luxury Apartment Complex, where I live. There's some land there that hasn't been developed yet and people like to drive in on Saturdays to party and change their oil. On Sunday mornings the ground is littered with oil, broken glass and party debris. But on this morning, in this spot, the trash was mine, I was embarrassed to notice. The ground glittered with broken glass and oozed spilled oil. The van had been towed away.

I stood, zero at the bone, at the spot where someone had tried to get rid of me. I was wearing my down vest, but I should have been wearing a down parka, too, because as far as I was concerned it had already gotten as cold as it could get. The Kid wore a sheepskin jacket an uncle had sent him from Argentina. He put his arm around me and, for a minute, I rested my cheek on the fleecy collar.

"The road is very straight here, Chiquita, like Avery said."

"Sometimes straight places are the most dangerous," I replied, "because that's when you let your attention wander and your guard down. The side door must have swung open when the van rolled over and thrown my purse out." We began looking for it in the scrub brush and tumbleweed, something the state police hadn't bothered to do. About a hundred feet from the wreck we came across the first track, a line of filter-tipped cigarettes, then the red flip-top box they had fallen out of. The trail made as the purse's contents were flung out told the story of my life and whoever had followed it could have learned a lot about me.

"Good you weren't smoking when you 'fell asleep,' " the Kid said.

Next were several wads of Kleenex, lipsticks, mascara, eyeliner, blush-on, a wide-toothed comb.

"You use all this stuff?"

"I carry it for emergencies," I replied.

Then there were the Spanish-language tapes I rarely listened to and some English tapes I had gotten for the Kid that he didn't listen to either.

"Your blood is red," I quoted, "your veins are blue. I speak English and so can you."

"Hey, Chiquita, here's your friend." The case had been flung open, the rubber derby plunked on the ground. I picked it up, an antique now, and put it back in its container to keep for sentimental value.

This trail we were following led directly to the highway; I wondered if the Kid had noticed. We came across my wallet, money and credit cards still intact; my key ring with my old nickname Nellie embossed on the plastic tag in gold letters; my address book with all the pages still inside; and scattered among all this, like rabbit droppings, light and darker brown M&M's. I found a notebook with a blue cover that I keep for records of appointments, mileage, meals, anything that might be tax deductible. The Aspen Inn was in there, some breakfasts and dinners. The last entry was the mileage to March and Katharine's house. The trip to Jimmy Brannen's hadn't been entered, but whoever had gone through my purse must have known I went there anyway and knew some other things now as well, but they hadn't found out what they'd hoped to—which was what I knew about them. And what was that? Subtle and unconscious clues might be more helpful here than the obvious. I had some parts, but I didn't have a whole. Now that I needed it, where was the jizz?

"Here's your purse," the Kid said. It was lying wide open in the ditch beside the road. "You want any of this stuff?"

"Just my wallet and address book. The rest is junk." But we walked back up the trail picking it all up, anyway, and stuffing it back into the purse. I didn't like all these pieces of myself biodegrading beside the highway.

"What kind of a guy is this 'April,' " asked the Kid, "who lets a woman go out and chase a murderer for him? I would never."

"Kid, he's in prison; he can't do it for himself. Besides he's not letting me, he's paying me. It's my job."

The Kid didn't say anything. He didn't have to, his shoulders did it for him.

"When it comes to my work I'm not a woman, anyway, I'm a lawyer."

"You're a woman to me, Chiquita." For one minute he looked like he was going to ask me to pack it all in and go back to Albuquerque with him, but he got in the Rent A Wreck and revved the engine instead.

When we got back to Fire Pond we had a late lunch in the Aspen Inn Coffee Shop. The Kid ordered coffee and chili. "The coffee is disgusting here and the chili is probably worse," I warned him. Chiles are hot red, green or yellow peppers, where he comes from. Chili as we know it in North America, a bean and/or meat mess, doesn't exist in Mexico. Close to the border they at least use chiles in their chili, but the further away you are the weirder it gets. I heard of a case where a woman in Minnesota who was hyperallergic to peanuts died because she unsuspectingly ordered chili that had peanut butter in it.

The Kid ordered it anyway. I decided on a tuna sandwich on whole wheat and a glass of milk, something the coffee shop couldn't mess up. But the bread looked like it had been inflated with a bicycle pump; there was more air than there was wheat and the tuna smelled like Puss 'n Boots. "How's the chili?" I asked the Kid.

"Good," he said.

"Do you think maybe it's a little bland?" What do they know about picante in Montana? When I made chili I made it hot enough to make your eyes water and when that wasn't hot enough I threw more jalapeños in.

"I like it." How could a person take pride in her cooking with an audience like that?

"Some guys over there are talking about you," said the

Kid, watching over my shoulder. "Do you know them?"

I turned around to see the third-best-looking man in Fire Pond—the prince—although taking his wealth into the equation some might elevate him to number one. Elegant as always in his creased Ralph Lauren jeans and a pair of cowboy boots that were probably made of ostrich hide, he was striding across the coffee shop trying to keep up with a long-legged cowboy. That guy was big enough without wearing cowboy boots and six inches of Stetson. He also wore a Western jacket, a string tie and a silver belt buckle with a great big turquoise in the middle. Dwight Stillman, the very biggest legal representation. Who else?

"Ms. Hamel," the prince said. "A pleasure to see you."

"The pleasure is mine."

"I would like to introduce you to Attorney Dwight Stillman."

"Attorney Neil Hamel here," I replied. "And this is . . . Mauricio Babilonia. Prince Sahid, Dwight Stillman." The *"mucho gustos"* and the "pleasures to" circled the table.

"May we sit down?" asked the prince.

"Why not? What brings you two to the Aspen Inn?"

"Attorney Stillman is staying here. It's a convenient location." Convenient, maybe, but not the very best. The prince had reserved that for himself.

"How was your stay in the Fire Pond jail?"

"Very limited. I made my one phone call to my attorney and he reminded the officials that I have diplomatic immunity and I was released shortly. It was very amicable."

"And Heinz?"

"Heinz is managing." The prince smiled. "He has been in this situation before."

"I imagine you and Attorney Stillman will find some way to get him out."

"We're working on that, ma'am." If they couldn't do it by legal means, Heinz could always try his luck at buying his way out of the Fire Pond jail. The legal superstar was lighting up the coffee shop with his illustrious presence, but it was all for my benefit. To everyone else in the place he was probably just what he looked like, a great big cowboy. It would be an interesting confrontation, I thought: the overconfident Stillman versus the uncertain Betts. In this case I'd put my money on the weak; they try harder.

"How's the chili, son?"

"Great," replied the Kid.

"Maybe I'll get myself some."

"You going to be sticking around?" I asked the prince.

His long elegant fingers mirrored each other as he twisted them, peering deep into his invisible ball. "If all goes as planned, I will be leaving in the Sparhawk on Saturday."

Stillman's chili arrived; the Kid was finishing his up. I decided my tuna was fit for cats, not humans, excused myself and went back to the room to call March.

"Are you feeling okay?" he asked.

"Pretty good, but I think I need a nap. If you don't mind, maybe I'll come by tomorrow instead. We went out to the accident scene this morning."

"Did you find anything?"

"Not really, a lot of broken glass. My purse had been searched, but nothing was taken. There wasn't anything to take."

"Katharine was here, by the way, and she told me about seeing you."

"We need to talk about that and my visit to Jimmy Brannen as well. I'll come by tomorrow. I promise."

"Okay." There was a lot of jail-cell ennui in his voice. He needed a visit, but I needed sleep.

"I just ran into the prince and Dwight Stillman. Stillman's staying here and representing Heinz. The prince told me he is planning on flying the Sparhawk out of here Saturday, 'if all goes as planned.' "

" 'If all goes as planned.' What does that mean?"

"Your guess is as good as mine. See you tomorrow."

"Okay."

There was a knock at the door. It was the Kid, the very best looking man in Fire Pond, although the poorest of the top three contenders. I let him in and we took a long siesta together with the curtains drawn. "Watch out for the rich guys," he said in one hazy moment, "they have more to kill for." But I don't know why he said that because where he comes from they're just as likely to do it for love.

Nobody waited under the elk horns at the Fire Pond Airport. The birders had gone home and now the Kid was leaving on the ten o'clock flight, which would get him into Denver around midnight and to Albuquerque very early in the morning. At least he'd had a nap. He wore jeans and his sheepskin coat and carried the well-worn and much loved *Cien Años*. Joan once told me that she'd had an aging relative who had gotten so foggy brained that she kept rereading the same book. When she got to the end she had forgotten the beginning, so she started all over again. But the Kid never forgot anything. He flipped through the remaining pages.

"I finish by the time I get to Albuquerque," he said.

"Easily," I replied. "Thanks for coming, Kid."

He shrugged—it was nothing.

"I should be back home soon," I told him.

He touched me lightly on the shoulder. "I know you, Chiquita. I know you won't leave until you finish here, but watch out and remember . . . drive careful."

"Don't worry," I said.

I watched while he went through the metal detector and walked down the corridor toward the plane, watched his long, skinny legs until they turned a corner and disappeared from view, and then I went to the Rent A Wreck counter and paid his bill, making it tax deductible. As I was now without wheels, I arranged to have the car transferred to me.

"No problem," said the clerk, whose name tag identified her as Rowanda Moore. Rowanda wore a white blouse and a gold vest. She had long, plum-lacquered, dagger-shaped fingernails that my secretary, Anna, would have envied and her puffy champagne blond hair looked suspiciously like it had been teased; obviously like it had been dyed. Light golden blond tinged with pink is a color rarely seen in nature. She handed me the papers to fill out.

"Do you happen to rent trucks or four-wheel-drive vehicles?" I asked her.

"Yes, ma'am, we do. We get a lot of customers looking for campers and 4 × 4s they can take into the back country. You interested?"

"Yes, but not in renting exactly." It was worth a shot. Just about everybody in Montana drove a four-wheel-drive or pickup, but that didn't mean somebody who lived elsewhere couldn't get his hands on one, too. "Has anybody turned one in with a dented fender? The other night someone ran into me and, well, I was wondering if it could have been one of your rental vehicles that did it."

Although Rowanda was practiced in the art of physical deception, she was honest about Rent A Wreck. "No, ma'am. We haven't had any accidents reported." That eliminated one possibility, but only one. Maybe it hadn't been turned in yet, maybe it had been rented at Budget or Avis or Hertz.

"Well, thanks anyway," I said.

I walked through the airport, past the Welcome to Big Sky Country booth where brochures advertised log homes, backpacking expeditions, rafting and hiking trips, hunting trips, fishing trips, boating trips that followed the path of Lewis and Clark and Sacajawea, their Indian maid. From a vending machine an upstate newspaper announced the Montana news: a man had been arrested for buzzing grizzlies by helicopter in Freezeout, an Indian named Kills on Top had been charged with a barroom murder.

My next stop was the Frontier Airlines ticket counter but no one was in attendance. I waited quietly for a few minutes, noisily a few minutes more. I coughed, cleared my throat, tapped on the counter. "Anybody work here?" I asked, slipping into impatient attorney voice. A boy with floppy bangs came out of a back room where a sign on the door said AUTHORIZED PERSONNEL ONLY. He left the door open and I could hear a football game playing on TV.

"Yeah?" he said.

"I have an aunt coming in for a few days from the East. I wonder if you could tell me what the connections are from the New York area."

"We don't fly to New York." An unseen cheer went up as someone scored a touchdown.

"I know that. But you do fly here and I want to know what the connections are."

He reluctantly punched his computer. "We can connect with an American nonstop flight to Denver and get her here at eight P.M."

"That's too late. Don't you have a flight that comes in around three in the afternoon?"

He tapped into the computer again, the keys tickety-ticked. I could hear a commercial coming from the TV. Spuds, the party dog, knew the secret to having a good time was knowing when to say when. "That flight comes from Bullhorn," he said. "It's the only incoming flight we have in the afternoon and the return trip of a flight that leaves here at eight in the morning. To make that three o'clock flight you'd have to leave New York at six A.M., stop in Chicago, change in Denver, have a two-hour lay-over and change again in Bullhorn. It's out of the way and a terrible connection. You'd do much better on the later plane. When can I book her for?"

"Let me think about it," I said. "I was also wondering if you could give me the names of passengers on a partic-ular flight. I was out here about a week ago and I thought I saw an old friend get off that three o'clock flight from Bullhorn, but he went to get his luggage and I lost track of him. It's someone I'd kind of like to get in touch with again."

His look implied, "For *this* you dragged me away from football?" But he said, "We are not allowed to give out the names of our passengers."

"Well, thanks anyway."

I wandered back through the airport and ended up in an observation room with a large window that faced the runway. There wasn't much traffic at Fire Pond Airport and at the moment the runway stood empty, its bright lights beating back the night. The walls of the room were lined with model airplanes, a history of aviation. The Air Force's sleek fighting machines were represented: a Sabre jet, a Scorpion, a Delta Dagger, a Shooting Star, a Voo-doo and the jet of the moment, named appropriately the F-16 Fighting Falcon.

There was a time when flying was new and people stood in the window and waited for their loved ones to take off, half convinced they would never see them again. Now kids were shipped back and forth across the country willy-nilly without even a certainty that a parent would be at the other end to meet them. A plane rolled toward the runway, the lights twinkled at the ends of the wings. I couldn't tell whether it was the Kid's flight or not from where I stood. My business concluded, I was ready to return to my home-away-from-home motel efficiency, but I hung at the window a little longer. If it was the Kid, I'd watch him leave. It was one of those instants where time and space connect, when a vacuum caused by a coming event sucks the breath from the present, a dark still moment before the whoosh of spontaneous combustion. Something at the dark end of the runway ignited while I stood there and burst into flame, its fiery tentacles reaching into the night. There was no way of telling what it was or how big it was, but most likely it was an airplane. What else was there to burn at an airport? A trap door dropped open beneath my rib cage and my heart hovered at the edge. At the same time my rational mind said, "It's not the Kid, the Kid's plane is on the runway." But you can't always trust the rational mind.

Word of the fire spread fast and people from all over the airport rushed to the window—a crowd for Montana. Some, like me, held themselves nervously in place, but most were thrilled. "Wow," said a little boy next to me. "Look at those flames." Obviously *he* wasn't worried about losing a lover. In the crowd I spotted a Frontier attendant.

"That couldn't be the Frontier flight to Denver, could it?" I asked. "I know somebody on that plane."

"No way," she said. "That's where the private planes are parked. Our flight is taking off just about now."

The waiting plane, not to be deterred from its schedule by a fire, sped down the runway and lifted off, giving its passengers a spectacular overhead view of the end of some-one's dream and the beginning of an insurance claim. I watched the taillights rise and move out. Now that I knew the Kid was gone, and it wasn't *my* private plane going up in smoke, the fire began to resemble a celebration, a pep rally bonfire or a campfire where kids sit around and roast marshmallows on sticks at the end of summer. There was no reason to linger any longer, but I stayed, fascinated by the fingers of flame. Apparently there was plenty of fuel to feed the blaze and it took the airport's ground crew a good fifteen minutes to get it under control. At my distance they were little stick figures, black silhouettes that moved back and forth in front of the flames. As the fire and excitement died down, I decided to head home. Among the crowd behind me I saw some sharp-eyed mountain faces, some placid faces from the plains, some watchful Indians and one face that I recognized all too well, the radiant, enraptured Katharine. Her expression approached bliss as she stared out the window.

"Katharine?" I asked.

She looked as if I had woken her from a dream and for a moment the dying flames reflected in the black centers of her eyes and they glowed red and feral like a coyote on the prowl. She smiled.

There was a disturbance at the end of the room. Someone was pushing and shoving his way through the crowd.

"That's her! That's the woman!" Even in haste and in anger the voice spoke of British schools and Mideast money—the prince. He was followed by two airport security guards who wore drab uniforms, but the prince himself was resplendent in a brown leather flight jacket with a white silk scarf around his neck. "That woman tried to blow me up," he said. "She wrecked the Sparhawk."

A guard lunged at Katharine and she threw up her arms to ward off the attack. He grabbed her and she fought and scratched back. The blissed-out look evaporated quickly and rage took its place. While the guard struggled to get control of her arms, she kicked her cowboy boot and nailed him right in the crotch. You had to admire her spirit.

"You bitch." The guy doubled over and Katharine began a broken field run, elbowing her way through the crowd. It was a gallant but hopeless effort. The other guard was right behind and, as she broke away and dashed across the slick-floored lobby, he tackled her. She landed flat and hard on her stomach and her breath was knocked out. Just to be sure she stayed that way, the guard sat down and straddled her back. It was an undignified position for a woman, but it had an impact. I'm not sure dignity was the issue when it came to Katharine anyway. Anger was. She pounded her fists against the linoleum and gasped for breath, never having been schooled, apparently, in the sixties protestor's art of going limp.

The prince walked up and stood next to her and his polished boots came to rest very close to her head. In spite of his British manners he came from a barbaric country, a place where you have the choice of killing your attackers outright or letting the state's executioners bury them up to the neck in sand while they throw stones at the protruding heads until they splatter like grapefruit. The prince studied Katharine's livid face carefully, looked at his boot as if he'd decided she wasn't worth bloodying it, then turned and walked away, leaving the suspect to the guard. Katharine recovered her breath enough to spit at the spot where his foot had lingered. "Bastard," she yelled.

If that was courage, she had plenty of it. But to me it looked like a mad monkey had gotten control of her mind, and once you let him in it's hard to get rid of him. He was a screeching, hyper monkey with no regard for anything but his own need to express. It's a type of abandonment and rage that I see exhibited nowadays more often by women than men, and men usually have to be drunk before they let it show. With women it is closer to the surface. Anything—an annoying husband, a bratty child—can set it off. Domesticity and marriage are its natural habitat, but not the only one. It is the raw nerve of anger, and if you scraped at it, all you'd find underneath would be another, redder layer. What could be the source of such a rage, but the illusion of helplessness? Wouldn't a person with perceived options and confidence find a more productive way to obtain a goal? It made one wonder what had been accomplished in the last twenty years. I suppose it was a sign of progress that women felt free to let it out in public, but it was depressing that they needed to.

"So Attorney Hamel," the prince said, parking his shiny boots next to me. "We meet again."

"What happened?" I asked him.

"She sabotaged the Sparhawk." The ball was between his hands and he squeezed them shut, squishing the air out. "I saw that woman walk away from the area, but I didn't think much of it. For all I knew she had a reason to be there, maybe she had a plane of her own on the field. I like to fly at night—the nights are so big and peaceful here—and I was taking the Sparhawk out for a short flight to amuse myself. I got in, turned on the starter, but there was something in the jet that jammed the engine and *whoosh* the plane went up in flames. It was very fortunate that I got out alive."

"Well, be grateful for that." You couldn't feel *too* bad for the guy; he hadn't even been singed and besides there were lots more Sparhawks where that one came from. "How could she sabotage a jet?" I asked.

"It's not very hard. You just throw something into the engine. Usually I cover the jet engines, but I took Attorney Stillman for a flight this afternoon and I planned to cover them after I finished tonight. A large rock would destroy an engine, so would just about anything else. You could empty your suitcase, that would do it: running shoes, jeans, a down vest, even a fur coat would destroy an engine."

"If it was a fur coat, it wasn't Katharine."

"Katharine? Do you know her?"

"Yes. She's March Augusta's girlfriend."

The prince, widening his hands like he was stretching out a note on an accordion, reinflated the ever-present ball. "Indeed. Her lover kills Sandy Pedersen, then she tries to kill me. Can someone please tell me why?"

"Well, first of all, as I already told you, March didn't kill Sandy Pedersen. Secondly, I don't know that she did try to kill you. If she did sabotage the Sparhawk maybe she just wanted to prevent you from leaving and make a statement in the process." Which raised the question of how she knew he *was* leaving.

The prince brushed some imaginary lint from the arm of the jacket, which looked like a old flight jacket but was made of butter-soft leather, much finer quality than any bombardier ever wore. It probably came from some boutique in London, one of those elegant stores where black-veiled Saudi women spent millions of dollars on clothes and jewels to be seen by nobody but other members of the harem. "Why should she care whether I left or did not?" the prince asked.

"She didn't want you to take the gyrfalcon."

"The gyrfalcon. What concern is that of hers?"

"She cares about birds, as do a lot of people." It was a possibility that the prince had somehow fulfilled his dream and gotten ahold of the gyr, but if she had been in that plane the only flying she was doing now was as a wisp of smoke. "You didn't have the bird in the plane, did you?" I asked him.

The prince stopped picking at the lint. "I'm afraid not," he said and changed the subject. "What is wrong with women in your country anyway? They have everything they want, but it hasn't made them happy. Why are they

167

so angry? Women in Saudi Arabia don't act like that."

"How would anybody know? They are invisible in their black veils."

"That is not true. They have power in the home. They can scream and yell just as well as an American woman, but they don't."

Katharine was screaming and yelling pretty well as the guards dragged her out of the airport. "Bastards," she screamed. "Bastards, bastards, bastards. You're letting the poachers, the real killers, go free while March is stuck in jail." All eyes were on her, but her face, deranged with anger, was not a pleasant sight.

I'd been in Montana long
enough now to know what there was to get angry about:
predators who were free to kill, predators who weren't;
poachers who illegally took raptors from the wild for money,
poachers who did it for the federal government; people
who were imprisoned for crimes they didn't commit, people who committed crimes and went free. There was
everything in Montana to get angry about and nothing.
The everything is easy, the nothing is hard, unless you're
a Buddha. Anger can be useful when it is under control;
it can also be a mad monkey that climbs into the mind and
throws sense out. Some societies (Latin and Arab for start-
ers) reward angry behavior. If a crime is committed in the
heat of passion, the criminal may go free, particularly if
the person who commits the crime is a man, and the person who supposedly provokes it is a woman. Even in the
U.S.A. we make a distinction between crime that is premeditated and crime that is impassioned, but I've never

been able to figure out why a crime that requires thought and planning is more reprehensible than one that is impulsive. A person who acts without thinking is far less predictable and far more dangerous to the ordinary uninvolved citizen than one who is motivated, plans ahead and knows who they're after.

As I drove through Fire Pond I was struck once again by its placid facade. It was hard to imagine a crime taking place here, planned or otherwise. What could go wrong in a town where the mountains were far enough away to impress you with their beauty without oppressing you with their shadow, a town with perfectly straight streets numbered and lettered in sequence, with no traffic problems even at nine o'clock in the morning, a town where cars stopped to let a pedestrian go by? It was another deep-blue-sky, crystalline-air day, a day of brilliant sunshine and clearly defined shadows. I was on my way to the massive stone building that now housed a gentle man, a black marketeer and an angry woman.

March and Katharine were under the same roof again. How long that would last could well depend on Wayne Betts. The prince's plane had been parked at a municipal airport and had not been on federal land so the supposed sabotage wouldn't actually be under Betts's jurisdiction. It wasn't a federal crime, but if Betts could establish that it was related to the federal crime (the killing of a government operative on federal land) he might be able to involve himself in Katharine's bail hearing, which would probably take place this afternoon.

I had a client once in Albuquerque whose bookkeeper robbed him blind and spent the money on drugs and sugar. The money she took came from his employees' withholding. Instead of paying the IRS she paid herself, and the penalties the IRS imposed when they caught up to him forced my client into bankruptcy. He got wise to her when she left the office one day to try to recover a repossessed car and he opened the mail to find a dunning letter from the IRS. We had her arrested on a Friday morning; she was out on Friday afternoon. "We don't like to keep women in jail over the weekend," the judge told me. "Then we have to feed 'em." Betts was probably liberated enough to have no compunction about keeping a woman in jail and feeding her for two days or twenty years if he thought she'd interfered with his sting operation.

The way to be a good lawyer, they say, is to see things through your opponent's eyes. How would Betts's swimming-pool blues see Katharine's unstrung behavior at the airport? I wondered. Would it indicate to him that she had also been involved in Pedersen's murder? She hated poachers, she had wolf-wipers in her shed, she was capable of violent acts.

I'd made an appointment to talk to Betts later. My concern at the moment was March, who sat across from me in the visiting room of the Fire Pond jail. He didn't look good; his hair seemed limp and drab, as if his curls had lost their spirit in captivity. His eyes were dull and he was badly in need of a change of clothes. Was he depressed for Katharine because the wild bird was now imprisoned between these stone walls or could it be because Katharine was no longer on the outside fighting his battles for him? March was the still center around which we had revolved. While he had been locked up passively in here, I'd been chasing a murderer for him, as the Kid put it. But still it was a job, I was gaining some experience and getting paid for it. What about Katharine? Was she acting out some submerged, possibly violent impulse for March? I didn't believe he was capable of killing Pedersen or of asking Katharine to do it, but maybe she'd been angry enough that she wanted to. She was openly angry, he wasn't, maybe that was enough. Maybe it was Katharine's violence that made it possible for him to remain so calm. Was she the falcon in this situation and he the falconer? Or, like in many relationships that had gone on for a while, had the roles blurred? Although the burden of proof wasn't on me, I was ready to believe Katharine had sabotaged the prince's plane. The more interesting question was what else she had done.

"What kind of a day is it?" March asked me wistfully.

"It's beautiful, crisp and clear and the sky goes on forever."

"It won't be long before we have the first snow. I'd love to be out there making tracks in it," he sighed.

"I know."

"I'm glad to see you," he said and for a moment the amber light came on and warmed his eyes. Even with his jailhouse pallor, he was a great-looking guy, and gentle, too, but gentleness could turn to Jell-O in here.

"I'm sorry I wasn't able to get back sooner. It's been quite a week; a murder, a car wreck, now this."

"What happened with Brannen? You never did tell me."

"He didn't tell me anything, but it wasn't long after I left his place that I was run off the road."

"I can't believe Jimmy would do something like that."

Hard for March to believe that anybody he knew was capable of doing anything he didn't like. "Maybe he didn't, maybe he called someone else who did. Have you seen Katharine yet?" I asked.

"Only briefly."

"How is she doing?"

"Not too well," he said. "She hates it here."

"Does she have a lawyer?"

"Yes, someone who has represented her before."

"What happened?"

"She found out the prince was planning on leaving on Saturday . . ."

"How did she find that out?" It was the question I'd been afraid I'd have to ask.

He picked at the tear in his jeans, which had widened at least an inch since I saw him last. A sliver of white leg peeked through. "I told her."

And that was the answer I'd been afraid of. "You *told* her? March, I asked you not to talk about what I told you with anyone and that included Katharine, especially Katharine."

"We live together . . . when we're not in jail together." He smiled slightly. "It's hard not to tell her what's going on in my life."

"You're not going to have much of a life if you don't cooperate with me." My voice was rising, but I couldn't help it. He'd given Katharine the opportunity to screw up my case.

March picked at his jeans some more. Another week in here and the hole would be big enough for his knee to fit through. "I'm sorry. I didn't realize it was so important."

"Of course it's important. I don't know whether Katharine sabotaged the prince's plane or not. I'm going to see Betts later and it would be better if I didn't know. However, he is likely to think that a woman violent enough to try to ground the prince is capable of killing or aiding in the killing of Pedersen. There's no point in my helping him to reach that conclusion. If he can find a connection between the two crimes, he'll keep you both in jail."

"He can't keep Katharine here. Being imprisoned would kill her."

"If he can't, there is a good chance the state can. She should have thought it through before she lost control and acted so irrationally."

"That's not fair."

Fair? What did that have to do with it? I was right.

"Katharine's been through some hard times," he said.

"You know someone who hasn't?"

"It's been worse for her than most. Her parents split up when she was only a kid. The father took off and her mother had a succession of boyfriends. One of them molested Katharine and locked her in a shed when she threatened to tell her mother. The shed was cold and dark; it was a terrifying experience. Because of that Katharine has a horror of being locked up. She can't stand to see any living creature imprisoned. It has freaked her out even to visit me here. It's going to be hell for her in jail."

A bad childhood experience—that might explain it, it might not. You could say she was traumatized by her childhood. You could also say she came into this life with a difficult karma to work out, a residue of bad deeds from past lives which was attracting violence to her in this one. It depends which side of the sixties you're on. Whatever the cause of it, there is a certain amount of repetition in life. A person who has been a victim of violence in childhood is all too likely to experience the same later on. Only sometimes the roles change, the victim becomes the aggressor when the violence is repeated. Abused children can become abusive adults. If Katharine was violent and out of control enough to have thrown something into the prince's jet engine, the next question would have to be, Had she been violent enough to have set the trap for Pedersen? Had March been accurate about the number of wolf-wipers in their shed? If so, had she gotten another one from Jimmy Brannen?

Next question, Had she run me off the road because she feared Jimmy Brannen had blabbed or maybe just because she wanted to? A lot of people were willing to peer over the abyss now and then; Katharine jumped right in. Maybe she had an elastic rope that she counted on to bring her back. If so, the person who held the other end of it sat across from me. If anyone knew what Katharine was capable of it was March so I asked.

"March, I don't like to do this, but there's a question I have to ask you."

"Shoot."

"Did Katharine set the trap for Pedersen?"

He hesitated and then he said "No," very softly. His amber eyes, however, had a blank and puzzled expression.

"She's an unguided missile. Who really knows what she would do?" I was thinking out loud, which is a mistake when someone else is listening.

"You never get angry?" asked March.

"I don't let it get out of control."

"Nobody's perfect." He was, in fact, getting a little edgy himself.

"What's that supposed to mean?" The acrimony in this conversation was escalating quickly.

"Your drinking, for example. Do you have *that* under control?" He was making a good case for the notion that depression is anger repressed. His hair curled right up as his own temper began to show.

"Drinking? What are you talking about? Have you ever seen me drinking?" This "drinking" business was getting overworked. I had a tequila now and then. So what?

"Actually, the only place I ever see you is right here. It was just something Joan mentioned once. She worried that you were drinking too much." He smiled ruefully, de-escalating already, indicating he either had a whole lot of control or only a little bit of anger.

"Joan? What did she know about my drinking?" It pissed me off. Here I was trekking all over Montana finishing up her business, working for him, and *they* accused me of drinking.

"I'm sorry, Neil. Don't be angry." The deer-in-the-woods

look had come back into his eyes. I was the attorney, he was the incarcerated client. We had the same goal—getting him out of here. There was a lot at stake and someone had to back off, which was something he did better than I. I'll admit it. It came with the territory. I don't know of anyone who ever paid an attorney to back off.

"Angry?" I asked. "Who's angry?" I looked at the large clock on the wall that ticked off the prisoner's precious visiting hours. "I should get going. I have to see Betts." Actually it wasn't time to see Betts—that appointment wasn't until this afternoon—but it was time to get out of here. When you get right down to it, I'm not crazy about being in jail either.

"What are you going to talk to him about?"

"Just some information about his sting operation I'd like to check out."

"Let me know what he says." He didn't push it, which was just as well; I didn't want Katharine attacking any more suspects if she got out on bail.

"Of course."

"Neil." He looked down at his jeans. "I really appreciate all that you're doing for me. I want you to know that."

"Thanks," I said.

"You're not angry?"

"Didn't I say I wasn't?"

"See you soon?"

"You got it."

I left him staring morosely down the long hallway that led to his cell.

On my way back to the Aspen Inn I made a stop at a nearby mall because I was out of Marlboros. Back in the Pontiac I lit my cigarette and began negotiating my way out of the parking lot. The exit onto B Street was blocked by a Chevy Blazer trying to make a left turn. The driver was a woman with neat blond hair. The Blazer had New

Mexico plates, which made her a neighbor I guess. It also had one of those bumper stickers you see in New Mexico that ask, "Are you prepared to meet your maker?" She thoughtfully chewed a piece of gum while she pondered her move and pondered it some more, afraid to take the plunge. There was some traffic on B Street, but not that much, and the blond just sat there chewing her gum, blocking my exit and letting opportunities go by. I sidled up on her right and tried to squeeze through, but it couldn't be done without scraping the lone strip of chrome off my no-frills rental car. I tapped my horn politely after she let one more opportunity pass, but there was no reaction. Granted a left-hand turn is tougher than a right, but if she was afraid to cross one lane and turn into another, she could have just turned right and gone around the block like a thinking person. Being trapped behind a gum-chewing Baptist in an oversized 4 × 4 was getting on my nerves. Maybe she was preparing to meet her maker in the parking lot, because she sure wasn't making any effort to get out of there. She had to be from the southern part of the state to be that slow. I checked the fine print over the zia sign on the red and yellow license plate. Ruidoso, the noisy city. If she came from northern New Mexico, she'd have learned not to hesitate in traffic and to stay alert in parking lots. I beeped again louder. She turned and smiled as if to say, "What can I do? It's in God's hands."

"Move it, bitch," I said.

When I got back to the Aspen Inn, the movable letters had been removed from the sign, indicating, I supposed, that the Rebekahs and Odd Fellows had gone back to their nests. As I eased my way between the yellow lines in the parking lot, a pickup truck pulled in next to me, a beat-up brown model with rust spots on the side and a lot of nicks and dings in the fenders. The blue letters on the license plate said TALL; Leo Wolfe stretched his legs slowly, stepped out and ambled over.

"Your truck looks like it's seen some hard driving," I said. If he wasn't stupid enough to show up at the Aspen Inn in a truck in which he'd tried to run me off the road, he might be arrogant enough.

"It gets a workout," he replied. "If you've got a minute, I'll buy you a cup of coffee."

The desk clerk flagged me down as we entered the lobby to give me a message from Marie, Tom Mitchell's secretary, saying she'd like to talk to me today. Leo took off his cowboy hat when we entered the coffee shop, and, since there was no peg to hang it on, he carried it to the booth. He sucked in his gut, squeezed himself behind the table and lay the cowboy hat on the seat next to him. Once we had ordered our caffeine (coffee for him, tea for me), he shook his mane and congratulated himself.

"Well, I was right about that sting operation, wasn't I?" Although he'd given the L and the W equal billing on his gate, I'd seen a lot more of the L so far than I had of the W. Unlike the bold and boastful lion, wolves are supposedly the shyest of creatures: sleek, swift, furtive, but nurturing pack animals. Only the leaders, the alpha pair, breed, but the whole pack participates in raising the young.

"You were right." I was willing to give him credit—not the same thing as giving him praise, but the difference was wasted on him.

"Betts pulled in some big international dealers, I hear. He was wasting the taxpayers' money by going after guys like me who keep a Mimi for a hobby when he had international operators and a Saudi Arabian prince." The waitress plopped a cup of coffee in front of Leo, a cup of water with a tea bag floating in it in front of me.

"Maybe he just set out the bait and waited to see who bit," I said. I took the tea bag out of the cup and put it on a napkin—there was no saucer—where it left a brown stain. I prefer weak or better yet herb teas; they're more colorful, but the New Age in tea bags hadn't made it into the Aspen Inn yet.

"A trapper wants to know what he's after when he sets a trap. The kind of predator you're after tells you where to set up, how to set up, what kind of bait and lures to use."

Trappers seemed to like to emphasize the word "predator" when they talked about their kills, I noticed, as if killing a killer made killing all right.

Leo poured some white sugar into his black coffee. "They sell lures for every kind of animal you'd ever want to trap. Did you know that? They've got lures for coyote, fox, mink, coons and beavers, lures that will appeal to their hunger, their curiosity, their sex drive—those are a mixture of musk and glands and in-heat urine. My personal favorite has always been Cat Man Do. It's kind of loud, but it'll pull in a coyote every time. They can't get enough of it. Now the use of urine is interesting. The smell of it will pull in the animal and it will also disguise the human odor. Some guys put trail scent packs on their boots with red fox urine scent in 'em when they hike to the trap. Covers up their smell. But in my experience if you're trying to pull in people, the best lure is money. It's more effective even than glands. Although that Kate's got a nice musky scent; I might walk a mile to get into her boots." He cradled his coffee in his large hands, sipping away without waiting for it to cool.

"Well, I suppose if someone were setting a trap for a human and intended to use his own urine as a lure, a man would be more likely to do it than a woman. It's a lot easier for a man to unzip and piss outdoors."

"Not if the woman's wearing a skirt it isn't. It's easy enough for a woman to squat down and pee with a skirt on."

His dumb macho act was about as unappetizing as a slab of raw and bloody meat, but he wasn't altogether as stupid as he liked to pretend. Since I was stuck with him at least until I'd finished my tea, I decided to take advantage of what knowledge he had. "Suppose you got it in your mind to trap a bird, how would *you* go about it?"

"There's a couple of ways. One is you make yourself a

headset, a wire frame that will fit over your head and shoulders, and you cover it with weeds or leaves, whatever it takes for camouflage. You conceal yourself. Dig a shallow trench if you have to and cover yourself with dirt. You take a pigeon, tie a string to its leg, hold it in front of you and move it around to attract the hawk. Of course, you've got to have some reason to think the hawk's gonna show up there. If she does, you wait until she attacks the pigeon and then you grab her around the legs. The other way is set up a spring-loaded bow net. It's a small net and you conceal it carefully. Again you hide yourself in a blind and use pigeons to pull in the hawk. But handling a bow net can be tricky when you've got a hawk coming at you. Kind of like pulling a trout out of thin air." He put down his coffee and flicked his own wrist in a fly casting gesture that was fluid and surprisingly graceful considering the size of his hands.

"I don't suppose just anybody can do it."

"Well, it takes a lot of skill to handle a bow net, but it takes more patience than skill to hide yourself and grab a hungry hawk around the legs." He brought his hands back to the coffee cup and the conversation back to a favorite subject—Katharine. "So Kate's been pulled in for blowing up the prince's jet plane. It was a beauty, too, I hear."

"The razor's edge of the performance envelope."

"That's good. I like that." He grinned. "She's a wild woman." He shook his head in admiration. "She's not gonna like prison, but Betts will want to keep her there. The way he'll put two and two together, if she'd blow up a prince, she'd trap a poacher."

"She's got a lot of traps in her shed, too," I said.

"That's right."

"Why are you so eager to pin Pedersen's murder on Katharine?" I asked him.

"The way she's acting she's doing it to herself."

I'd have to agree with him on that one.

"How's March doing?" he asked.

"Not great. He's miserable in prison."

"The poachers been hassling him?"

"Not any more. They think he's a hero now that it has come out that Pedersen was a government operative."

"If Betts can pin the murder on Katharine, March'll get out."

"Could be he won't pin it on either one of them. Pedersen was pretty careless, you told me so yourself. Seems to me a more likely murderer would be someone who realized he was being set up. Someone Pedersen had talked to, someone he had the goods on."

"Like I told you before it wasn't a falconer. They get all the excitement they need just from watching their birds." He finished his coffee, put his cup down, waved at the waitress to get some more. "More for you?" he asked me.

"No," I replied. My teacup was still almost full. "Any falconer who ends up in the Fire Pond jail isn't going to be seeing many birds."

"*If* Betts can make the charges stick."

"Did you come all the way into Fire Pond just to talk to me about that?"

"No. I came in because the Fish and Wildlife Service asked me to. You a birder?"

"Me? No way. I can tell the difference between a raven and a crow, though."

"Yeah? How's that?"

"It's a matter of a pinion."

He laughed at the joke, the first person in recent memory to do so. You never know from what barren range a sense of humor will spring. "If you're not a birder, what brought you to Montana in the first place?"

It wasn't hunger, it wasn't sex, it wasn't even money. "Curiosity," I said. "Why did the Fish and Wildlife Service ask you to come in?"

"Because I know a hell of a lot more about raptors than they do, and they have some sick birds in their custody, some that their operatives brought in, some that they took from poachers. They've already had to destroy five Finnish goshawks that a Canadian smuggler had because they'd gotten rickets from starvation diets. They've got sick falcons, birds with broken wings, birds that need care, and the Fish and Wildlife Service doesn't know how to do it.

"They're the FWS, not the FBI. They hired incompetent agents, guys who don't know a falcon from a duck, to go into the wilderness and take fledglings and even eggs from the nests. Between the great horned owls and the coyotes, a young falcon hasn't got but a twenty-five to fifty percent chance in the wild anyway. And now they've got government agents to deal with. A falcon's egg is a delicate thing. Some heavy-handed government operative took peregrine falcon eggs from a nest, I hear, and broke them. It kind of annoys me that the government can get away with that when it's illegal for me to take a passager bird, train it to return to me and watch it fly and hunt like . . . like what? There's nothing in the world you can compare a falcon to. Everything else that flies gets compared to them."

"What else has got a plane, a car, a TV series and a movie named after it?"

"A football team, too. The gyr is a beauty—talk about the outer edge of the performance envelope."

"You've seen her?"

"I've been out to the aerie, sure. It was no secret where she was once March took you all out there and Pedersen got bumped. Just because the Fish and Wildlife Service says I can't touch don't mean I can't look. She's the biggest, whitest, swiftest bird I've ever seen."

"You'd love to have her, wouldn't you?"

"Wouldn't you take Robert Redford if you had the chance?"

"I could live without him."

"Some people think March is a great-looking guy."

"Not that great," I said, putting down my teacup and bringing the conversation back to where *I* wanted it to be. "Wouldn't it bother you to see a wild and free spirit like the gyr in captivity?"

"If she were mine, I'd treat her well. A good falconer will feed his bird and tend it better than it would ever be in the wild. Some birds in captivity live to be thirty years old. They'd never make it that far on their own."

"Yeah, but in captivity they spend most of their lives tied to a perch."

"They get to fly, they get to hunt. A falcon is wild and stubborn as hell. It's not a dog you can train to roll over and bark on command. In fact, you could beat the shit out of it—if you were inclined that way—and it still wouldn't do anything it didn't want to. It comes back to its trainer because it's lazy, because it gets fed, because it's a creature of habit. It's on its own when it's flying, there's nothing to make it come back but habit and hunger."

He hadn't, I noticed, mentioned love and devotion.

"A hawk in the wild doesn't do anything, anyway, unless it's hungry. It just sits on a perch and hangs around till it's empty enough to kill." He finished his second cup of coffee, put the cup down, and laid his big hands on the table, the kind of hands that would coddle, protect and smother, if you let them. He got to the point of his visit.

"Now that Betts has called in his sting operation the Fish and Wildlife Service is stuck with the bunch of birds they brought in for evidence. Only they don't know how to take care of them, so they want me to help." He shook his head. The irony of it wasn't wasted on him. "It's a big job and I could use some assistance. I was wondering if any of the birders are still around who know something about raptors."

"John King has gone," I said. "But Avery is still here. He knows something about everything, maybe he could help."

We tracked Avery to his room, where he happened to be taking a nap, although he'd be the last to admit it. As a nocturnal being, midday wasn't his best time. His fine white hair had enough natural electricity to crackle even before he tuned in, but his eyes blinked slowly awake behind his thick glasses and his skin had the rumpled texture of sleep. He was tucking his shirttail in as he answered the door. It made him seem not old exactly but vulnerable, to predation, maybe, or just to time.

His door had a sign on it that said it was a no smoking room, which immediately instilled in me a desire to light up. His room had the same mottled wall-to-wall and plaid sofa as mine but it seemed more like a nest. It was the pile of books on the end table, I guess, the maps opened up and spread across the floor, or maybe the clothes he hadn't bothered to hang up.

"Neil," he said. "Good to see you." He did his happy little two-step again and made me feel that if I offered my hand, he'd kiss it.

"Avery, this is Leo Wolfe. He's a falconer."

"My pleasure," said Avery. "What kind of bird do you have?"

"Kestrel."

Do lions and wolves eat owls? I wondered. Was Leo's ego massive enough and Avery old enough that Leo would patronize him just like a woman?

"I need some help," Leo said and he told Avery about the birds. He could dispense with the macho bullshit when he wanted to, but then Avery had the ability to bring out the best in people.

"The birds are with a vet in town," said Leo, "but he doesn't know zip about hawks. You want to come on over with me and take a look?"

"Be glad to," said Avery. "Why don't you come along, Neil? You might find it interesting."

"What time is it?" I looked around the room, but Avery—like me—didn't seem to wear a watch or keep a clock either.

Leo glanced at his wrist where some red numbers flashed. "Twelve-thirty," he said.

"I have an appointment with Betts at one-thirty. I guess I could come for a little while."

"You might tell Betts what I think of his sting operation when you see him," Leo said.

"It did seem to be a misguided effort," Avery agreed. That was putting it kindly. Avery had lived a long time, had seen a great deal and had ended up kind. It said a lot for the man.

Leo Wolfe hadn't lived as long or ended up so kind either. "On second thought," he said, "maybe I'll tell him myself."

They left in Leo's truck and I followed them to the vet's office, which was in a Victorian bungalow on Q Street, neat and tidy looking outside but smelly as an old dog within. Avery and I waited in an examining room while Leo went to get a wounded peregrine.

"Peregrines are the most elegant of birds," Avery told me. "As they get older their wings become slate gray, their breasts are white and they have a chiaroscuro that reminds me of Fred Astaire in his tux."

The peregrine that Leo brought in was about eighteen

inches tall, brown and beige with a mottled breast and wings and black markings around her wary eyes. Leo's large hand held her by the legs.

"She's a young one," he said, "trapped by some government operative in Utah to use as bait to put falconers in jail."

"What's wrong with her?" I asked.

"Broken wing." As if on cue, the falcon tried to flap her wings. One wing opened up, the other bent and flopped over.

"Jesus," I said.

The peregrine's eyes changed from wary to panic-stricken as her wing failed her, the same desperate expression seen in the eyes of the grounded oil-slicked birds in Alaska's Prince William Sound. Leo tried to calm her by stroking her breast gently with his finger.

"What will become of her?" asked Avery.

"We'll set the wing but most likely she'll never fly again. Makes you good and mad, don't it, that some government jackass could do a thing like that to a falcon?"

18

I'd been to Betts's office enough times to know the route by now. I knew that even-numbered streets went one way, odd numbers another, but, wrapped up in my thoughts and puffing on my Marlboro, I made an error and turned down Fourth Avenue the wrong way. Nobody was on Fourth at the moment and I cruised along unaware until suddenly a Subaru whipped around a corner and swung wide to avoid me. The driver waved frantically. Another car came up right behind him and another. A light must have turned green somewhere downstream releasing this tide of traffic. There was a lot of horn beeping and irritated gesturing. "Okay, okay," I said, pulling into a driveway and smashing my cigarette out in the ashtray. "I get the point."

Wayne Betts awaited me at his large desk. As anticipated he had put two and two together and he didn't waste any time telling me about it. While it was interesting to hear his views on Katharine, it wasn't really why I had gone to see him. There was something else I wanted to discuss. Although his hands had been on the table when he'd talked to me before, his cards hadn't.

"This is not the first time we've had trouble with Katharine Conover," he said. "She's an animal . . . rights . . . activist."

The pauses indicated that "animal rights activist" was one of those phrases beloved by right-wing types who prefer slogan to thought. Obviously, it was supposed to stimulate me into some salivating, Pavlovian response, but my answer was to stare at Betts just as blankly as he usually looked at me. "So?"

"Animal rights activists are sick and violent individuals. Do you know what she did?"

"No."

He leaned back in his chair, stretched his legs and gave his knuckles a little squeeze, looking just like a Texan about to spin a tall tale. Considering the circumstances, I accepted what he told me as the truth, but it was one of those true stories that are weirder than fiction. Like a lot of weird stories, it involved Californians. "Well," he said. "There was a beaver farm in Crono, about fifty miles southwest of here. Some investors from California were trying to set up a business raising beavers for their pelts just like people raise mink. They had hundreds, maybe thousands, of 'em. Some people value beaver skins, but they're not the nicest animals to keep around. They're mean and smelly, not exactly household pets."

I didn't know much about beavers in general except that they worked hard and sharpened trees up like pencil tips. However, I had once made the acquaintance of a particular beaver when I was a law student at UNM and had a boyfriend who liked to hike in the Pecos. We had a favorite lake we hiked in to to swim nude. Anybody else who hiked in there swam naked, too, so that was no problem. The water was icy, high mountain cold, but by the time you got to it you were hot enough so it felt good for a little while. It was a favorite spot and the summer the romance peaked we spent a lot of time there. The next year the romance had begun a terminal downhill slide, but we hiked back up once anyway to try to recapture the feeling. It was a mistake. A beaver had taken over the pond and built himself a lodge at one end. The once-clear mountain lake was already starting to silt up, but we were hot, took off our clothes and leapt in. The beaver swam out of his twig hut, his rodent face just visible in the track he cut as he cleft the pond. He swam across the lake once, then came back again, edging a little closer to the spot where we stood. He head was slick and brown, and there was nothing cute or Disneylike about it. His broad, flat tail came up into the air and smacked down hard and loud as a gunshot against the water as if to say that pond was his now and he intended to be the only one in it. Who were we, uneasy lovers, to challenge him? I never went back there again.

"Unfortunately," Betts continued *his* beaver story, "the investors weren't well capitalized. They ran out of money and went back to California leaving the beavers with nobody to feed and care for them. It was not a pretty sight; the animals were sick and starving. Many of them died. Katharine's group petitioned the government for permission to go in there and feed the beavers until the case could be settled. Permission was granted to feed and care for them—that's all. But the next time the Fish and Wildlife Service went back to check up the beavers were all gone, every last one. Those people took it upon themselves to release them. They rented a bunch of vans from Rent A Wreck and turned them in in Boise, Idaho, but the vehicles had been destroyed. The beavers had ripped them to shreds and defecated all over the place. They'll never get the smell out. It was disgusting."

"What happened to the beavers?"

"Unless Katharine and her buddies turned them in to pets, they released them somewhere between here and Boise. Most of those beavers were raised in captivity and they didn't know zip about surviving in the wild. Sometimes these soft-hearted do-gooders are soft headed, too. People get pretty irrational when it comes to wildlife."

"What would you have done?" I asked.

Betts sat up straight in his chair. "Fattened 'em up, slaughtered 'em and sold the pelts to pay off the creditors." He looked at his watch. "I believe Katharine Conover is a violent menace to society and that she should not be released on bail."

Betts's record had been admirable so far, but unless there were some witnesses I doubted he'd be able to pull this one off. Katharine had walked through an airport, something destroyed a jet engine, she'd lost her temper under duress. There wouldn't be any fingerprints; the evidence had gone up in smoke. Maybe she'd broken some people's code for female behavior, but you still need evidence to prosecute someone in America. If that's all they had, it wasn't much except for the supposed connection between March and Pedersen and the real connection between Pedersen and the prince, March and Katharine.

"It's also quite likely she and March were in complicity in the Pedersen murder," said Betts.

"Why would she do something that would endanger her lover?"

He widened his eyes, the butterflies drifted up. "Women do crazy things."

"Men don't?"

"This particular woman has committed very irrational acts."

Next he'd tell me she'd been on the rag and recommend the PMS defense. Well, who was I to defend Katharine? She had her own attorney. "Actually, I didn't come here to talk to you about Katharine Conover. I'd like to talk about someone else—Cortland James. I assume you know who he is."

The blues fluttered down and lighted on me. "An Easterner, the head of the Conservation Committee. He was here with your birding expedition."

"Maybe, maybe he was here before the birding expedition. As the Irish say, a man can't be in two places at once unless he's a bird. When Cortland was supposedly still back East, he could well have been here. The flight he arrived on came from Bullhorn and didn't connect with any flights from the East. I think he flew out of Fire Pond on the Frontier flight to Bullhorn on November twelfth and came back on the return trip."

"So?"

"You could get the names of the passengers on those flights."

"What would that prove? Maybe he flew under an assumed name."

"He seems pretty fond of the name he has."

"Maybe he had business in Bullhorn." Once again there was that sense of something lurking behind the darting butterflies. Were we going to have to go through the discovery routine again?

"Do I really need to remind you that if you have information that will affect my client you are required to disclose it to me? All of it."

Betts fondled his knuckles, looked out the window as if he wished he were on the other side of the glass, and then he fessed up. "We don't need to check the passenger lists. Cortland James was here before the afternoon of November twelfth."

"He was negotiating with Pedersen?"

"Yes."

"Well then, I suppose you have it all on tape."

"Not exactly." He had the kind of fair skin that was also an indicator, and the flush it exhibited right now indicated to me that the government had screwed up so badly even *he* was embarrassed by it. "Some of the tapes are missing. Someone broke into Pedersen's apartment the day of the murder and took them."

The day of the murder. The day Cortland supposedly stayed home sneezing into his embroidered hanky. There's more than one way to induce a runny nose. "Someone broke into Pedersen's apartment the day of the murder and you didn't tell me?"

Betts shrugged. He had more nervous habits than George Bush and something similar to be nervous about, another dubious government cover-up. "There were no fingerprints, no witnesses, nothing to tell. It could well have been one of the falconers who negotiated with Pedersen. It could have been Katharine. Her whereabouts haven't been established for that day."

"Was Cortland James's tape taken?"

"All the tapes in the apartment were taken. Tapes of some falconers were missing, too."

"What about your men in the phone truck? Weren't they recording everything?"

"Not everything. Some of the falconers would only meet Pedersen in places we couldn't get close enough to record. In those instances he wore a body recorder about the size of a cigarette pack taped to his calf." He bent over to demonstrate on his leg where the recorder was affixed. It was a child's trick, trying to divert you from the major misdeed by plying you with irrelevant details.

"Didn't he copy those tapes?"

"He was going to. We planned to pick them up Wednesday."

Trust the federal government to set up an elaborate, expensive sting and fuck it up.

"We have no reason to suspect Cortland James of murder or of taking the tapes. He is a wealthy, prominent citizen, the head of a prestigious conservation organization, not a falconer."

"He was negotiating with Pedersen, he must have wanted the falcon. Why? To add to his life list?"

"We don't know." He used the royal "we." It was "I" when the government did something right, I noticed, "we" when they didn't. "But we have no reason to believe that Cortland James would kill for a bird."

"Maybe he didn't kill for a bird," I said.

Betts blinked his eyes and looked at his watch again. "Are we finished? There's a bail hearing in fifteen minutes," he said.

"We're finished," I replied.

I went next to see Marie, Tom Mitchell's crackerjack secretary, in the office on Third Avenue. The pace had picked up since the last time I'd been there. No longer sitting still at her desk staring wistfully toward the Dakotas, Marie was bustling around, shuffling papers, and the phone rang several times during our brief interview. It's annoying to be talking to someone who keeps taking phone calls, but I had it under control.

"How's it going, Neil, you making some progress?"

"Some," I said.

"The reason I wanted to talk to you is that Tom called this morning to say he's coming back Monday."

"You seem relieved."

"I am. I hate not having anything to do. Anyway, Tom said he's ready to take over March's defense."

"Have you talked to March about it?"

"I wouldn't do that. He's your client now."

"I'll think about it," I said, even though I already had. Would I like to go back home and sleep curled up behind the Kid? Yes. Was I still pissed with March for talking to Katharine? Maybe. Would I leave Montana with an unresolved case, without even finding out who had run me off the road? No. Could I persuade March to keep me on the case? "I'll talk to March over the weekend and call Tom on Monday."

"Give him my best," Marie said, taking another call.

"Be glad to," I said.

It felt like a night to go home to my motel efficiency and plot my next move while I curled up with a Cuervo Gold and some Lean Cuisines. As I had plenty of the former but none of the latter, I stopped at Albertson's on my way back. I picked out a zucchini lasagna and a cheese cannelloni, got into the checkout line and read the headlines on *People* and the *National Enquirer* just to stay in touch.

A courtly silver-haired gentleman got on line behind me. "Elvis Presley is alive," I told him. "He was seen buying Lean Cuisines in a supermarket in Oregon. He's still trying to lose weight, but he'd do better if he limited himself to one. The trouble with Elvis is he never learned when to say when."

"You can read that far?" asked the gentleman.

"Only when I wear my contacts," I replied.

"I have glasses," he said squinting toward the tabloid headlines, "but I hate to wear them."

"How do you find your way around this place? It is rather large."

"I've been here so often I know where most everything is. I wanted to make myself a cheesecake, but I think they've moved the mix. You haven't seen it, have you?"

There was a sign over aisle four clearly visible through my lenses, CAKE MIXES, it said. "Aisle four, right over there," I told him.

"Thanks."

He was back with his mix before he'd lost his place in line. I paid for my groceries, he paid for his. He followed me outside.

"You're not from around here, are you?" he asked.

"New Mexico."

"Welcome to Montana. I hope you'll enjoy your visit."

"Thanks," I said. I watched him get in his truck, not bothering to put on the glasses he hated to wear, and, squinting narrowly, pull out of the parking lot. I waited a few minutes to put some distance between us. If you're going to have a collision, you might as well have one with a gentleman, but it's better not to have one at all.

There are those who focus on the far away in Montana, those who keep their eyes on the middle distance, those who can only see what's up close. The time had come to look up close, to go out to the aerie and search for the black line, the thread that led out of the rug.

19

When I got back to the Aspen Inn, I put a quarter in a vending machine in the lobby and took out the *Fire Pond News*. The name of Kills on Top, the Indian who had been accused of a barroom murder, had been spelled Killsontop in this paper, which made him seem a lot less culpable. The selection of stories about wildlife-related crimes rivaled the *National Enquirer* today. A man in Silverton had been treated for rabies after having had sex with a raccoon. He defended himself against charges of animal cruelty on the grounds that the raccoon was already dead.

It was an early edition paper and the news I was looking for wasn't in it yet. I checked the weather. A winter storm watch was in effect for Sunday afternoon, as a major low pressure system was coming in bringing snow, several inches of it, which could easily close Freezeout for the winter. Tomorrow, Saturday, could be my last chance to get to the aerie to look for evidence and to see the gyr. It could also be somebody else's last chance to take her, my only chance to prevent it.

I stopped by Avery's room and found him sitting on the floor reading maps. Some people read the *National Enquirer* for amusement, some read the phone book, some read maps.

"I was thinking I might drive up to The Pipes Sanctuary tomorrow. Want to come?" He pointed the spot out to me on the map. Map readers need to see a place before they go there and have an image in their mind of where it sits relative to all the other places they have (or haven't) been. I could understand it, having once been a map reader myself, but then I discovered legal briefs and phone books.

"Actually, Avery, I was going to ask you if you'd go back to Freezeout with me. I'm not getting any cooperation from Wayne Betts. I still feel that something is missing and that if we look at the aerie hard enough we'll find it. I know what you said about not leading another predator to the nest, but it could be a case of keeping other predators away from the nest. Everyone knows where the bird is now anyway, where Pedersen fell. There's a storm predicted for Sunday; it could be the last chance to get out there this year. I think we should do it."

"Be glad to," said Avery.

"How did it go with the birds?"

"Depressing. A lot of them are not going to make it, but they're in good hands with Leo."

"Big hands, anyway."

"But surprisingly gentle. It's quite something; unusual in a man with such a . . ."

"Monstrous ego?"

Avery smiled. "Blustery manner. There were some lovely birds, but nothing to compare with the gyr. She's one in a million, one in a billion maybe."

"There are still people out there who want her badly. Can't anything be done to stop falcon poaching?"

"A volunteer watch could be set up. It's been done before. In Vermont they did that to keep people from hiking down a trail that led to the first pair of peregrines to come back to nest. I've heard that in Germany they've set up watches to keep disreputable falconers from taking the birds, but that would be difficult in a place as remote as Freezeout. Amazing, isn't it, the lengths we go to to save our wildlife? But we may never match the lengths some are willing to go to destroy it. In Africa the game wardens have taken to tranquilizing rhinos and filing down their horns so poachers won't kill the animals for them. It's unusual for the gyr to hang around so long, sooner or later she's going to go further south or head back north. If we find her there, maybe we could convince her to leave sooner just in case the storm doesn't close Freezeout. There's no guarantee she'll find a safe place, but wherever she goes is likely to be safer than here."

"I'm game. How do we do it?"

"Scare her off somehow. Let me think about it a little bit."

"While you do that, I'll go watch the news. You'll call me when you wake up?"

"First thing. We should get an early start."

I turned on the TV when I got back to my room and got a local station that gave in-depth reportage of high school football games—anything to fill an hour. Next they got to the weather and talked about the upcoming storm. A news reporter came on the screen finally and told me what *I* wanted to know, which was that Katharine Conover had been released on bail. Betts had struck out on this one; the wild bird was free again. He still had Heinz, however. Tomorrow was Saturday, the day the prince was to leave Fire Pond "if all goes as planned." He'd shown little respect for our criminal justice system so far, maybe he'd lost confidence in his expensive attorney as well. He'd have to leave the Sparhawk out of his plans but he might well include the gyr and/or Heinz. He cared plenty about the gyr—enough to find some way to trap her? It was questionable how much he cared about Heinz and whether he could (or would) spring him.

The rest of the news was too boring to watch, even for the mood I was in, so I preheated the oven, precooled my glass. When that had been accomplished, I put the Lean Cuisines in the oven and poured the Cuervo Gold over the ice in the glass. I flipped through the channels. A dying John Huston was on one of them, breathing through an oxygen tube and complaining about the colorization of his movies for cable TV. It was some kind of entertainment news show, but Sylvester Stallone came on next and forced me to shut it off. There wasn't much else amusing in my stucco-walled, mottle-carpeted room, nobody in Fire Pond to call and I'd already read the phone book. I began thinking about words:

> **raptor:** a bird of prey;
> **rap:** a kind of jive talk, the knock of spirits against a
>   table;
> **rapacious:** covetous, subsisting on prey;
> **rapid:** fast, a place in a river where the water moves
>   swiftly but is blocked by obstacles;
> **rape:** to violate by force;
> **rapture:** a state of ecstasy;
> **rapport:** an affinity;
> **rapprochement:** a state of cordial relations;
> **rapier:** a two-edged sword.

I played monkey at the keyboard until the Lean Cuisines were done: His rapture over raptors and his rapport with them were a rapier. He raped the environment rapidly, rapaciously and repeatedly but never rapped about it because it would destroy the rapprochement.

I poured another drink, ate dinner, cleaned up by throwing away my plastic fork and tin dishes, then lay down on the fold-out sofa. I opened Joan's journal to the end of the Raptor section, where she quoted again from her favorite book, *The Peregrine* by J. A. Baker:

> Like the seafarer, the peregrine lives in a pouring-away world of no attachment, a world of wakes and tilting, a sinking planes of land and water. We who are anchored and earthbound cannot envisage this freedom of the eye. The peregrine sees and remembers patterns we do not know exist: the neat squares of orchard and woodland, the endlessly varying quadrilateral shapes of fields. He finds his way across the land by a succession of remembered symmetries. But what does he understand?

What does any living creature understand of any other? was my question, even those that walk the same paths and speak the same language. What do we have to go on? Eyes, expressions, body language, words, words that are spoken and words that are written, words that reveal the essence of someone, words that do not.

There was nothing left to read now but Personal. I turned to this:

> Like a haggard falcon, having gotten used to solitude, I have come to prefer it. I have lived alone for many years. What love I have is at a distance, and companionship has sometimes been lacking, but there is a still, clear center to my life, a clarity that no one can give or take away from me. Moments come, moments pass, the sunlight dances on moving

water. An unnoticed moment is gone, an observed one lives. What matters is not that the moment passes, but that it is observed. Birdwatching has brought much joy and beauty to my life, it has taught me to be still, to listen, to see.

In the outer world there is always imbalance, every measure requires a countermeasure, every relationship, another, a check, a balance. My students take excitement in each new romance, each new adventure and when it ends, another comes that is to be everything the previous adventure was not. My niece, Neil, how busy she is with her law practice, her romances, caught up in the turning wheel. She smokes, she drinks too much, she has inappropriate lovers. If she were my daughter, I would tell her that I worry. If she were my daughter, she wouldn't listen. Her way is her way, not mine. So be it.

Ultimately it is not so important what fate one has, as that one truly lives it. All paths have merit, all paths lead to the same end. Any life has meaning, if it is lived fully. I am an observer, but that doesn't mean I haven't lived. I have seen a sunrise on the ocean, I have heard the cañon wren, I have smelled a cedar in the forest, I have touched the green velvet moss on a rock.

I have watched peregrines—those rockets of birds—fly at Burnt Mountain, the female saw-toothing along the escarpment and inscribing vertical eights in the air turning upside down at the top of the loops. I saw her rise up and up until she was only a speck in the sky and then fold her wings and stoop with breathtaking speed and grace. I heard the wind rip through her feathers as she plunged by. I saw her diving into the wind, rolling over and over, reveling in the turmoil of the air, the power of her flight. The falcon lived these moments without thinking. I, who observed them, live them again.

The falcon can spot me at a distance, long before I am able to see her, but what does she see? An aging lady with silver hair and binoculars, who moves carefully, but never carefully enough. She fears me and flies away. Younger people see a woman with an unlived life. Maybe they see their future in me and fear me, too. But all around me I see adventure, risk, daring. I don't fear, I don't envy, I am content to be me.

It was the end of the journal. I closed it and laid it on the floor. One question had been answered anyway—on Joan's terms she had lived.

As for me, I had a murder to solve, a cliff to climb and an early morning wake-up call. I finished my drink, ground my cigarette out, hugged the pillow that my absent and inappropriate lover had slept on and turned out the light. The wheel would be spinning when I woke up tomorrow. So be it.

Let it be.

20

I was still asleep when Avery called. I didn't mind being woken up by him, but he wasn't pleased with himself.

"It's late, Neil. Damn it. I've slept in."

"Don't worry. You've earned the right to sleep late now and then."

"But not on a day when I'm going to see a gyrfalcon."

"What time is it, anyway?"

"Seven-fifteen."

Late to him, but early to me. "We've got lots of time," I said.

"Not enough," he grumbled.

We agreed to meet in the lobby in forty-five minutes. Everybody gets grumpy now and then, even those with a "still, clear center." But it probably happened to Avery less than most; maybe he'd had a bad dream.

He was waiting for me by the coffee urn wearing a pair of serious hiking boots and a white nylon poncho over a wool sweater, a down vest and wide wale corduroy pants. His electrically charged hair made a white aureole around his head. Behind his thick glasses his eyes were keen. He looked fine, but just to be sure, I asked him. "Are you all right?"

"All the better for seeing you," he replied.

"Didn't you sleep well?"

"It was nothing, a heavy foot stomping on a dream. That's all."

"Whose foot?"

"Ah, if you could tell me that, we'd have something. There's nothing wrong that being outside for five minutes won't cure. Have you looked out yet?"

"I usually don't until I've had a Red Zinger."

"Would you settle for coffee?"

"I'll try."

"Here." He poured me a styrofoam cupful. "Sugar?"

"Never."

"Cream?"

"A little." I took a couple of sips and picked up a muffin for the road. "Let's go."

Avery had a large overnight pack with a metal frame and he hoisted it on his back. I picked up my fanny pack and we stepped outside. The sky over the Aspen Inn parking lot was as big as ever, maybe bigger, but it was a watercolor gray, with light streaks where the paint had washed and dark ones where it had settled. The air was heavy, still and ominous; winter was coming in. "Snow," I said.

"It's a fast-moving storm. Now they're saying it will hit after midnight tonight or early tomorrow morning and predicting a couple of feet in the higher elevations. If that happens, it'd be rough to ski in there, so it's probably now or never. What do you say?"

"Now."

208

"I'm with you."

We took the no-frills Rent A Wreck and I drove, thinking that would give Avery a chance to go back to sleep if he wanted to. He did eventually but first he talked. "I'm glad to see you're wearing your down parka today," he said. "In iffy weather like this, it's wise to be prepared."

It was colder than it had been on our first hike, but still November and not as cold as it could get, so I hadn't worn my down vest. "Is that why you brought the big pack?" I asked him.

"It is."

"What have you got in there anyway?"

"Food, of course, I have some cheese and bread, fruit and trail mix and some freeze-dried beef stroganoff just in case and a pot to cook it in. I have water, a down sleeping bag, my Swiss army knife, a tarp, waterproof matches, a flashlight, USGS maps . . ."

"Avery, we're only going for the day."

"Now you're talking like a New Mexican. You get too much sun down there to have any respect for the weather. Spend a lot of time outdoors in a state like Montana and you learn about bad weather. How often have you heard of people dying suddenly in the Sangre de Cristos or the Jemez?"

"Often enough. There was a boy who walked up a trail from the Santa Fe Ski Basin last winter wearing nothing warmer than a windbreaker. It was sixty degrees when he left. When they found his body a few days later his tracks had led round and round in a circle."

"Hypothermia. It causes irrational thinking. It probably wasn't any colder than twenty or thirty when he froze to death. You can survive easily in those temperatures, but you have to be prepared. People don't often freeze to death in Montana and the reason is they are prepared. We probably won't see any snow or have any problems, but we're ready if we do." He looked at my New Balance light hiking boots, cleat bottoms, fabric uppers.

"I wish you'd worn something heavier on your feet."

"I don't have anything heavier."

"I bet you don't have a hat either."

"Nope."

"You'd be amazed how much heat escapes from the head. Well, not to worry, I've got an extra hat and wool socks, too." He opened up a package of trail mix and poured me some. For a few minutes he stared silently at the big gray sky and the clouds hanging over the Rockies, and then he said, " 'But thou know'st winter tames man, woman and beast . . .' " His brain was like one of those new computers that come equipped with the complete works of Shakespeare. All you have to do is tap in a word, and they pop up an appropriate quote.

"Shakespeare?" I said.

"You're right. *Taming of the Shrew.*"

"Easy guess. Shakespeare was wrong, however. Winter may have tamed the man, but it hasn't tamed the woman, and probably not the beast either."

"You're not talking about Katharine, are you?"

"Maybe."

"You don't much like her, do you?"

"Running around throwing foreign objects into jet engines isn't going to help me get March out of jail."

"Suppose you do get him out and Katharine goes back to jail, what then?"

"He'll probably go back to running his guide business; the falconer will become the falcon."

"You're not thinking like the falcon Diana of taking her place, are you?"

Of sleeping in the handcrafted bed with the white spread, with a naturalist's soft red beard hanging over me? "Of course not."

"I liked the Kid. He's a good person."

A sweet person, a decisive person, a person who *would* use a condom if you asked him, a person maybe you shouldn't need to ask. "You're right," I said. "He liked you, too." But what had we come out here for anyway? To resolve the unresolvable contradictions of love? To catch a snow cloud and put it in a jar? We'd come out here to see a bird.

"Do you think we'll find the gyr when we get there?" I asked him.

"She's hung around this long. I think our chances are good she's stayed a while longer. Let's hope we can convince her to move on."

"That's not what I mean, Avery. Pedersen's dead, Betts has pulled in his net, but there are still people out there who want that bird badly."

"Poaching, the scourge of wildlife. When will it ever end?"

"March told me he thought the trophy hunters were the worst of all; there was no justification for what they did."

"He's got a point. It is a little harder to blame a starving African village. A white gyrfalcon is a once-in-a-lifetime occurrence. I'll be very disappointed if you don't get to see her, sick if someone has taken her."

"So will I."

Avery yawned, rested his head against the seat and fell asleep. I drove the rest of the way in silence and woke him when we reached Freezeout. He blinked his eyes, shook his head and recharged his hair. "Here already?" he asked.

He directed me to a different access road than the one March had taken. It was a bumpy and rutted one-lane dirt road, heavily wooded on both sides, a road where you wouldn't want to meet another vehicle because it was so narrow one of you'd have to back out before you'd find a place wide enough to pass.

"I know it's not much fun driving this road," he said, as we bounced off a rut, and I yanked the steering wheel in an attempt to keep us out of the ditch, "but it's the best way to get to the aerie. We're going to take the Spider Woman trail, which will bring us out at the top of the ledge. March took us by the scenic route where we had the lake view and the gyr across it. Also, I don't think he wanted people to know that the gyr's nesting place is accessible. This trail is shorter and will get us there faster."

The trailhead was about a mile up the access road marked by the omnipresent Freezeout sign to watch out for bears and an indentation between trees, room for the Pontiac and one or two other vehicles. We parked and got the packs out of the trunk. It was cold, colder than downtown Fire Pond, the kind of cold that bites your nose and makes your eyes tear. The kind of cold where your breath precedes you and your brain waves escape out of the top of your head, that focuses what's left of your mind on one thing—comfort. The sky was as gray here in the mountains as it was in Fire Pond, but not nearly as big, only patches of it were visible between the green branches of the red cedars and the bare black arms of the tamaracks that scratched at the sky. The drabness of the sky muted the colors of the forest. The trail itself was kind of a brown earth bled to neutral. The lack of visual stimuli seemed to heighten the other senses. The cedars smelled pungently, the silence was deep and heavily laden.

"It's unbelievably quiet here today," I said.

"Maybe the depth of the silence correlates to the strength of an upcoming storm," Avery replied. "The Indians have a saying that a wolf's hearing is so acute it can hear the clouds passing overhead. I bet an animal whose life depends on it has a very good idea what kind of weather is coming. Their senses are so much sharper than ours. It could be they're all hiding already."

He zipped open one of the flaps on his pack, pulled out a knit hat and a pair of Thinsulate gloves. "Here," he said, handing them to me.

To set a good example, he put a hat on his own head. It was (or had once been) white, sheepskin with fleece-lined ear pieces that flapped over his ears. The sheepskin came to a point on the top of his head.

"This is my Peruvian Andes winter birdwatching hat," he told me. With the hat on and his white poncho flapping around his arms and knees, he looked like a snowflake. He lifted his pack, hitched it over his shoulders, shook himself to settle it, set the bear bells attached to the metal frame jingling, took a few quick two-steps and started down the trail. He hadn't gotten very far before he turned around and said: " 'I have always known that at last I would take this road / But yesterday I did not know / It would be today.' "

The words dropped into the silence as precisely and delicately as needles from a tamarack tree.

"Zen Master Dogen, thirteenth-century Japan?" I asked.

"Narihara, eleventh."

" 'The unspeakable in full pursuit of the uneatable.' " It was my turn to scare the bears away.

"Shakespeare?"

"Oscar Wilde, nineteenth-century England."

"What was he talking about? Poaching?"

"Fox hunting."

"That's good, I like that." We began to hike, slowly at first because the beginning of the trail was uphill and steep. It helped to keep warm, but slowed down the conversation. I could see the wisdom of dressing in thin layers, like all the outdoorsmen recommend. My down parka soon got too warm. I wished I could take it off, but I didn't have room to stuff it into my fanny pack, and Avery's pack was already full. I unzipped it, took off Avery's hat and put it in my pocket. He marched on ahead of me, the bells on his backpack jingling. I hoped the bears were all off in a den somewhere preparing for a long winter's sleep because it was hard to imagine anything being frightened by Avery or his bells. We strode on one foot then the next, up one steep incline after another through a Little Red Riding Hood kind of forest, full of intrigue and imagined danger with big bad villains skulking behind the trees. The trail was lined with cedar trees and behind them more cedar trees, perfect cover for anything that was lurking or hiding or watching. The only sound other than footsteps and jingle bells was an occasional bitching squirrel. This trail was three miles to the aerie, Avery had told me, half a mile less than the other route, a full mile round-trip, not that big a difference. It was after noon when we stopped. We sat on a log and ate some trail mix, some hunks of cheese and bread and an apple each. Avery consulted a map.

"Pretty soon we're going to break out of this cedar forest," he said, "and when we do we will be at the top of the ridge. From then on we will be in the open. Move slowly and carefully. Try not to do anything sudden or unpredictable that would startle the gyr should she be watching. Be as quiet as possible and always remember she fears you. I'll climb along the top of the ledge and look for the best place to descend. When I find it, I'll wave you on. Okay?"

"Okay," I said.

When we got to the top, an enormous view opened up. Over the edge of the ridge I could see the lake and the opposite ridge where we had stood with March. The lake, reflecting the cold gray sky, had lost its jewellike brilliance. The clouds had closed in and the tops of nearby peaks were disappearing into the gray. The snow seemed very close to falling. I felt that if I held out my tongue, a flake would drop on it. I did, it didn't. Avery took out his binoculars and slowly scanned the sky. "She's not there," he whispered. Considering my last experience with binoculars, I let him be the eyes. He put out his hand and motioned me to be still and then he walked out of the forest in stalker mode, alert as a predator, but not as hungry. The years, which had a tenuous hold on him anyway, fell away as he skirted the ledge.

The precipitousness of this place reminded me of the Mayan temples in Central America where the jungle rolls away like ocean swells and you don't dare look down. The steps of those temples are so steep, you could put your foot down solidly on the first one and still have the sensation you were stepping into the abyss. Supposedly an elevated level of consciousness is connected with high places, but the pleasures of living in them escape me. I suddenly remembered a dream I had as a child where someone was annoying me with a toy that buzzed at my heels. To escape it I jumped up and sat on the sky. I wanted to tell Avery about this dream, but he had disappeared over the edge. The tip of his Peruvian hat poked up and then a gloved hand waved at me to follow.

It wasn't quite as bad as it looked and I wasn't eighty-two years old and carrying supplies for a winter bivouac on my back either. There was a trail of sorts, and when there was no trail, there were rocks to climb over and latch onto, and when there were neither of these, there were foot holes in the rock, and branches of those bushes that grow in the most inaccessible places to grab.

"If Avery can do this, so can I," I told myself. It kept me occupied and finally we landed on a ledge about as wide as Avery's pack. On one side of us was a rock wall, on the other a sheer drop that I'd say was about five hundred feet. It ended in the rocky pool where Pedersen had taken a dive. Avery gave me a thumbs-up. "Good work," he whispered.

He began negotiating his way around the narrow ledge, trying to find some way to get the pack off because the next step was to crawl under the overhang where the wolf-wiper trap had been. He twisted and danced around, moving dangerously close to the edge. Finally, he backed up to the abyss, turned around, slid the pack down his back over the edge and pulled it back up. He found a place to lean it against the wall and we scrambled around it. He'd kept his binoculars with him, of course, and he scanned the gray sky once more. He shook his head—no gyr. Maybe she was long gone and this was a fool's errand. Maybe there would be no traces, no black line that led out of the rug, no evidence that would change the already made-up mind of Wayne Betts. There wouldn't be any footprints on the rock, I could see that.

"You ready?" Avery whispered happily. The tougher the going got, the younger he became.

"Ready as I'll ever be."

He went first, crawling into the opening that was about as high as a wolf or a large coyote. I followed. There was rock above us and to our right, on our left was a long way down. We crawled across like other predators with our noses to the ground, but unlike the others our senses had been dulled by centuries of abuse and neglect. If any prey had peed or been in heat here, the appeal of it was wasted on me. I didn't have a predator's keen vision either, able to spot a marmot on the ground five hundred feet down, or a fish leaping in the lake, or the bloodstains on the rock where Pedersen had landed. If I hadn't been wearing my contact lenses I would have barely been able to see the soles of Avery's hiking boots. I could see well enough, however, to note that my hands and knees were dangerously close to the edge, that there was nothing between me and the rocks but the aforementioned five hundred feet. Four-legged predators know fear, fear of us, fear of each other, but the precipitousness of that drop so close to their paws wouldn't fill them with the same queasy terror that sickened me. What did they care? They are surefooted and their instincts for self-preservation impeccable, but a human's instincts are always questionable. We're too removed, maybe, from the basics. People are capable of extremely destructive acts, self or otherwise, and the bottom line is you never really know what you'll do until you are faced with the chance to do it and even that depends on how much sugar you've eaten and where the moon is on a particular day. This was no time to be having an acrophobia attack, but that seemed to be what I was having. Acrophobia isn't the fear of heights, it's the fear of depths. There was nothing keeping me out of the abyss but myself; it didn't make me feel any better.

"Don't look down," Avery said.

"Thanks," I replied.

I could always divert myself from phobias by fear of the real thing. We were approaching the end of the overhang where the cedars grew. Their shimmering green needles filled the opening, the rusty dead ones covered the ground. It had to be where the wolf-wiper had been concealed; it was the only place there was any cover and the needles and fallen branches beneath the tree provided it. Pedersen must have put his hand right into it and detonated the cyanide. "Careful, Avery," I whispered.

He turned and winked at me. "Piece of cake," he said. He crawled into the branches. I followed, trying to put my hands and knees exactly where he had placed his. I pushed my way through the branches and saw Avery's corduroy pants and hiking boots as he stood up, and then I stood, too. I brushed myself off and took a look around. The view was still enormous, the drop still precipitous, but the ledge, I was happy to notice, had widened by about fifteen feet. Avery walked around the cedars and away from the edge. I followed. He stopped suddenly and stared at the ground.

He was looking at a bloody broken-necked pigeon lying flat on its back in the last convulsions of death. There was a string attached to its foot and it made a path through the bird shit and bones that littered the ledge. It led to a two-legged predator semicamouflaged by tree-bark pants, a jacket with deep pockets and a headdress attached to a metal frame that had cedar branches sticking out of it at peculiar angles. The stark reflecting glare of the face hidden behind the branches had been further concealed by camouflage netting pulled down like a thug's stocking with holes cut through for the eyes, nose and mouth. The human predator wore an elbow-length gauntlet on one arm and on it was balanced a large, white falcon.

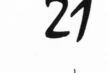

We'd come face to face with
the falcon of legend and of kings and the man who managed to be two places at once. Despite his protective color-
ing, the man was approximately the same size and shape
that I'd expected, about five foot six and built like a boy.
He wore L. L. Bean hiking boots on his feet.

"Cortland James," I said.

"What are you doing in that ridiculous getup?" asked
Avery.

"Hello, Avery," replied Cortland.

The gyr was very large, almost two feet tall. Pigeon
blood stained her fiercely hooked beak and her piercing
talons. Her breast and leg feathers were pure white and
thick as warmup pants around her legs. You might have
expected the object of so much male desire to be softer,
but there wasn't a wasted ounce of fluff on this bird, or
the slightest inclination to compromise. She was streamlined, functional and efficient, the ultimate in performance

and speed. Fierce and regally beautiful, she was captive but unbowed. Her head was held high, her bearing erect, her wings at her sides. Her eyes were huge, black and dense, so large that they made her rounded head seem small in comparison. Although momentarily still, she was not tranquil and appeared to be taking the measure of her situation. Cortland had already attached jesses to her feet and they bound her to his wrist. It was clear why someone would pay a fortune and travel a great distance to see her, but to capture or kill her, never. I wanted to stare into her black eyes long enough and hard enough to enter her pouring-away world of no attachment, but in her world a stare was preliminary to an attack. I'd fallen under the spell of her alien essence; it was broken by the sound of bickering men.

"I thought you went back to Connecticut. What in God's name are you doing here?" asked Avery.

"Isn't that rather obvious?" Cortland replied.

The voices caused the bird to raise her wings and hiss an angry warning.

"You're the twisted, modern-day Audubon, aren't you?" I said. "The man March told me about who takes rare and endangered birds from the wild and stuffs them for his collection. The gyr is another rare bird for your list—your death list."

"That's despicable," said Avery.

"I have an extraordinary collection," Cortland said. It wasn't often, I supposed, that he had the opportunity to brag about his illegal hobby. "You would be quite impressed by it, Avery. I have a magnificent quetzal, the most elegant male in the bird kingdom, and now I am going to include this fierce female. Isn't she splendid?" His voice, muffled somewhat by the camouflage, still managed to express his enthusiasm. His mouth, an opening cut through the camouflage netting, was an obscene hole, the mouth of a pervert sucking on a forbidden pleasure.

"I'm impressed by birds in nature," said Avery, "not in somebody's den. What gives you the right to take a bird from the wild? After a hundred fifty million years of life on earth who are you to decide what lives and what dies? Your father is one of the world's most respected conservationists, and here you are a common poacher. If he knew about this, it would break his heart."

"That's probably why he does it, Avery. It's a secret thrill, an arrested adolescent's rebellion against an overpowering father," I said.

Cortland laughed a short and bitter laugh. "What do you know about it?" he asked me. "My father, the respected conservationist, had all the time in the world for conservation. I was supposed to grow up just like him, but how could I do that when I saw more of him in the newspapers than I did at home? As for your question, Avery, species are vanishing daily with or without *my* interference. At least when the birds are all gone I will own a valuable record of the magnificence that was. You might say it's an investment, an investment in our desolate future. My father's conservation efforts are a joke. He was going to cut me off unless I came home to run his stupid organization. So I'm doing it, and I've learned one thing for my trouble—that his efforts are futile, a finger in the dike against man's hunger, stupidity and greed. We buy up our little bits of land to preserve habitat, islands of green surrounded by pollution and scum, and the world goes on losing rain-forest habitat and species daily. This," he raised the arm that held the gyr, "is the only way left to preserve wildlife."

"Giving into despair is a self-indulgent cop-out," Avery said. "As long as there is one person on the globe who cares and fights, there's hope. Let the bird go."

"I've gone to an inordinate amount of trouble to get her.

I'm not going to give her up now." Cortland's eyes no doubt had a brilliant but deadly sparkle as they caressed the gyr.

"The trouble includes setting the trap for Pedersen and trying to eliminate me by running the van off the road. Doesn't it, Cortland?" I said.

He didn't answer, just watched the falcon.

"You mean he attacked you and killed Pedersen to get this bird?" asked the incredulous Avery.

"Not exactly," I said. "To say he did it for his reputation and to keep his father from discovering what he was up to would be more like it. To him, it was a matter of self-preservation. Cortland made the mistake of negotiating with Pedersen for the gyr. He probably had a considerable reputation in the black-market bird world which led Pedersen to contact him. Maybe Cortland wasn't confident of his abilities to trap the gyr, maybe he was afraid of being spotted by March or another birder at the nest, maybe once you start negotiating in the black market they won't let you stop. In any case Cortland fell into the government's sting operation. Pedersen, who wasn't known for being subtle, taped their conversation; Cortland discovered that."

"Clever," said Cortland. The gyr hissed and fixed him with a cold eye.

"He probably tried to get or buy the tape back but Pedersen refused. Since Pedersen now had the means to ruin his reputation, his fortune and his collection, Cortland got ahold of a wolf-wiper, killed Pedersen and stole the tape. He was planning to use the birding expedition as a cover for his activities. When the gyr disappeared who would ever suspect a birder and conservationist was the cause of it? But the prince and his agent, Heinz, whom the government wanted badly to entrap, came along and forced his hand. It was what I'd suspected, but I hadn't been able to prove it."

It was the last straw for Avery. "That is contemptible. Let the bird go." As he stepped toward Cortland, his poncho caught a gust of wind and billowed around him, altering his shape and startling the gyr, who cakked shrilly, a harsh, loud and primeval sound.

"Back off! You're frightening her."

"Be careful, Avery," I said.

"*Ke-a, ke-a,*" the gyr screamed a warning.

The man who lunged at Cortland wasn't eighty-two years old. He was a young man armed only with a passionate commitment; it wasn't enough. Cortland's free hand came up out of the deep pocket holding a pistol, and, as Avery reached for the arm that balanced the gyr, the gun went off. The sound echoed horribly around the canyon. I screamed and my screams echoed, too.

Enraged by the sound of the shot, the smoking gun, the white tremor of the too-close hand, the gyr leaned forward and with her sharp and fierce beak bit Cortland's finger. "Damn," he swore, shaking her off and dropping the gun, which clattered across the ledge. In the fractions of a second in which I had to act, I pounced on it and picked it up.

Avery had taken the shot in the middle of his chest, and the force of it knocked him backward. A red spot appeared on the front of his poncho and the blood spilled over his fingers as he staggered across the ledge clutching at his chest. As he came to the edge, he was already beyond knowing where he was. The gyr screamed, "*Ke-a, ke-a.*"

"Please, Avery," I cried.

"*Ke-a, ke-a,*" the cakking echoed. Avery's glasses fell off and his ear pieces flapped while he struggled to stay erect. His eyes widened incredulously as he teetered for a moment on the edge of the cliff. I lunged for him and grabbed onto the tail of the poncho, but it slipped through my fingers as he fell. The white fabric billowed around him, his hat fell off and his hair spread out. He looked like an otherworldly snowy owl that had been attacked in midair and was falling backwards, but no falcon waited below to pluck him up. He was probably unconscious before he smashed and split open against the rocks. I hope so.

"You killed Avery," I said stupidly to Cortland, turning the weapon over in my hands.

"He attacked me. The gun went off."

"Self-defense?" I replied. "You shoot an unarmed, eighty-two-year-old man, while in the act of committing a felony, and your argument is self-defense?"

"It was an accident. I didn't mean to kill him, but think of it this way, if Avery had had the chance to choose his own death it's the death he would have chosen, isn't it? Quick, practically painless, in the wilderness, fighting for something he loved and believed in at the peak of his powers. What lay ahead of him anyway but old age and decrepitude?"

The gyr, at the apex of her own powers, flapped her powerful, aerodynamically perfect wings and tried to lift herself out of the human mess, but the jesses bound her to Cortland's arm. The force of her struggle knocked her over and she fell backwards, hanging upside down from the jesses, bating with wild ferocity, as if she would harm or even kill herself rather than be taken by him.

"Careful, careful. I want you to be absolutely perfect," Cortland said. With his bloody free hand he reached to help her back up.

"Let her go, Cortland," I said.

"I can't. She's too precious. I'll never find another like her."

I stepped toward him, straightened my arm and lifted

the gun. The trigger felt smooth beneath my finger. "Now."

Cortland unwrapped the jesses from his arm. He held the gyr's legs carefully with one hand, lifted her to an erect position with the other and took the jesses off. And then, as slowly as was humanly possible, he let her go. She flapped her powerful falcon wings, wings that were better equipped for flight than anything else man or nature has ever created. She *ke-a*'d once to celebrate her freedom, and then with rapid wing beats she circled higher and higher and higher, pure white against the darkening sky. As I watched her become a streamlined silhouette, then a dark speck, I hoped that her brief contact with our species would teach her to avoid us forever. But she hung in the air, hovering above us, and then like a thunderbolt she shot down again, folding her wings up close to her body and plunging back to earth with devastating speed motivated by a prey visible only to her keen eyes, by some impulse to protect her nest or maybe just because she knew how. She swooped within inches of Cortland's head, startling him so he tripped and fell. She swept by me so close I heard the wind rip through her feathers. She plummeted down, down toward the lake and then she opened her wings and lifted gracefully up again, inscribing vertical loops as she rose. Higher and higher she flew while Cortland and I watched in awestruck silence and then she was gone.

I stepped to the edge of the ledge, picked up Avery's glasses, put them in my pocket and took one dreadful look down at his bloody and lifeless body. To Cortland I said, "Halloween is over; you can part with the costume now." If Avery hadn't been lying dead on the rocks below us, I might have enjoyed this part, although Cortland dawdled and took his sweet time about taking off the cedar boughs and the camouflage netting, until his deliberation got on my nerves. "Now," I said.

I could practically see the clouds sliding down the peaks

beyond the lake. A cold, wet drop smacked my lips and then a snowflake landed on the arm of my parka. The flakes were full and fat and meant business. The storm hadn't waited long enough to prove the forecasters right—it had begun.

It wouldn't be much fun to climb out of here in a blizzard burdened by a foot-dragging felon. There was a cliff face to climb, a narrow path to follow. The visibility would get poor, the trail slippery. Cortland would be looking to make a break and add the only witness—me—to his death list. If he succeeded, it might be springtime before I was found by humans, if there was anything left to find. He'd dawdle—he'd already proven he could do that. It would get dark by four-thirty. He'd try to trip me or slip away in the darkness and falling snow. Why should I subject myself to the risk? Why not just kill him now? The gyrfalcon killed day after day after day. It was her nature to kill; she had to to eat, but she'd also kill in self-defense without a thought. Why have to kill him later in the heat of fear and passion, why not be rational, plan ahead and get it over with? Cortland had killed Avery; the time had come for him to pay his debt. The pistol, which already had at least one notch in it, felt steady and firm in my hand. The target was only a few feet away. All I had to do was point and squeeze. It was probably even the natural thing to do. Self-defense, I could argue, and why not?

Killing a man had to be like stepping off the dark edge and swinging far out over the abyss. Once you'd done it, what was there to bring you back? Cortland himself had killed twice now, once in premeditation, once in haste. If he'd put on any power with the knowledge, it didn't show.

I steadied my arm, squeezed hard on the trigger and sent a bullet off the cliff. Cortland jumped. I'd scared him, but I hadn't killed him. It wasn't what I'd been trained to do. "Let's get out of here," I said.

Already the pace of the snowstorm had picked up so I could see the white drops separating Cortland and me. There was only one way off the ledge, the same way we had come in. I made Cortland empty his pockets and take everything out of his backpack. A Swiss army knife fell out. I took it. Some chocolates and fruit. I took those, too. I told him to disassemble the headdress and put that and the mask in his backpack—evidence for Wayne Betts—and made him precede me under the overhang. I pushed his backpack along between us. I wondered how long it would take before the snow claimed Avery. It was a death he might have chosen, outdoors with winter and nightfall coming on, but he would have chosen not to die at all. He was dead; there wasn't anything good to say about it. He had lived; there was plenty to say about that.

. As I crawled along behind the soles of Cortland's Bean boots with the gun in my hand, my hands and knees were just as close to the edge as they had been coming in, the rocks were still five hundred feet below, but the fear of falling or diving was gone; I'd found out what I couldn't do.

Cortland stood up clumsily when he got out of the overhang, bumping into Avery's pack and knocking it over the edge. I watched it tumble down and smash into the rocks. It sickened me to see all of Avery's careful preparations for food, shelter and warmth get trashed.

"What an asshole you are," I said to Cortland. I didn't trust him behind me. I didn't trust him in front of me either—he might be stupid enough to fall backwards—but at least I could see him there. I made him put on my pack and I carried his with the evidence. We climbed the natural steps in the cliff face—Cortland first—crawled around the rocks and up the trail.

When we reached the top he wanted to go down to the trail that circled around the lake, the way he had come, but I motioned him into the woods. It was a shorter route, as Avery had said, my rental car was waiting at the end, and besides I was familiar with the trail; Cortland was not. It gave me an edge.

There is often the sensation when you go to an unfamiliar place that it takes a long time to get in, and no time at all to get back out. But I had the feeling this was going to be a long afternoon. The cedars were dark sentinels in the snow, the path was already white and getting slick. Winter had returned once again and was claiming Freezeout.

Cortland turned just before we entered the woods and made me an offer. "This business is going to be extremely upsetting to my family. Couldn't we just forget the whole incident? You can't be making very much as a lawyer in Albuquerque, and I can afford to pay you very well."

The money lure. To me it had about as much appeal as coyote piss and in-heat urine. "Just keep walking," I said.

22

     And so we began, one foot in front of the other, one tree after another. We happened to be in the north woods at a time of year when night fell in the afternoon. I was already regretting the loss of the flashlight in Avery's missing backpack. There would be no moonlight to guide me either, and once we reached the Pontiac it was at least a mile to the main road with no guarantee the car would get through the snow. Cortland's Bean boots cut black hollows in the snow; my hiking boots stepped on them. It was a confused trail that we left, footprint on top of footprint. The sky got darker, the trail whiter, the snow deeper, my mood blacker, but something kept me hiking down the trail to justice with a gun on Cortland's back—conditioning more than instinct.

  Avery's death was a black hole. You could rationalize it by saying he was an old man who'd lived a full life, fulfilled his potential and died in an action he believed in. You could also say he'd been brutally and senselessly mur-

dered by a scumbag of a poacher. A lot of people might
not have thought Cortland was capable of committing
murder, but he'd risen to the occasion. His father, no doubt,
would be more surprised than anyone at the slime hidden
in his son; parents are often the last to know. Cortland had
an unblemished preppy veneer, one of those white chocolates you pick out of the box that is smooth on the outside
but filled with a disgustingly inedible mess. Weaklings kill,
too, maybe more than anyone else, and poaching is a dangerous occupation—not only for the wildlife. Poachers get
used to killing, birds at first, maybe, then small mammals,
larger ones, moving on up to human beings. There must
be some sense of power, a thrill in the killing; they get to
like it too much. I supposed whatever sense of power
Cortland had had in his life was perverted. Apparently
everything had been given to him, including his job, so
there was no sense of pride in that. The thrill of deceiving
his father by participating in an activity he despised, walking the tightrope of discovery, the excitement of negotiating on the black market, of buying the birds—it must have
made him feel like a grown-up.

The prep himself was barely five feet ahead of me drag-
ging his heels, scuffing the snow over his boots. I could
have asked him what twisted pleasure he had gotten from
his activities. It was the perfect opportunity for a confession, with his eyes straight ahead he wouldn't have had to
see the confessor, but Cortland didn't volunteer and I didn't
ask. The only words I had for him were "move it" and
"faster."

We trudged along like this for a mile or so, the hunter
contemplating the prey. I should have fallen into a hiker's
trance by now aided by the snow dropping relentlessly in
front of my eyes and tap-tapping on the trees, by the hypnotic effort of picking up one foot and putting it down
again, but the rhythm was broken by Cortland's efforts to

slow down and mine to speed him up. In a hiker's trance I might not have noticed that the squirrels that had been squawking intermittently as we passed had picked up the beat of their complaint. A branch cracked loudly back in the cedars and cracked again. The squirrels bitched louder. Maybe I should have asked for his confession, because Cortland and I certainly hadn't made enough noise to scare a bear away. There was a chill in the center of my bones caused by the sensation that I was being watched, if not stalked, that something out there was contemplating me. The fear of a bear's enormous jaws closing on me, of being half-eaten and left mangled and bleeding to die in the snow, was primitive and irrationally worse than anything I could imagine from my fellow man. Cortland James and I had that in common, we were the same species. If there was a bear out there, we might end up in this together.

The gentleman stopped suddenly and bent over. "What are you doing?" I asked.

"Tying my bootlaces."

"Fuck your bootlaces. Get up."

"Just a minute."

"I said get up, asshole." Maybe the angry voices would scare anything lurking out there away, maybe not. I had the sudden and distinct sensation that at the shadowy gray periphery of vision, something large and furtive had moved.

Cortland sprawled in the snow. "What are you doing?" I asked. "Making angels?"

"I tripped. Give me a minute to get myself straightened out."

"No minute. Get up now."

As I closed in on him with the gun in my hand, he rolled over, scooped up a handful of snow and threw it in my face. The snow stung my skin and landed in my eyes. For an instant I was blinded and lost in a whiteout. In that instant Cortland James jumped up, grabbed my wrist and knocked the gun loose. Taking a lesson from Katharine, I kicked at the direction where I thought his crotch should be. It wasn't there, but the kick threw me off balance and I slid and fell in the snow, pulling him down with me. We rolled over and over, bringing back flashes of wet mittens, icy hard snowballs and a little girl who didn't play with tea sets and dolls, who spent her time roughhousing with the big boys, who never learned whatever little girls used to learn about not punching boys out. Although it had been a while since I'd been in this kind of wrestling match, I remembered enough not to let some snot-nosed preppy get the best of me. Rolling with the force of our fall, I managed to end up on top. My vision had cleared up enough so I could see the gun had landed just out of reach. I couldn't get to it and hold on to Cortland at the same time, so with one hand I pushed down on his neck, with the other I punched. He twisted and squirmed beneath me gasping for breath. I punched his face again and again. It was a lot more satisfying than holding a gun that was too deadly to fire. Something else came back to me from my tomboy days—never take your eyes off an opponent, watch every blow as it lands, every bruise that forms.

Cortland was getting some nice welts, especially around the eyes, when he suddenly stopped squirming. Playing dead? Offering his neck in a submissive gesture of surrender? I held my punch. His pale eyes widened, he gasped, and at the same time I felt a large paw grab my shoulder and shove me aside. I rolled in the direction of the gun and managed to grab it before anything else did.

Against an enraged bear a pistol is supposedly a far worse strategy than playing dead, but that didn't stop me from picking up the gun and pointing it. It was the natural thing to do. The predator grabbed Cortland by the neck, yanked him up and faced me across the barrel. It was Leo Wolfe.

"Jesus Christ," I said. "What are you doing here?"

"I suppose I could ask you the same question," he replied, keeping a firm grip on Cortland. "You two come all the way out here for a roll in the snow?"

"That person you are holding on to is Cortland James. He killed Avery."

"If you killed Avery, you're going to answer for it, friend. He was a fine man. I came across his body on the rocks back there and that was something I would hope I'd never lay eyes on in my lifetime. It wasn't a sight it'll be easy to forget either. I followed your tracks here one on top of the other, noticing who was stepping on who."

"She killed him," Cortland said. "I saw her do it." It was a futile effort, and Leo gave it all the respect it deserved—he laughed.

"I know this lady and I know she didn't kill Avery. Now why don't *you* tell me what happened?" he said to me. "And while you're at it, why don't you give me that gun?"

"What happened, yes, the gun, no. Why don't you tell me what you're doing at Freezeout?"

"I came out to get one last look at the gyr before winter settled in and she took off."

"A look?" As he'd said himself, goodness was a rough trail.

"Just a look." Leo was wearing a down parka that made him seem even bigger, but he wasn't carrying a backpack. Whatever he needed to take a look was in his pockets; there was no place to carry the nets or camouflage or guantlets or whatever else was required to trap a falcon. "I'd feel easier if you'd stop pointing that gun at me," he said.

I looked down at my arm, which had gotten the shakes; the gun was trembling violently and pointing right at Leo. I turned it toward the ground.

"Now I suggest that we get a move on because there's still a fair piece of trail ahead and it's getting dark. You can tell me your story while we walk," he said.

I did, although I didn't feel much like talking. My voice wavered, my face stung and my arm ached from pounding Cortland. I was cold, deep winter cold, as cold as I ever wanted to get. The trail was downhill from here on out and you couldn't get going fast enough in the snow to warm up. The cold had worked its way right down into the center of my bones and it looked like it was planning to stay until spring. I wished I had my down vest. I was glad I had the hat that Avery had given me; at least I could keep the brain waves in.

"If you and Avery had come along just a little bit later, he'd have gotten the gyr," Leo said when I'd finished.

The falcon of legend and kings. "It was a thrill to see her," I said.

"Isn't she something?"

Cortland was dawdling again. "Get the lead out," I told him.

"I can't see," he whined, "my eye is swelling shut."

"Tough shit," I replied.

We finished up the final leg in silence. Cortland scuffed along sullenly. I was numb.

When we got to the car, Leo agreed to drive. I said I'd keep the gun on Cortland. We put the pack and evidence in the trunk. "It's all downhill. I think I can get her out of here all right," Leo said. We made Cortland take off his belt and put his hands behind his back. Leo wrapped the belt tight around his wrists and bound them together. We put Cortland in the backseat; I watched him from the front.

Leo turned on the headlights, put the car in first gear and cranked up the heat. With his foot to the pedal, he rammed the Pontiac through the snow. Like he said, it was all downhill. There was a lot of slipping and sliding on the way out. The snow fell steadily in the track of the lights. It landed on the windshield and a wiper ticked and scraped it away. It settled softly on the road, the tamarack/larches, the red cedar trees. It fell on the squirrels, the hawks, the marmots, and on the rocks where Avery lay.

As if he had read my mind Leo said, "Don't worry about Avery. Clears up in a day or two they'll get a helicopter in and haul him out of there."

"I think after a day or two it might be better to leave him be." There were a lot of hungry predators out there whose habits had been disrupted by the snow.

"Maybe, but it always makes a family feel better to have a body."

The James family wasn't going to be pleased with the body we were delivering. Their fair-haired son squirmed in the backseat and twisted his hands around as if trying to undo them, maybe to brush at the bangs that were falling across his forehead. He was getting the beginnings of a purple shiner under his right eye.

"My eye hurts," he complained.

"Sue me."

"Just settle down there," said Leo. "You got a weapon aimed at you."

"This belt is unbearably tight. It's cutting off my circulation."

"Ain't that a pity? He's a whiny little son of a bitch, ain't he?" Leo said to me.

Cortland didn't look like anything special curled up in somebody else's hunting clothes in the backseat of the car, except for the bitter light in his pale eyes. Those eyes were the wild blood in the James family; they gave me the feeling that if he cried hard enough the color would wash out.

"Good thing I came along and rescued you when I did." Leo could move as lightly and furtively as a wolf when he wanted to, or roar like a lion if he wanted to do that.

"Excuse me?"

" 'Good thing I came along when I did and rescued you,' I said."

"Rescued me? What are you talking about? I had Cortland under control. As a matter of fact, I was just getting warmed up. A few more minutes and I would have punched his brains out."

"Could be. Could be that's what I rescued you from," said Leo.

23

Wayne Betts was convinced, even though the tapes were never found. A check with Frontier Airlines showed that Cortland James hadn't flown from Fire Pond to Bullhorn and back again on November 12, but James Audubon had and he'd paid cash. There was no record of Cortland James, Jr., on any incoming flight. The truck he'd rented from Rent A Wreck was found with a badly dented fender in the lower parking lot at Freezeout right beside Leo Wolfe's pickup, which had a few dings of its own.

The prince's father had taken a turn for the worse and he went back to Saudi Arabia. There wasn't enough evidence to prosecute Katharine for sabotaging the Sparhawk and the charges were eventually dropped. Attorney Dwight Stillman had a pressing case in Oklahoma, and one of his associates began representing Heinz Hoffman. Even though I had solved the murder of their operative Sandy Pedersen at no cost to the federal government (my fees being borne entirely by my client), they didn't ask me to work for them again.

The prince came to see me before he left. He was flying by commercial airline out of Fire Pond to Denver then New York and on to Riyadh. He had dressed the part in a beautifully tailored suit and silky tie—the richest man in Fire Pond and the most elegant.

"So Heinz is still in the Fire Pond jail," I said.

The prince smiled and lifted his invisible ball. "Unfortunately, getting him out wasn't as easy as we thought."

"What will happen to him?"

"Attorney Stillman will do his best." He shrugged. But now that the prince was leaving the country, Attorney Stillman apparently considered Heinz a second-rate criminal worthy of a second-rate defense. He would have been better off representing one of the falconers. Some of them were prominent citizens, none too happy about having government agents walk in on them with loaded guns and walk out with birds they didn't know how to care for. More birds died—Leo Wolfe couldn't handle all of them. The falconers had romance on their side and got a lot of publicity for their cause. It was the kind of public case at which Dwight Stillman excelled, but he'd made a commitment to publicity in Oklahoma. He couldn't be in two places at once either. Even though his associates might try valiantly to fill his shoes, few had such big feet.

The prince placed the ball on the table and looked at me with his dark Arabian eyes. "Did you see the gyrfalcon?" he asked.

"I did."

"Tell me about her, please."

What was there to say? She was beautiful, regal, white with a magnificent stoop as fast and deadly (to some) as a thunderbolt. A swift and powerful flyer, fierce and angry when threatened, probably full of fear but she never let it show. I told him.

"Oh," he said. "She would have given such joy to my father." It brought tears to his dark eyes. In Saudi Arabia they still care about pleasing and honoring their fathers; I'll give them credit for that. But if it's fierce, fast and white females they want, they could just take off the black veils and let their own women cut loose instead of coming over here and stealing ours.

The prince was already looking ahead. "Maybe she'll be back in the spring, or next fall," he said wistfully, "if someone else doesn't get her first."

The American way: grab it now, because if you don't someone else will. By next fall there would probably be another poacher out there skilled at taking wildlife for a buck for the prince or anyone else willing to pay. Another year, another poacher hawking his wares, another species in trouble or gone, another large step backward for mankind. The proliferation of species had probably peaked in wild and wonderful abundance around the time that the Old World discovered the New. Now species were being erased from the map one after another and the pace could be expected to escalate until the world got back where it started from—primeval ooze with an oil slick floating on top.

"What time did you say your plane left?" I asked the prince.

He was wearing one of those sleek, astronomically expensive gold watches with a face that only the cognoscenti could read. "Soon." He sighed. He squeezed the air from his ball, folded it up and put it away. "I must be on my way." He reached to shake my hand. "It was a pleasure to meet you."

"*El gusto es mio.*"

"Excuse me?"

"My pleasure," I said.

I had dinner with March at a nouveau Wild West saloon in Fire Pond, a place with lots of cut-glass mirrors, a brass foot rail at the bar and ferns everywhere, some fake, some real. The menu offered beef in all its variety: chopped, sliced, grilled, roasted; and potatoes in some of theirs: baked, French fried. There was also a salad bar, but it looked like it hadn't been changed recently. We both ordered the teriyaki chicken, the only fowl on the menu. March asked for a beer, I got a Cuervo Gold, but before we even got a chance to sip at them, the manager, Ruthie, brought over a bottle of California champagne and gave March a big hug.

"*I* knew you didn't kill anybody," she said.

So did everybody else in the place, because when Ruthie raised her glass they all stood up and toasted with her. "To March," they said.

He was moved, and his soft-up-close eyes got perilously moist, but he deflected the praise by turning it on me. He stood up and raised his own glass. "To my lawyer, Neil. Without her I'd be dining in jail tonight."

"To Neil," they said.

And then we sat down to finish up our business, but there wasn't much to finish up (he'd already paid my bill in full) and the champagne was beginning to make it seem irrelevant anyway. March looked great. He'd changed to a plaid shirt and jeans with no holes in them. His hair had been washed recently and the red-gold curls bounced.

"Who would have believed that Cortland James would turn out to be a poacher and a murderer? The guy ran a conservation organization." He shook his head; the curls sprang out and settled down again. "What made you suspect him?"

"A couple of things: the cold that cleared up right away, the fact that he didn't have a discount fare. He seemed like the kind of nickel-and-dime Eastern rich who would never pay full fare. There was also his lack of enthusiasm about the Conservation Committee. A real conservationist would be passionate; Cortland acted like he didn't care about anything but his exotic sightings. Jizz, I guess."

"Why didn't you tell me you suspected him?"

Why indeed? "Because you never want to believe anything bad about anybody," I said.

"That's exactly what Katharine says," he replied. "But it's not true. I was willing to believe that Pedersen was a poacher, wasn't I?"

"The evidence *was* overwhelming."

"Was I so wrong about Leo?"

"Okay, he turned out better than I expected. His ego is out of control, but he's not a poacher. There's Jimmy Brannen, however. He must have sold Cortland the wolf-wiper, then told him I'd been there."

"Okay. I'll reconsider Jimmy."

"What a pity that Avery is dead and the taxpayers will have to support Cortland James's life in jail," I said.

"It should be a relief to Avery's family that the helicopter rescue crew was able to get his body out of there."

Maybe, but I hated to think about the tracks in the snow that must have led them to the body. "If it had been my choice I would have left him there. Freezeout seems like the right place for Avery; he loved it."

"It's a terrible loss to the birding community. First Joan, then Avery." Not one to let a conversation get maudlin, March changed the subject. "Well, I guess you got a taste of Montana in the winter."

"I did. It was cold out there and getting colder by the minute."

"But not as cold as it will get."

"I'll be back in New Mexico when it does."

"I'd like to get down there one of these days, take a look at some of the petroglyphs, see how efforts to reintroduce the Mexican wolf are doing."

"You're invited."

"Thanks. One advantage to the kind of winters we have is that it slows down the poaching activities for a little while."

"I suppose someday we'll reach the point where the only wildlife left will be in the Arctic. What do *you* think? Does wildlife have half a chance?" I wanted to know how someone as optimistic as March Augusta, someone who never liked to dwell on the negative or believe the worst of human beings, would answer that question.

He poked at his teriyaki chicken. "A chance," he said. "The trouble is that poachers aren't always slobbering idiots. They're people with good and bad qualities just like you and me, people who are hungry, people who are trying to please their fathers or screw them, people who only see their self-interest and don't stop to consider the global view."

Spoken by someone who'd never had to go to court and take away someone's child or life savings, someone who'd never released a farm full of starving beavers, either. If you couldn't convince yourself of the rottenness of people in some professions, you'd never be able to act.

We ate our dinner and drank our champagne while March accepted congratulations from just about everybody who passed by. Katharine was supposed to be joining us for dessert, but she arrived early. I think her watch was regularly set for daylight savings time and in October she'd made the mistake of moving it back another hour. She blew into the room and spun around, stopping at the tables of everyone she knew. When she got to us she kissed March, gave him a little squeeze and sat down. To me she said, "Hello, Neil." Her hair had been washed, as well, and it was a wild mass of curls. They had that in common. Her brief time in captivity hadn't broken her spirit, either— she was radiant. I doubt if she'd been habituated any better to civilization, however.

"Well, congratulations, you did it, you got March out of jail," she said to me. "I'd say you went even above and beyond the call of duty."

"Let's just say I did my job." I smiled, she smiled back. We had our desserts. When it was time to go, March stood up to give me a hug and I had the pleasure of feeling his soft, red beard.

"Thanks again," March said. "Maybe sometime in good weather you'll come back to Montana and we can go to Freezeout and pay our respects to Avery."

"I'd like that," I replied.

By the time I left Denver, the big quiet of Montana was just a memory. Someone at Frontier Airlines liked Whitney Houston and she whined over the loudspeaker all the way to Albuquerque. I thought earphones existed so passengers could make their own choices about music.

To take my mind off Whitney's voice I took some phones out of a plastic bag, covered my ears up and started thinking about birds, trained ones to be exact. I'd come late to birds and observation, but, thanks to Joan, not too late. I was returning to the nest myself, but unlike a hawk I brought no trophy from the hunt (with the possible exception of March's check). That made me think of Blanca, the pigeon, returning to her Kid. The coop that awaited me had gold shag carpeting, stucco walls and a view of elephantine mountains. The lure, maybe, was the dinner the Kid was bringing from Baja Tacos since my refrigerator had gotten empty once again.

Training birds is a risky avocation and a trainer could easily give his heart and have it broken. The first time he releases the bird there must be great uncertainty. Will she remember where the coop is and that she has become habituated to it? If it's a falconer, has he stroked his bird, fed her fresh meat, given her reason to come back? There must be intense relief when the bird returns from her first free flight. After each subsequent flight doubt lessens, and the falcon's fate becomes more deeply entwined with the falconer's, although no one can ever remain totally certain of his ability to call in the wild. But suppose that time after time the falcon does return; it becomes a repetition, a habit, finally a marriage. Does the repetition make the possibility of an ultimate break less certain or more? No matter how comforting the lure of what is known, how snug the nest or warm the meat, there is still the tug of the winter wind, the lure of the wild—to some birds anyway. There must come a moment when that kind catches a lift and hovers on it weighing the call of what is against what is not. But suppose the curiosity lure isn't that strong, suppose the bird is a pigeon; she comes back day after day, year after year, relinquishing her freedom to one person, her trainer. And then one day she returns to find it's the trainer who has left and she's rewarded for her faithfulness with a thumb in her throat and a broken neck.

Even though it was dinnertime when I got to Albuquerque, the sun was still shining. I watched the herding elephants as we made our approach to Albuquerque International, gray humpbacked mountains that would probably be around long after the real elephants were gone. As I'd driven myself to the airport, I drove myself home. My Rabbit (*el conejo*, the Kid calls it) was in the economy parking lot about a half mile from the terminal. They have a bus, but it seldom shows up so I walked to the lot. At least I didn't have a blizzard to contend with.

I arrived at La Vista Luxury Apartment Complex a few

minutes before the Kid. Time enough to stash my suitcase, pour myself a Cuervo Gold, sit down on the sofa and
put my feet up. Back in the Sunbelt again. The Kid
knocked, but the door was already unlocked and waiting
for him. "Come on in," I called. He carried an enormous
bag of food, a six-pack of Tecate and some limes—I already had the salt. He gave me a kiss, put the bag down
on the coffee table, sat down, popped open a Tecate, poured
on some salt, squeezed a lime and opened the bag.

"Welcome back, Chiquita," he said.

"Thanks, Kid."

"They had a special on tacos today."

"I guess." The tacos exited one after another from the
bag, followed by little containers of zinger salsa. In Albuquerque they know what picante is.

"You gave that guy a black eye?" the Kid said, biting
into his first taco.

"At least one." I shook some salsa on my taco and bit
in. The flames licked my throat while the tears from my
eyes tried to put out the fire. Either they'd put more jalapeños in, or I'd been gone too long.

"I didn't like that guy," said the Kid.

"That doesn't surprise me." I quickly swallowed some
Cuervo Gold.

"He's rich, right?'

"Yup."

"You have to watch out for them." The Kid shook his
head and picked up his Tecate. "I feel bad about Avery.
He was one something special person."

"You're right. The best."

We ate tacos without speaking for a while and then the
Kid asked, "What happened to the other guy, the one who
was in prison?"

" 'April'?"

245

"Yeah, him."

"Betts released him. He went back to his girlfriend and his guide service."

The Kid nodded as if to indicate that was the right place for them. We finished up the tacos and cleaned up by throwing the papers and the bag in the trash.

"Listen, Chiquita, I want you to show me how you gave the rich guy a black eye," the Kid said.

"You want to see that?"

"Sure. Show me."

"Okay, it went like this." I had him lie down on the gold shag carpet on his back and then I straddled his skinny body. "You're a lot taller than he is, Kid."

"Go ahead. Show me."

I put my left hand on his throat and then I raised my right arm, made a fist, brought it down hard, pulled the punch and tapped him on the eye.

"You did that, Chiquita?"

"I did."

The Kid tried to shake his head, I loosened my grip. One thing led to another and pretty soon our clothes were on the floor. Without even being asked he got up and went to the drawer where I'd put the condoms. A man and a woman might arrive at an understanding where it wouldn't be necessary to use condoms. A couple could even get to a place where it wouldn't be necessary to use a diaphragm. The Kid didn't suggest it. Neither did I.

TABLE OF CONTENTS

LIST OF FIGURES AND TABLES

ACKNOWLEDGMENTS

This book was long in the making, and I express my deepest thanks to all those who helped me to get it over the finish line. I thank David McBride and Oxford University Press for the motivation to set some thoughts to paper in this volume, as well as Holly Mitchell, Leslie Johnson, Liz Davey, and Bob Land for their editorial assistance.

I thank my colleagues and friends for their continual encouragement—and supportive critiques—of my work. Particular thanks go to my colleagues at Harvard—especially Archon Fung, Iris Bohnet, and Dean Doug Elmendorf for providing me the time to complete this manuscript during my first two years in Cambridge. My Kennedy School colleagues Cornell Brooks, Dara Cohen, Marshall Ganz, Nancy Gibbs, Douglas Johnson, Jennifer Lerner, Samantha Power, Sushma Rahman, Hannah Riley-Bowles, Mathias Risse, Dani Rodrik, Eric Rosenbach, Maya Sen, Wendy Sherman, Kathryn Sikkink, Stephen Walt, and Jay Ulfelder are constant sources of encouragement and food for thought. I am also deeply grateful to all of the students in my course, Civil Resistance: How It Works, which I taught during the Spring and Fall semesters in 2020. Our stimulating and lively discussions helped me to sharpen the ideas presented in this book. I especially thank Zesean Ali for his careful review of the completed manuscript, as well as the five 2020 HKS Topol Fellows—Anikó Bakonyi, Enrique Gasteazoro, Niku Jafarnia, Morgan Pratt, and Inayat Sabhikhi—who provided incisive and constructive comments on each chapter.

I am grateful to Richard Jackson and the University of Otago's National Centre for Peace and Conflict Studies, which provided me with a William Evans Fellowship for writing, engagement, and reflection during New Zealand's summer of 2016. I am also grateful for the chance to have presented these ideas at many different fora over the years, which has allowed me to understand "what everyone wants to know" about civil resistance. I appreciate opportunities to discuss this work among scholars at Uppsala University, University of Oslo, Harvard University, Columbia University, University of Massachusetts–Amherst, and Wellesley College. I also appreciate many productive conversations and debates with activists at numerous community-centered events in Denver, Little Rock, London, Berkeley, Oakland, Nashville, Cambridge, Santa Fe, The Hague, Nairobi, Portland, Memphis, Boston, New York, and beyond.

When I started the book, I was a professor at the Josef Korbel School of International Studies at the University of Denver. I thank my colleagues there, especially Debbi Avant, Marie Berry, Rachel Epstein, Cullen Hendrix, Oliver Kaplan, Julia Macdonald, Tricia Olsen, and Timothy Sisk, for their support. I also thank Cassy Dorff and Evan Perkoski for numerous enriching conversations that helped me think through this book while they were fellows there. And I thank my Korbel School students, particularly Joel Day, Sooyeon Kang, Maria Lotito, Pauline Moore, Jonathan Pinckney, and Christopher Shay, for engaging so eagerly with the topic of civil resistance—as well as for their assistance in developing the data used to support this and other projects. I am also grateful to Allyson Hodges and Mohammed Otaru for their help assembling references and summaries of cases.

I also wish to convey special thanks to the International Center on Nonviolent Conflict (ICNC), which in the past has provided me resources for data collection, access to scholars and activists interested in civil resistance, and exceedingly fertile ground for a lifetime of learning and discovery on this topic. I am especially grateful for numerous exchanges with and support from Hardy Merriman, Maciej Bartkowski, and Peter Ackerman. I am also grateful for the opportunity to learn from scholar-practitioner specialists like Howard Barrell, Shaazka Beyerle, Victoria Bin-Hui, Steve Chase, Howard Clark, Veronique Dudouet, John Gould, Tom Hastings, Mary Elizabeth King, George Lakey, Rev. James Lawson, Jason Macleod, Ivan Marović, Michael Nagler, Sharon Nepstad, Jamila Raqib, Chaiwat Satha-Anand, Janjira Sombatpoonsiri, Gene Sharp, Maria Stephan, Stellan Vinthagen, Stephen Zunes, and many others. I truly stand on the shoulders of giants.

I am immensely grateful for the keen editorial skills of E. J. Graff, who graciously stepped in as an editor at the end of the drafting process. E. J.'s professionalism, substantive expertise on the topic, penchant for accessible writing, and encouragement were essential to finishing the project. Thanks as ever to Charlie Porter, who helped pull the references into shape in the final hour. John Ahlquist organized a group to read and comment on the final manuscript, and I thank him along with Sarah Barr, Martin Epson, Hunter Gatewood, Mike Uy, and Sherry Wong for their helpful suggestions on the draft.

Next, I thank the millions of activists around the world whose tireless and dedicated work provides the inspiration for my own. There are many organizers and activists who have shared with me vital lessons and continually motivated my work in this area with a sense of humanity and urgency. This has taught me more than I ever could have learned from books, articles, films, and music about historical cases. They are too numerous to count, but they know who they are. I am particularly indebted to Farida, Viri, Jeannette, Max, Carlos, Paulina, Isabella, Nelini, Eli, Erin, Rachel, Paul, David, D.J., Katrina, Cybelle, Austin, Anthony, Dominique, Kazu, Kifah, Marium, Ankur, Daniel, George, LaTosha, Evan, Julie, Nada, Srdja, Rivera, Jamie, Victor, Dana, Jessica, Adam, Edna, Roger, Kathy, Alice, Greg, Stephen, Kai, and countless others who have humbled, challenged, and encouraged me over the past few years. I'm in awe of you, and I thank you for your unwavering insistence on justice. I will forward any royalties generated from this book to the activist organizations and communities who are on the frontlines and have taught me so much in the struggle for a better world.

And, as always, I am most grateful for my loving family and the countless ways that they have supported me throughout my life and career. To Kathe and Courtney—thanks for always being there, no matter what. To Spring, Richard, and Julia—thanks for being such curious, enthusiastic, and loving supporters. To Andrea and Bo—thanks for supporting me and always helping me to not take myself too seriously. To Grammy—thank you for your unconditional love and for nurturing my passions for learning, service, and justice. To my parents, Richard and Marianne, to whom I owe everything—thank you for your constant encouragement, love, and faith in me. And to Zoe, love of my life, intellectual heroine, partner in all things, and perpetual inspiration for my moral imagination—thank you for giving me the courage, motivation, clear-eyed and incisive feedback, time, and support to follow through on this modest contribution to justice.

As I finished drafting this manuscript, the global COVID-19 pandemic claimed the life of my beloved grandfather, Alan Abel. Throughout his life he was motivated by a commitment to justice, fairness, and service to others. His spirit was with me as I completed the manuscript, even as I remained constantly aware of the profound loss his passing created for my grandmother, my family, and the many lives he touched. This book is my tribute to his memory. I hope the result would have made him proud.

PREFACE

In June 2006, I stumbled into the study of nonviolent resistance as a skeptic.[1] Like many others in my field of international relations, I was concerned primarily with questions about why people pursue political violence—terrorism, communal violence, civil war, and insurgency—and how to contain it. Most of us start from the assumption that people turn to violence because it works. Numerous examples from history suggest that violence is the only way to seriously contest power—and that violence often pays. The French Revolution, the Algerian Revolution, the Chinese Revolution, the Vietnam War, the Soviet-Afghan War, and many other examples suggest that armed insurrection by militarily inferior forces has often defeated powerful states.

But that summer I attended a workshop organized by the International Center on Nonviolent Conflict that introduced me to civil resistance, its theoretical and strategic dimensions, and the ways people power movements had accomplished in many cases what violent rebellion could not. The books and articles we read made the claim—sometimes implicit, other times explicit—that civil resistance was as effective or even more effective than armed struggle in achieving major political concessions. These arguments were largely based on cases like Serbia, where the Otpor movement had initiated the downfall of Slobodan Milošević; Poland, where the Solidarity movement had successfully challenged the entrenched Communist Party; the Philippines, where the People Power movement had removed Ferdinand Marcos from power; and the US civil rights movement, where lunch counter sit-ins, boycotts, and marches had initiated the desegregation of many southern cities and created the base for a broader campaign.

I thought these cases were probably exceptional. For every case like Serbia, Poland, or the Philippines, I could recall a case like Tiananmen Square, Hungary 1956, or Burma 1988 in which popular uprisings were crushed. After all, even Mohandas Gandhi's effort to expel the British from India had ushered in a period of violent turmoil, punctuated by India's bloody partition with Pakistan. Moreover, I suspected that successful cases could be explained by other factors—weak states incapable of suppressing unarmed actors; international actors willing to patronize nonviolent movements; moderately democratic institutions that accommodated them; social, economic, or demographic characteristics that predisposed some populations to embrace nonviolent action where others would turn to violence; or plain old government incompetence in shutting down a popular uprising.

Maria Stephan, who was at the workshop, challenged me to develop a research approach that could prove my skepticism. So she and I teamed up to design a study that could assess—systematically and empirically—the relative success rates of nonviolent and violent mass movements, as well as the underlying causes for these successes. Drawing on thousands of source materials—including encyclopedias, bibliographies, case studies, historical documents, news reports, and other scholars' published lists of popular revolutions—we developed a list of cases of nonviolent mass mobilization featuring at least one thousand observed participants seeking maximalist (country-level) goals from 1900 to 2006. We did not count smaller campaigns, or reform movements.

After two years of data collection and vetting with subject experts, I ran the numbers. I was shocked. More than half of the campaigns that had relied primarily on nonviolent resistance succeeded, whereas only about a quarter of the violent ones did. Moreover, when I ran a variety of regression models that included features of the regime as control variables, I could find no systematic statistical association between structural features of the country and the outcomes of the campaigns. Generally speaking, nonviolent campaigns were succeeding more often than violent campaigns *despite* a variety of structural factors—like geography, wealth, military power, or demographics—that we typically associate with predetermining such outcomes.

Stephan and I published our findings in 2011, which coincided with the height of the Arab Spring.[2] In the ten years since, many scholars have further developed research on how civil resistance campaigns develop, why they succeed or fail, and how they change the societies in which they emerge, producing important new debates and consensus about key questions. What's more, scores of new mass movements around the world have expanded the range of places where civil resistance is shaping history. This has refined our understandings of how nonviolent resistance works.

Although many cases don't make headline news, the past decade—2010 to 2020—has seen more revolutionary nonviolent uprisings around the world than in any other period in recorded history.[3] In fact, there have been more such campaigns in the first two decades of the twenty-first century than there were during the entire twentieth century. From Armenia to Sudan, from Belarus to India, from Chile to Hong Kong, from Thailand to Burkina Faso, large-scale movements have fundamentally reshaped the political landscapes of dozens of countries around the world.

The United States has been part of these trends as well. The past ten years has seen a dramatic increase in mass mobilizations in the US. From Occupy Wall Street to United We Dream, from Black Lives Matter to Standing Rock, from the Women's March to Families Belong Together, from #MeToo to Protect the Results, from Justice for Breonna Taylor to Joy to the Polls, people power has affected the past decade of American politics in unprecedented ways.

During this time—due in part to my research interests, but mostly to compelling moral crises—I have evolved from being a detached skeptic of civil resistance to becoming an invested participant in nonviolent movements. I now study the history and practice of resistance with much greater urgency, for the sake of my own democracy and in solidarity with human rights defenders around the world. In particular, crackdowns against recent movements have led me to study more intently the historical campaigns led by oppressed peoples all around the world, as well as the lessons of Black, Indigenous, and queer people leading ongoing campaigns for justice in the US. As a participant or ally in antiracism campaigns, the movement for immigrant rights, the sanctuary movement, the climate movement, the LGBTQ+ rights movement, and the democracy movement in the United States, I've learned a great many lessons from skilled activists and organizers. As a result, my own understanding has grown about the ways that people power campaigns develop, unfold, resolve, and transform. These lessons provide both inspiration and cautionary tales. This book may therefore read both like an appeal and a warning.

In particular, several emerging patterns are cause for concern for people invested in achieving social, political, and economic justice. The first is a disturbing global wave of rising authoritarianism, with countries like India, Poland, Hungary, Turkey, Brazil, Thailand, the Philippines, and the United States all backsliding toward autocracy over the past decade. In these and many other countries, aspiring demagogues have rolled back or eliminated civil rights protections for marginalized groups, assaulted judicial independence, threatened political opponents with imprisonment, bullied or persecuted journalists, carried out brazen attacks on elections and the voting process, and turned a blind eye to armed vigilantes attacking their domestic opponents. Indeed, this slide toward authoritarianism is exactly what has provoked so many mass movements around the world to rise up in defense of democracy and basic rights.

The emergence of digital authoritarianism itself is a cause for particular concern. The digital age has created the semblance of social connection, while empowering autocrats to better surveil, control, and disrupt perceived political opponents. China, Iran, Russia, and Saudi Arabia have used digital tools to silence opponents, spread propaganda and disinformation, and sow polarization and division among their rivals. So, too, have regimes in smaller countries, like Togo and Bahrain, relied on digital surveillance to curtail civil society.

Recent trends among mass movements also show some cause for concern. Even though nonviolent resistance is now ubiquitous as a leading strategy for creating change worldwide, the data also suggest that governments are defeating revolutionary nonviolent movements more often than in prior decades.

Data on these movements suggest that this apparent decline in movement effectiveness may be related to changes in the ways that these movements have developed and unfolded in the digital age. There are four key changes in particular, which I discuss in more depth in Chapter 5:

- Contemporary movements are smaller in size than their historical counterparts.
- Contemporary movements seem to rely more on street demonstrations than other methods of nonviolent action, such as mass noncooperation, like work stoppages, walkouts, rolling strikes, boycotts, or general strikes. Symbolic displays of resistance do not necessarily weaken the opponent's sources of power.
- Contemporary movements tend to embrace "leaderless resistance" instead of establishing accountable leadership structures that can assist with coordination and strategy.[4]
- Contemporary movements are increasingly characterized by less disciplined nonviolent action. This is important because fringe violence tends to alienate supporters, polarize societies, and increase harsh repression by the state rather than expanding the movement's bases of support and alliances or building transformative power.

Moreover, there are some persistent myths about whether and how civil resistance works, which also might undermine its general appeal and effectiveness. These myths include the ideas that:

- Nonviolent action is weak and passive.
- Violence is the quickest and most reliable path to liberation.
- Nonviolent resistance is impossible or ineffective against extreme injustice.
- Nonviolent resistance cannot produce genuine social, political, or economic transformation.
- People use nonviolent resistance—and promote it to others—when they have convenient access to power, and that this method of resistance is unavailable to marginalized communities.

- Movements win when their causes are righteous, regardless of which technique of struggle they use.

Despite these common myths and critiques about nonviolence, civil resistance is an idea whose time, again, has come. This book engages directly with questions that observers, colleagues, students, activists, friends, journalists and the general public have asked me about civil resistance over the years I've spent studying it. I try to lend a perspective grounded in synthesizing the best evidence available to help further dispel myths and misconceptions about the empirical record of nonviolent resistance, and to reveal its potential power.

How to Read This Book

I hope this book can be a continuing conversation. The question and answer format is dictated by the What Everyone Needs to Know® series itself, but this format has a few key benefits. First, the Table of Contents reflects the pressing questions people have asked me regarding what civil resistance is, how it works, and why it's so important for everyone to understand. I've done my best in each section to address what we know—and what we don't know—about them. Second, the book unfolds in a fairly sequential way, with each chapter picking up where the last one left off. This means that you may encounter concepts and historical examples in multiple parts of the book when they are relevant to multiple questions. However, you can also jump around to different sections that address your most pressing questions without necessarily missing out on vital background.

This book is a basic empirical introduction to what I think everyone should know about civil resistance, discussing patterns of civil resistance in fairly general terms. The book focuses on global trends, patterns, and dynamics rather than in-depth accounts of specific historical examples of nonviolent resistance. Although I use examples of civil resistance campaigns to illustrate different points from time to time, I defer to other experts for those interested in specific knowledge about in-depth theoretical and conceptual discussions, as well as detailed knowledge about the workings of particular campaigns. The book is not a chronicling of everything that *is known* about civil resistance—many in-depth studies are available that parse various findings, nuances, and controversies, and I point readers in the direction of these resources throughout the book. I urge serious students to avail themselves of the full bibliography; those who want a few additional citations will find the "Selected Resources" section sufficient. The book is designed to serve those who are curious about people power but have never studied it, and to offer some novel insights for seasoned veterans of nonviolent movements as well.

Second, this book is not intended to be the last word on the subject. Civil resistance is an emergent phenomenon, and the world is changing rapidly. Ten years from now, one might write an entirely different book on the subject, revising many of the tables, charts, and substantive conclusions I've drawn from them. The book focuses on what practical implications we can draw from historical cases and global trends. The best way to read this book, then, is to see whether the text resonates with your own observations, intuitions, and experiences; to take what is useful and leave the rest.

Third, many of the ideas I offer in this book have been published in different articles, op-eds, blog posts, and other formats. I note that in endnotes where it applies. Much of my knowledge emerges from my repeated interactions with frontline activists and intellectual giants in the field, some of whom I name in the acknowledgments. But this is the first time I've put my thoughts together in one place, and in a format intended to reach a large audience. I am grateful to those whose knowledge and contributions to the field have cultivated my own, and to those who have encouraged me to synthesize and communicate these insights more broadly.

And fourth, despite the Q&A format, I don't necessarily intend for anyone to read this book as a prescriptive manual on how to *do* civil resistance. People who are waging nonviolent struggle are always in the best position to decide for themselves the best course of action to take. There is no generalizable recipe for effective resistance anyway. But there are distinct lessons from the past that could inform the present and the future. Therefore, although I don't give advice, I do tell readers what I make of the available evidence, with caveats appropriate to each instance. Where there are low levels of confidence about certain findings, I try to articulate that clearly. Where there is fairly robust agreement in the field about certain findings, I likewise express degrees of consensus.

The book has a progressive political orientation, which is deliberate. My hope is that readers will come away feeling more informed about civil resistance—its role in human history, its role in our world today, its controversies, and the empirical realities of its strengths and limits. My goal is to serve those seeking broader understanding about the realistic alternatives to violence in our world, to counter those whose view of civil resistance is shaped more by polemic than by real-world evidence, and to make people who read this book feel more equipped, prepared, and empowered to make a difference in the global fight for justice.

CIVIL RESISTANCE

WHAT EVERYONE NEEDS TO KNOW®

CIVIL RESISTANCE

A BRIEF INTRODUCTION

Ring the bells that still can ring
Forget your perfect offering
There is a crack, a crack in everything
That's how the light gets in.

—Leonard Cohen

Civil resistance is a form of collective action that seeks to affect the political, social, or economic status quo without using violence or the threat of violence against people to do so. It is organized, public, and explicitly nonviolent in its means and ends. This book summarizes some of the main takeaways from history about the ways that civil resistance campaigns have formed, strategized, organized, and mobilized.

This chapter introduces you to the impressive history of civil resistance over the millennia, but it also grapples with some of the key controversies that persist regarding how to define civil resistance and how to understand its impact on the world around us. But before we discuss this technique's development over the centuries, let's define our terms.

Why call it "civil resistance" and not something else?

I've titled the book *Civil Resistance* because that term best captures the historical legacy out of which people have developed and refined the technique. The term itself has only been in use for about 100 years. Mohandas Gandhi coined the term while struggling against British colonialism in India. Over the years, many academics and practitioners—from Gene Sharp to Rev. James Lawson—came to adopt the term to describe this emergent phenomenon.

Civil resistance is a method of active conflict in which unarmed people use a variety of coordinated, noninstitutional methods—strikes, protests, demonstrations, boycotts, alternative institution-building, and many other tactics—to promote change without harming or threatening to harm an opponent. In English, the term "civil" derives from the Latin *civis*, meaning "citizen." In contemporary usage, the term "civil" conjures a sense of public responsibility, in which people collectively assert their rights and needs on behalf of their communities. The term "resistance" derives from the Latin *resistere. Sistere* is a strong form of the verb stare, "to stand." The prefix *re* adds intensity to the word.[1] Through civil resistance, people from all walks of life come together to take a stand, with great intensity and strength, and demand justice and accountability of others.

Some civil resistance methods can be, and often are, incredibly disruptive and confrontational—like gluing oneself to a major thoroughfare, deliberately overcrowding jail cells, or refusing to vacate an official's office. People or institutions targeted by nonviolent mobilization often feel deeply threatened; such resistance jeopardizes their power, status, and comfort without giving them many straightforward options for resolving the conflict. They respond accordingly, with attempts to suppress nonviolent dissidents using arrests, imprisonment, targeted killings, torture, and other forms of coercion. Those using nonviolent resistance often expect and prepare for violence by their opponents. But nonviolent dissidents avoid using violence themselves, because violence is less effective than these other tactics against entrenched armed power. Not all proponents of civil resistance believe in or endorse pacifism, though some do. And not all pacifists use civil resistance, though some do.

Because this approach is so often misunderstood, it's worth examining each element of the definition a little more closely.

First, civil resistance is a *method of conflict*—an active, confrontational technique that people or movements use to assert political, social, economic, or moral claims. Civil resistance actively promotes conflict, creating disruption and amassing power to affect, alter, or transform the status quo. It is about fighting back when people believe they have been mistreated by powerful individuals, organizations, governments, or political systems, and building up new systems that address underlying injustices. Civil resistance is an antidote to passivity and apathy.

Second, civil resistance is waged by *unarmed civilians without directly harming the opponent*. The people who are making changes are ordinary people equipped with their own creativity and ingenuity—along with their various sources of social, economic, cultural, and political leverage—with the goal of influencing their communities and societies. Also civil resistance undertakes actions that are not violent. For most scholars and practitioners, the "civil" part of "civil resistance" explicitly means rejecting armed or violent actions in this mode of conflict. Of course, definitions of "nonviolent" and "violent action" are themselves controversial. For our purposes, people waging civil resistance do not use weapons or physical attacks like punching, trampling, assaulting, or killing while they are directly confronting their opponents. But the term "civil" does not necessarily mean "friendly," "respectful," or "polite." On the contrary, scholars typically classify interruption, rude gestures, turning one's back, heckling, shaming, stigmatizing, and ostracizing opponents as nonviolent behaviors that, when used in combination with other methods, can impose costs on their opponents and their supporters.

Third, civil resistance involves *coordinating a diverse set of methods*. This approach to struggle is deliberate and premeditated, and purposefully uses a variety of methods—like strikes, protests, go-slows, stay-aways, occupations, noncooperation, and/or the development of alternative economic, political, and social institutions, among others—to build power and leverage from below. Just because people are protesting in the streets does not mean they are engaging in civil resistance. Spontaneous, improvised street actions that are not coordinated across various civic groups as part of a broader strategy rarely have staying power or capacity for long-term transformation. Nor does organizing a one-off protest or strike qualify a group as part of a civil resistance movement. Civil resistance is neither spontaneous nor purely symbolic, but rather involves a protracted struggle with the same coordinated groups—civic associations, youth groups, unions, religious institutions, and other civil society groups—working together over time toward the same goal.

Fourth, civil resistance involves *noninstitutional actions*. In other words, civil resistance is deliberately disobedient, acting outside of existing institutions, laws, and larger systems that have become widely viewed as unjust or illegitimate. Civil resistance often works to openly challenge, contest, undermine, subvert, divide, or replace such institutions. Voting, holding campaign rallies, writing and collecting petitions, lobbying, calling one's member of Congress, and organizing legal advocacy campaigns are typically not considered civil resistance—since all of these actions occur within the system. Some tactics that *are* considered civil resistance, because they take place outside official channels, include the following: holding an unauthorized or illegal march, violating "unjust laws," holding strikes and work stoppages, tax refusals, and direct actions such as blockading banks, boycotting products, or occupying a politician's office. All are typically considered extra-institutional. There are hundreds—if not thousands—more examples.

Of course, in practice, many civil resistance campaigns combine both institutional and unauthorized action. The US civil rights movement, for instance, involved various forms of civil resistance—marches, bus boycotts, lunch counter sit-ins, consumer boycotts, silent processions, public prayer and worship, mass demonstrations, the deliberate overloading of jails, and many other methods—alongside more traditional political methods like issuing public statements, legal advocacy, lobbying the White House and congressional elites, and supporting antiracist candidates for public office. However, movements that rely *only* on institutional action, like rallying for political candidates or writing letters to public officials, are typically not considered civil resistance movements.

Finally, the goal of civil resistance is to *affect the status quo*. Civil resistance tends to seek change—often revolutionary change—within a broader society. Civil resistance tends to have a popular or civic quality, involving groups or coalitions working together to make collective claims about political, economic, social, religious, or moral practices and concerns—on behalf of a larger group. For instance, Black activists during the civil rights movement did not act to secure rights for movement participants alone; rather, they sought to eliminate the entire system of segregation, racism, and white supremacy in the United States, for everyone. The Sudanese Revolution, which toppled the dictatorship of Omar al-Bashir in April 2019, eliminated a brutal regime to bring democratic change to all Sudanese people.

In reviewing what civil resistance is, understanding what it isn't can be useful. First, civil resistance is not the use of a single technique, like protest. Recall that civil resistance tends to involve many different nonviolent techniques—like demonstrations, strikes, stay-aways, blockades, the creation of alternative institutions, and other forms of noncooperation—sequenced intentionally to dislodge entrenched power. The technique implies organization and coordination. Civil resistance campaigns often have individuals or coalitions in leadership roles, helping to coordinate and guide the campaign's strategy. Protest can be part of civil resistance, but protest can also happen spontaneously, without significant organization, and without a civil resistance campaign's shared goals, strategies, or organizing committees. People who take to the streets to respond to a particular instance of brutality or an offensive and newly announced policy are voicing their rage. But they are not necessarily engaged in civil resistance, which implies continual, coordinated, collective action using a mix of techniques toward a decisive outcome. In fact, as we see later in this volume, isolated protests' effects are typically quite different than the effects of protests that are associated with broader civil resistance campaigns.

Second, civil resistance is not necessarily about peaceful conflict resolution. In a very real sense, civil resistance constructively *promotes* conflict. That said, conflict resolution has a role in many civil resistance campaigns—either as a way for movements to deal with their own internal disputes and conflicts, or as a way for them to prepare for bargaining once they bring their opponents to the negotiation table. After the Zapatista movement in Chiapas, Mexico, moved away from armed struggle and embraced political resistance in 1994, for example, members have developed a number of internal processes for handling conflict related to and within the movement, including its own autonomous judicial processes. And in Poland in 1989, one of the ways that the Solidarity movement dislodged the Communist government was the movement's historic Round Table Talks with Communist Party elites. In these, between February and April 1989, over thirty Solidarity and opposition movement leaders succeeded in persuading the government to allow free and independent trade unions, to establish a presidency instead of rule by the Communist Party's general secretary, and to establish an elected senate. Several months later, Solidarity swept the national elections, deposing the Communist Party from its authoritarian rule over Poland. It was the beginning of the end of Soviet-aligned Communist control over Eastern Europe. And Solidarity managed to bring the government to the table only because it had run such a successful civil resistance campaign over nine years, including strikes, factory shutdowns, protests, establishing underground universities, and printing and circulating an illegal newspaper called *Solidarność* (*Solidarity*), from which the movement got its name.

Third, civil resistance is not necessarily equivalent to nonviolence, although it might use that approach. Commitment to the concept of nonviolence, rather than civil resistance, grows from moral arguments about how nonviolent action is the most righteous approach to political action—both its means and its ends. Principled nonviolence prohibits the use of violence on moral grounds. Similarly, pacifism is a principled position that unconditionally rejects the use of violence, seeing violence as immoral. While many pacifists are convinced that nonviolent alternatives work better than violent ones, their primary commitment is to the moral righteousness of the means and the justice of the ends.

That's not quite true for those committed to civil resistance; they may be primarily concerned with strategy, not morality. Most proponents of civil resistance see this technique as a functional alternative to violence, and therefore they tend to be interested in when and whether civil resistance works—remaining agnostic about whether it is morally superior to violence. That said, many people who study or advocate strategic nonviolent action are themselves pacifists, even though they frame their discussion of civil resistance in utilitarian terms—hoping to convince nonpacifists of its viability.

However, many related terms could have made a decent alternate title for this book, including nonviolent mobilization, nonviolent action, nonviolent struggle, people power, unarmed insurrection, "war without weapons," strategic nonviolence, nonviolent struggle, political defiance, Satyagraha, positive action, nonviolent revolution, or mass uprisings. Many people use these terms somewhat synonymously, although others see crucial differences between these concepts. Although I do use these terms largely synonymously through this book, I've avoided the word "nonviolent" in the title because many people tend to interpret that term as equivalent to words like "passive," "submissive," "inactive," "peaceful," or "resigned."

Doing so conjures in many readers' minds such possibilities as resignation, submission, passivity, or playing nice in the face of profound injustice. That's not what this book is about.

How has civil resistance developed?

Civil resistance techniques have been recorded as long as humans have been keeping histories—from ancient Egypt to ancient Greece to the early Roman Empire. For instance, the first recorded strike in human history happened in around 1170 BC, when Egyptian laborers building burial chambers for King Ramses III refused to work until they received stable food rations.[2] Many early Christians refused Roman imperial military conscription, usually paying for this objection with their lives.[3] The first known feminist rebellion in North America was a sixteenth-century civil resistance campaign by Iroquois tribal women to end unregulated warfare within the Iroquois nation. Men exclusively controlled declarations of war, along with other political powers. Iroquois women coordinated a sex and childbearing strike, refused to harvest and prepare crops, and refused to produce moccasins necessary for war-making. Ultimately Iroquois women won the power to veto war declarations.

Even though people have used civil resistance methods throughout history, the technique did not have a name until Mohandas Gandhi popularized the term "civil resistance" a century ago.

Yet the root of civil resistance entered the lexicon in 1848 when writer and philosopher Henry David Thoreau delivered a lecture in Concord, Massachusetts, called "Resistance to Civil Government." The lecture was published as a pamphlet in 1849, which came to be known as *On the Duty of Civil Disobedience*. In that tract, Thoreau argued that citizens ought to disobey government laws or policies that violated their own moral conscience—to avoid becoming agents of injustice themselves. He also began to theorize about transgressive, noninstitutional action he believed to be occasionally necessary to restore basic freedoms, liberties, and justice.

Thoreau was writing in opposition to slavery and to the Mexican-American War of 1846–1848, which abolitionists and anti-imperialists generally perceived to be an immoral conquest. But Thoreau's writings inspired several generations of dissidents and philosophers who followed him—not least among them was Gandhi, who read Thoreau during his first time in jail.

When he encountered Thoreau's writings, Gandhi was already a skilled practitioner and scholar of resistance, having been inspired by numerous worker and anti-colonial rebellions taking place around the world. But he was really the innovator of civil resistance as a way to prosecute organized, civilian-led conflicts against militarily superior opponents. From 1893 to 1914, Gandhi worked as an attorney in South Africa, where he was troubled by discrimination, segregation, and other racist policies that applied to nonwhite inhabitants of South Africa under the colonial system. At various points, he was kicked off a train for trying to board in first class, pushed off a footpath reserved for whites, and ordered to remove his turban—and he also witnessed many other forms of discrimination against migrant laborers. He wanted to end these injustices and developed a series of practices he called *satyagraha* (truth-force or soul-force) as a method of refusing to cooperate with injustice while developing just alternatives. Gandhi had also been impressed by the anti-tsarist rebellion of 1905 in Russia, during which hundreds of thousands of Russians in the city and country alike had revolted against Tsar Nicholas II through a nonviolent general strike and various other demonstrations, leading the tsar to establish some democratic reforms. Gandhi was also deeply affected by the writings of Russian novelist and pacifist Leo Tolstoy, with whom he carried out a multiyear correspondence about the morality and necessity of renouncing violence in all its forms.

In 1907 Gandhi began his first official satyagraha to demand the repeal of the racist Asiatic Registration Laws (the Black Act), which required all Indians in South Africa to register and be fingerprinted by colonial authorities and to carry registration papers at all times. Gandhi organized migrant Indian workers to disobey the law, picket colonial offices, travel without registration papers, and refuse to work. In doing so, he experimented with what he called "passive resistance"—popular refusal to cooperate with unjust laws without using violence against the opponent—to lead communities to advocate for dignity and rights. Over the course of seven years, thousands of striking Indians were imprisoned, including Gandhi himself. But the laws were repealed in 1914, proving to Gandhi that nonviolent collective dissent could be an effective method even for people living under colonial rule.

By 1915, having achieved the repeal of the Black Act, Gandhi returned to India and began to imagine a new movement against British colonial rule there. It was there that Gandhi gave the technique the names many now use to describe it—civil resistance, nonviolence, nonviolent action, and nonviolent struggle. Organizing numerous satyagrahas against British colonialism in the 1920s, Gandhi built a mass following and a national leadership for noncooperation, civil disobedience, and self-determination. This culminated in the 1930 Salt March, during which Gandhi and tens of thousands of Indians marched 240 miles from his Ahmedabad retreat to the Arabian Sea to resist a monopolistic colonial law that prevented Indians from making and consuming their own salt. When the entourage arrived at the sea, Gandhi encouraged his followers to deliberately violate the law by boiling their own salt as a method to both resist colonial rule and claim self-sufficiency in producing the commodity. The movement escalated to include strikes, mass protests, mass noncooperation with various colonial laws, and a campaign to develop economic self-sufficiency so that Indians could free themselves from dependency on colonial products. Although Gandhi's movement against British colonial rule in India had many shortcomings, it showed millions of people worldwide that unarmed civilians engaged in collective noncooperation could wield enormous power.

Many people today have limited understandings of what Gandhi achieved, remembering only his strict moral positions against violence or meat-eating. Gandhi's messages still appear on bumper stickers, posters, and T-shirts—leaving skeptics to see his work as noble but naïve, inspiring but ineffective, laudable but futile.

Such cynics might be right if Gandhi's moral commitments were the only reasons he favored the use of civil resistance against the British Raj. But in reality, Gandhi was a fierce pragmatist. He abandoned the term "passive resistance" after realizing the term conveyed a sense of resignation and acquiescence, rather than active struggle and defiance. He also wanted to dissociate the technique from woman suffragists in England, who had begun to use the term "passive resistance" to describe militant tactics, including protestor violence, that Gandhi did not recognize as consistent with the path of satyagraha. Gandhi began to use the term "civil resistance" as a sort of mashup between "civil disobedience" and "passive resistance."

Although many people before Gandhi had used techniques of civil resistance sporadically, they had rarely done so in full consideration of its long-term potential as a political strategy for liberation. Gandhi's singular contribution to the theory and practice of nonviolent action was his self-consciousness about producing a comprehensive technique that combined noncooperation against oppression with the creation of alternative institutions that would alleviate poverty, discrimination, and injustice.

Other groups struggling against oppressive systems took notice of Gandhi's work. In the early twentieth century, Black activists and clergy from the United States began a decades-long interchange between the United States and India, hoping to draw inspiration and know-how from the Indian experience.[4] These activists were themselves experienced in building capacity for mass mobilization to confront injustice, but they were eager to learn from the experiences and successes of others struggling for equality. And so numerous Black pacifist activists traveled to India to learn from Gandhi and his successors. Martin Luther King Jr. had been exposed to Thoreau's *Civil Disobedience* while a college student at Morehouse, and he had learned about Gandhi's Salt March during a sermon by Howard University president Rev. Dr. Mordecai Johnson while King was a student at Crozer Theological Seminary. Several other prominent civil rights leaders also educated themselves as to the potential applications of civil resistance to destroy systems of racism in the United States.

Among these was James Lawson, a Methodist minister from Berea, Ohio, who visited Gandhi's old ashram in the 1950s to learn and develop new strategies for resisting injustice in the US. As a conscientious objector during the Korean War, Lawson had spent eighteen months in federal prison, reading, praying, and reflecting on Gandhi's practices. He studied Gandhi's autobiography and developed his own understanding of the steps necessary to prepare, provoke, and shepherd a successful liberation movement among ordinary Black people who lived their lives under constant threat of lynching and police brutality, discrimination, and the Jim Crow laws that enforced segregation across the American South. Gandhi's Salt March inspired Lawson and others to hold workshops on the theory and practice of nonviolent resistance in Nashville starting in 1958. Many local university and high school students attended these workshops and began planning and organizing a campaign to desegregate downtown Nashville. In late 1959 and early 1960, students—including John Lewis, C. T. Vivian, Marion Barry, James Bevel, Diane Nash, and Bernard Lafayette, and other key figures of the civil rights movement—launched a campaign that combined lunch counter sit-ins, marches, strikes, boycotts of downtown businesses, and voluntary imprisonment to overwhelm Nashville's jails and courtrooms. Their campaign ended enforced segregation in Nashville within six months. Ella Baker, Fannie Lou Hamer, Bayard Rustin, Vincent Harding, and others also drew from these experiences to catalyze people power and organized resistance against legalized segregation, racist voter suppression, economic injustice, sexism, militarism, and other social ills in the United States.

These experiments with civil resistance techniques likewise inspired many other anticolonial and antiracism struggles around the world, in spite of evidence that Gandhi himself harbored racial prejudice and discriminatory views.[5] Although many African anticolonial movements in the nineteenth and mid-twentieth century used both unarmed and armed struggle to fight for independence, people power movements in Ghana, Zambia, and elsewhere won independence largely through civil resistance.[6] Similarly, through an unrelenting combination of protests, civilian-led boycotts, strikes, and other methods of nonviolent action, Black South Africans successfully confronted and ended legal apartheid in that country. Moreover, many observers argue that the most effective period of the Palestinian National Movement was during the first eighteen months of the First Intifada (1987–1993), a struggle waged by a broad-based coalition of Palestinian civic groups that coordinated various nonviolent methods to push for Palestinian self-determination and independence from Israel.[7]

While the technique of nonviolent action has diffused globally, intellectuals and scholar-practitioners took notice. Pacifist thinkers from the 1920s and 1930s traveled to India to learn from Gandhi's experience. Upon return from India, the American philosopher and peace activist Richard B. Gregg wrote the first book outlining a systematic theory of nonviolent resistance. Called *The Power of Non-Violence*, it was published in 1934. The book influenced numerous peace activists throughout the 1930s and 1940s, including

A. J. Muste, a leading pacifist thinker in the United States; and Aldous Huxley, then leader of the United Kingdom's Peace Union. It also influenced many other academics in the aftermath of World War II, who saw the global arms race and advent of the nuclear age as major justifications to theorize realistic alternatives to violence.[8] This included feminist thinkers, like Barbara Deming, who wrote numerous books on the power of nonviolent action to both resist oppression and create a just and inclusive future.[9]

Gene Sharp, whom many consider to be the father of the field of civil resistance studies, served nine months in prison for protesting the draft during the Korean War. After working with various pacifists and researchers, he received his Ph.D. from Oxford University. From his work there, he wrote a three-volume opus, *Theory of Nonviolent Action*, published in 1973. The book articulated his own theory of how well-organized and well-prepared civilians could successfully build power, mobilize, and wage unarmed struggle—a topic we return to in Chapter 2. He identified commonalities across historical cases—such as Gandhi's movement, Dutch and Norwegian resistance to Nazi occupation, and the Russian Revolution—and generated a list of 198 methods of nonviolent action. That list—and Sharp's theories on nonviolent action—remain a prominent resource for many students and practitioners of nonviolent action today.[10]

Many of Sharp's writings were subsequently translated and disseminated around the world. Numerous organizations—such as the Albert Einstein Institution, the International Center on Nonviolent Conflict, Nonviolence International, and others—emerged during the 1990s and 2000s to systematize the theory and practice of nonviolent action. These developments jump-started an era in which activists and organizers around the world could access a proliferation of training manuals, documentaries, oral histories, and web resources about how nonviolent resistance works.

Today, a quick Google search of trainings, organizations, toolkits, manuals, and online bibliographies about civil resistance would turn up hundreds or thousands of relevant entries. Organizations like the International Center on Nonviolent Conflict have supported scholarly research on nonviolent resistance, held workshops for activists to meet with scholars, designed online courses, and amassed huge resource libraries for those interested in the topic. In the United States alone, groups like the BLACKOut Collective, Beautiful

Trouble, Training for Change, and the Sunrise Movement offer trainings, field guides, and collective wisdom for people learning how to wage struggle and organize their communities to build power.[11] More broadly, groups like Nonviolence International and CANVAS offer trainings and workshops for people learning how to organize for change and wage nonviolent struggle.

How successful is civil resistance?

The answer to this question might surprise you: compared with the alternatives, nonviolent resistance is a stunningly successful method of creating change.[12] Let's first look at the aggregate success rates of 627 revolutionary campaigns—violent and nonviolent—over the past 120 years. Revolutionary campaigns involve large-scale mobilizations seeking to topple governments or create new nation-states. In other words, these are hard to achieve. Violent revolutions are those in which the revolutionaries relied on armed insurgency, urban guerilla attacks, assassination campaigns, and other forms of armed struggle to achieve their goals—like the Russian Revolution of 1917, North Vietnamese insurgents' opposition to US military forces from 1960 to 1975, and the Cuban Revolution of 1959. Nonviolent revolutions are those in which the revolutionaries are unarmed, and relied primarily on methods like protests, demonstrations, strikes, nonviolent sit-ins and occupations, and mass noncooperation—like the Honduran pro-democracy movement of 1944, the Danish Resistance against Nazi occupation of 1940–1943, and South Korea's April Revolution of 1960. You can see a list of all 627 revolutionary campaigns in the Appendix of this book. For our purposes, I define "success" as the overthrow of a government or territorial independence achieved decisively because of the campaign within a year of its peak.[13] Applying this standard definition of success to both types of revolutions, over 50% of the nonviolent revolutions from 1900 to 2019 have succeeded outright—while only about 26% of the violent ones did (Figure 0-1).

That's a staggering figure that undercuts a widespread view that nonviolent action is weak and ineffectual while violent action is strong and effective. In Chapter 2, I explain why campaigns of civil resistance have succeeded more often than their violent counterparts—often overcoming incredibly difficult barriers to do so. And if you're wondering about the fates of such countries after their revolutions

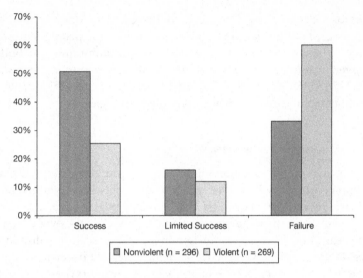

Figure 0-1 Success Rates of Revolutions, 1900–2019

end—like popular well-being, stability, or transformative political change—stay tuned for that discussion in Chapter 5.

What are some foundational examples of civil resistance?

Civil resistance has been used for centuries, in many situations, and toward many goals. Table 0-1 provides a brief summary of some highlights in the development of civil resistance as an approach. This list is not comprehensive by any means. But it should give you the impression that civil resistance has played an important part in world history—even if it can be difficult to conjure examples off the top of one's head.

American Revolution

American colonists waged a civil resistance campaign against British imperial rule from 1763 to 1775, before the Revolutionary War. While many people associate the American Revolution with the armed insurrection of George Washington's Colonial Army against King George's British regulars, this armed revolt didn't happen until after an extended period of effective civil resistance that made it all but impossible for the British government to govern

Table 0-1 A Partial List of Significant Examples of Nonviolent Resistance

Period	Locations	Description	Iconic Figures (where applicable)
1700s BC	Egypt	Midwives resist genocide	Shiphrah and Puah
1170s BC	Egypt	Laborers strike against Ramses III for food rations	
750s BC	Rome	Antiwar intervention by Sabine women against two warring factions of Rome	Sabine women
494 & 449 BC	Rome	Commoners in Rome engage in a general strikes and mass noncooperation (including secession) to win the right to elections and civil law	Plebians
AD 200s–300s	Roman Empire, including Numidia (contemporary Algeria)	Anti-Roman military conscription	Early Christians, Tertullian, Origen, Maximilianus, Martin of Tours
1100s–1309	Southern France	Anti–Roman Catholic Church	Cathars
1200s–1600s	Europe	Protestant Reformation	Waldensians, Taborites, Anabaptists, Mennonites, German Baptist Brethren, Quakers, Diggers
1500s	France	Antityranny	Étienne de la Boétie
1540s–1615	Americas	Anticolonialism	Bartolomé de las Casas, Guaman Poma de Ayala
Early 1600s	Iroquois Nation	Antiwar	Iroquois women
1765–1775	American colonies	American Revolution	John Adams, Benjamin Franklin, James Madison, Thomas Jefferson, Quakers

(continued)

Table 0.1 Continued

Period	Locations	Description	Iconic Figures (where applicable)
1832	Jamaica	Christmas Day Rebellion	Samuel Sharpe
1700s–1861	United States	Abolition movement	Harriet Tubman, Frederick Douglass, Sojourner Truth, William Wells Brown, Maria Stewart, Harriet Beecher Stowe, William Lloyd Garrison, Frances Ellen Watkins Harper
1815–1860s	United States / Europe	Peace movement	David Low Dodge, Noah Worcester, Henry Holcombe, Charles Whipple, Julia Ward Howe, Jean-Jacques de Sellon, Alexis de Tocqueville, Victor Hugo, Leo Tolstoy, Bertha von Suttner, Frédéric Passy
1871–1912	United States / United Kingdom	Labor movement	Eugene Debs, Helen Keller, A.J. Muste
1848–1929	United States / United Kingdom	Woman suffrage	Frances Ellen Watkins Harper, Mary Ann Shadd Cary, Mary Church Terrell, Nannie Helen Burroughs, Ida B. Wells, Sojourner Truth, Elizabeth Cady Stanton, Susan B. Anthony, Emma Goldman, Jane Addams, Emmeline Pankhurst, Sylvia Pankhurst
1867–1880	New Zealand	Anticolonialism	Te Whiti-o-Rongomai
1905	Russia	Revolution of 1905	Leo Tolstoy
1905–1911	Iran	Persian Constitutional Revolution	Mohammed Mossadeq

Table 0.1 Continued

Period	Locations	Description	Iconic Figures (where applicable)
1870s–1916	Ireland	Independence movement	Ladies Land League, Arthur Griffith
1909–1968	United States	Civil rights movement	Ida B. Wells, W. E. B. Du Bois, James Farmer, George Houser, Andrew Johnson, Rosa Parks, Martin Luther King Jr., Bayard Rustin, Fannie Lou Hamer, Ella Baker, Thurgood Marshall, John Lewis, Barbara Johns, James Lawson, Harry Belafonte
1914–1919	Global	Anti–World War I movement	Helen Keller, A. J. Muste, Bertrand Russell, Clive Bell, Wilfred Owen, Siegfried Sassoon
1919–1922	Egypt	Egyptian independence movement	
1919–1949	India	Indian independence movement	Mahatma Gandhi
1919–1940	United States	Workers' rights movement	W. E. B. Du Bois, A. J. Muste, A. Philip Randolph, United Auto Workers
1929–1930	Nigeria	Igbo Women's War	Madame Nwanyeruwa, Madam Mary Okezi, Ikonnia Nwannedia Nwugo
1920s–1940s	Ghana, Nigeria, Zambia	African independence movements	Kwame Nkrumah, Jaja Wachuku, Obafemi Jeremiah Oyeniyi Awolowo, Kenneth Kaunda
1930–1934	Northwest Frontier of India (contemporary Khyber Pakhtunkhwa in Pakistan)	Khudai Khidmatgar / Muslim Pashtun movement	Badshah Khan

(continued)

Table 0.1 Continued

Period	Locations	Description	Iconic Figures (where applicable)
1941–1945	Worldwide	Anti–World War II movement	Richard Gregg, A. Philip Randolph, Dorothy Day, Women's International League for Peace and Freedom, Ralph DiGia
1942	Norway	Anti-Nazi movement	Norwegian teachers
1943	Germany	Rosenstraße protests	German wives of Jewish men
1945–1980s	United States, worldwide	Antinuclear movement	Robert Oppenheimer, Albert Einstein, Andrei Sahkarov, Plowshares movement, Clamshell Alliance, György Konrád
1948–1994	South Africa	Anti-apartheid	Nelson Mandela, Desmond Tutu, Mkhuseli Jack
1965–1970	United States	California grape workers' strike and boycott	César Chávez, Dolores Huerta
1965–1973	United States	Anti–Vietnam War movement	Women Strike for Peace, Daniel Berrigan, David Dellinger, Students for a Democratic Society
1968	Worldwide	Student-led protests against imperialism, economic inequality, and authoritarianism	
1977–1980s	Argentina, Brazil, Chile, Uruguay	Latin American pro-democracy movements	Mothers of the Plaza De Mayo
1980–1989	Poland	Solidarity	Lech Walesa, Adam Michnik
1983–1986	Philippines	People Power Revolution	Cory Aquino
1988–1990	Burma	Pro-democracy movement	Aung San Suu Kyi
1989	China	Tiananmen Square	Student protesters

Table 0.1 Continued

Period	Locations	Description	Iconic Figures (where applicable)
1989	Czechoslovakia	Velvet Revolution	Václav Havel
1991	Latvia, Estonia, and Lithuania	Singing Revolution	Pro-democracy, pro-independence groups
1991	Soviet Union	Defense against a military coup	Boris Yeltsin
2000–2010	Serbia, Georgia, Ukraine, Kyrgyzstan, Belarus	Color Revolutions	Srdja Popović, Ivan Marović
2010–2013	Tunisia, Egypt, Yemen, Bahrain, Libya, Syria	Arab uprisings	April 6 Movement, Tawwakkol Karman, Ouided Bouchamaoui
2011	Worldwide	Occupy Wall Street	
2014–present	United States	Movement for Black Lives / Black Lives Matter	Alicia Garza, Patrice Cullors, Opal Tometi
2016–2020	United States	Resistance against Donald Trump	Women's March; Protect the Results; Choose Democracy; Hold the Line
2019–present	Hong Kong	Pro-democracy movement	
2019–2020	Lebanon, Chile, Iraq, Bolivia, India, Pakistan, Kashmir	October Revolutions	

Sources: Global Nonviolent Action Database; various others (see appendix).

the American colonies. Methods included boycotts of British goods; refusal to consume British-made goods; noncooperation laws requiring colonists to export raw materials from the American colonies to Britain; colonists' mass refusals to serve on juries under Crown-appointed judges; destruction of Crown property, as in the Boston Tea Party, and the creation of parallel economic, judicial, and political institutions—including the Continental Congress itself. In fact, after all this resistance, by the time the Second Continental Congress approved the Declaration of Independence and authorized a Continental Army, the colonies were already de facto independent.[14] As John Adams wrote in a letter to Thomas Jefferson, "What do we mean by the revolution? The war? That was no part of the revolution; it was only an effect and a consequence of it. The revolution was in the minds of the people, and this was effected from 1760 to 1775, in the course of fifteen years, before a drop of blood was shed at Lexington."[15]

Abolitionists

Abolitionists used civil resistance techniques against slavery throughout the nineteenth century in Britain, the Caribbean, and the United States. Coordinated work stoppages were a common form of unarmed collective action among people who were enslaved in Haiti, the Dominican Republic, and Jamaica, who used the withholding of their labor to secure more humane conditions from plantation owners. For instance, in Jamaica in 1831–1832, enslaved people organized a massive strike—a coordinated refusal to work—to press their demands that exploitative plantation owners begin paying wages and allowing greater freedoms, an action that became the Christmas Rebellion, also known as the Baptist War. Ultimately sixty thousand of Jamaica's three hundred thousand enslaved people joined in, making it the largest such uprising in the British West Indies. Although the organizers intended to use peaceful strikes, some groups armed themselves and began fighting British Dragoons and paramilitary groups. The uprising collapsed after eleven days, after which the last living rebels surrendered. In horrific reprisals, plantation owners killed at least five thousand enslaved people during the rebellion and its aftermath. And yet the rebellion—along with the plantocracy's disproportionate response—inspired and horrified people throughout Great Britain and intensified support for the abolitionist cause. Within two years, the British government passed a partial emancipation law; four years later, it fully abolished chattel slavery in all of its colonies. The Jamaican uprising was neither the first nor the last campaign in which people collectively withheld labor to win powerful concessions.

Nationalist and anti-colonial movements

People on every continent have undertaken struggles to reclaim their rights and autonomy from colonial authorities. For instance, during the Indian independence movement of 1919–1947, civil resistance techniques were used by both Indian Hindus like Gandhi and lesser-known Pashtun Muslims like Badshah Khan. Khan recruited a hundred thousand members to a "nonviolent army," who swore an oath to wage nonviolent struggle against British rule in contemporary Pakistan.

Indeed, history is full of notable anticolonial resistance during which people in Asia and Africa embraced civil resistance by refusing to purchase products imported from colonizing countries, pay imperial taxes, or mine local resources for export—including the Nigerian independence movement (1945–1950), the East Timorese independence movement (1974–1999), and the Ghanaian independence movement (1890s–1950s). In the last example, national independence leader Kwame Nkrumah followed Gandhi's example by experimenting with what he called "positive action."[16]

More recent self-determination movements have often relied heavily on techniques of civil resistance. That's true for the Palestinian national movement during the First Intifada (1987–1989), the Kosovo Albanian self-determination movement (1989–1999), and the ongoing movement against Indian occupation in Kashmir.[17] Civil resistance campaigns against military occupation have occurred in places as diverse as Nazi-occupied Denmark (1940–1943), Soviet-occupied Czechoslovakia (1967–1968), and Morocco-occupied Western Sahara (1999–present).[18] And many secession movements have embraced civil resistance techniques, including the ongoing Southern Yemen secession movement (2007–present) and the Catalan movement in Spain (2014–present).

Labor movement

One of the most potent methods of civil resistance is the refusal to work in unjust conditions. The global labor movement has long used civil resistance, among other techniques, to demand fair working conditions. Beginning in the nineteenth century, organized labor action worldwide effectively established minimum wages, pressed for laws against exploitation of child workers, established two-day weekends, capped daily work hours, demanded paid benefits and paid holidays, and more. Civil resistance has been one of labor's powerful tools for promoting and expanding labor rights, particularly as strikes or work stoppages became popular. A recent study suggests that the repeated use of general strikes in Europe led to Western European governments' concessions on issues like pensions.[19] There are many more recent examples. For instance, in 2018, hotel workers in the Unite Here Local 26 union in Boston won historic concessions from Marriott International. Enduring rain, wind, and snow on the picket line for forty-six days, they successfully used their collective power to win greater wages, better benefits, and job security protections. In 2018 and 2019, teachers across nine US states used strikes, walkouts, and protests to demand higher wages, increased support for staff, smaller classrooms, and other essential work protections. In West Virginia, Virginia, Colorado, California, and Arizona, these "#RedforEd" strikes and walkouts resulted in pay increases for teachers and staff, as well as a variety of other concessions. And during the global pandemic of 2020, medical staff, grocery store workers, and public servants walked out of their jobs to effectively demand more concerted government action on COVID-19; personal protective equipment like masks, gloves, and gowns; hazard pay; and paid sick leave.

Peace, antiwar, and anti-nuclear movements

In the 1960s and 1980s, the US peace movement and the US and European antinuclear movements used civil resistance methods. For instance, in the late 1970s and 1980s, the Clamshell Alliance, a coalition of peace and antinuclear groups in the United States, routinely undertook civil disobedience actions like members chaining themselves to nuclear installations' fences, setting up human blockades around nuclear power plants, holding mass demonstrations, and even occasionally dismantling or destroying equipment at nuclear facilities.

Racial justice movements

Movements for racial justice have emerged and grown in many different political, economic, and social systems, using civil resistance methods. As I mentioned earlier, Black students, clergy, workers, and civic groups relied on the technique during the US civil rights movement (1953–1968) and in South Africa by Black organizers and allies in their struggle against apartheid (1990–1994).[20] More recently, in the United States, the Black Lives Matter movement has used civil resistance techniques to demand an end to police or vigilante killings of Black people, to protest and the criminal justice system's failure to prosecute the perpetrators and to demand justice to Black communities affected by police brutality. Since it emerged in 2013 after the acquittal of Trayvon Martin's killer, Black Lives Matter and the Movement for Black Lives have deployed innovative civil resistance techniques and strategies against racism, police brutality, and structural violence against Black life in the United States. During the summer of 2020, after the killings of Ahmaud Arbery, Breonna Taylor, and George Floyd, tens of millions of Americans mobilized in what was the largest and broadest mass mobilization in recorded US history.[21]

Feminist movements

Beginning in the mid-nineteenth century and continuing to today, women's rights movements have used civil resistance in nearly every country in the world. In India over the past decade, antiviolence groups demand accountability and justice for victims of rape and femicide, organizing massive marches, pressuring police to investigate sexual assault allegations, and confronting alleged perpetrators with sit-ins and rallies. Started in the United States by organizer Tarana Burke in 2006, the worldwide #MeToo movement has encouraged survivors of sexual violence to speak up and identify their perpetrators, using such methods as coming out as a survivor of sexual abuse, naming perpetrators, organizing legal support funds for survivors, and engaging in rallies, protests, and vigils to fight patriarchal and sexist norms of silence and complicity in many different social settings.

Environmental justice movements

People increasingly use civil resistance to demand environmental justice. Indigenous communities across the world—from Brazil to West Papua to Standing Rock—have taken powerful stands against corporate exploitation of land, the privatization of natural resources, pollution, and the violation of autonomy and land rights. For instance, in 1999–2000 activist Oscar Olivera led a successful campaign in Bolivia against attempts to privatize rainwater in Amazon rainforests populated by Indigenous communities, a campaign called the Cochabomba Water Wars. And in 2016 in the United States, tens of thousands of people descended on the Standing Rock Indian Reservation in North Dakota and South Dakota to support the Standing Rock Sioux and help them to defend their territory against a planned Keystone XL Pipeline project, which was expected to destroy the natural ecosystem and poison their local water sources. Organizations like Greenpeace regularly deploy nonviolent direct action and civil disobedience to insist on environmentally sustainable approaches and to disrupt and prevent big corporations from extracting minerals and fossil fuels without regard for the climate or the local communities affected by hazardous by-products. The transnational Extinction Rebellion movement has challenged global inaction on climate change, bursting onto the scene on November 16, 2019, with a series of rallies, bridge and highway blockades, and acts of civil disobedience in London. Similarly, Greta Thunberg and countless other youth activists have faithfully refused to attend school on Fridays, engaging in a series of #FridaysForFuture strikes worldwide. In the United States, the Sunrise Movement uses various forms of creative nonviolent resistance to build a broader youth constituency to wage nonviolent struggle for environmental justice.

Movements for safety and security

Further, a number of different movements around the world have used civil resistance to demand civil stability, safety, and security in places where states, armed guerrillas, or organized criminal groups used systemic violence against some or all of the population. For instance, in the Colombian Civil War from 1964 to 2016, citizens established "peace villages" where residents refused to cooperate with either armed groups or the state. Mexico's Movement for Peace with Justice and Dignity, which mobilized from 2011 to 2013, was a response to the violence of Mexico's drug wars, committed by drug lords, gangs, and federal troops alike.[22] Between 2004 and 2011, in at least one Sicilian city, a mass refusal to pay protection money effectively ended the mafia's grip over that city's businesses.[23] And in the

Syrian and Iraqi civil wars, people in Raqqa and Mosul organized courageous resistance campaigns against various armed groups, including the Islamic State, by combining overt acts of defiance with everyday forms of resistance.

Anticapitalist movements

Movements have demanded revolutionary change to the ways in which capitalism has led to the concentration of wealth in the hands of a few at the expense of the many. Over the course of the twentieth century, numerous student, worker, and poor peoples' movements have demanded that their governments protect workers from exploitative corporate practices, harsh effects of globalization, and unfair workplace practices, while also demanding reforms to market capitalism.[24] Biennial convenings of the World Trade Organization have been disrupted by movements protesting globalization and demanding just economic practices, perhaps most notably in Seattle in 1999. In 2011, the Occupy Wall Street movement went global, inspiring hundreds of marches, work stoppages, citizens' assemblies, and tent-city encampments around the world. After months of mobilization, this movement had called renewed attention to economic inequality, corporate injustice, and excessive corporate influence on politics worldwide.

Prodemocracy movements

In the past century, hundreds of civil resistance campaigns have worked to depose authoritarian, antidemocratic, or corrupt regimes—at times struggling against counter-movements aiming to reinstate them. Such campaigns have ranged from Portugal (1974) to Poland (1980–1989), from East Germany (1989) to Egypt (2011), from Serbia (2000) to Swaziland (2011), from Tunisia (2010) to Togo (2013), from Georgia (2003) to Guatemala (2015), and from Brazil (1984–1985) to Burkina Faso (2014). In all of these cases—and hundreds of others—people power movements have tried to topple dictatorial regimes or defend democracies against authoritarian power-grabs. Over the past decade alone, powerful movements have erupted in countries as diverse as Turkey, Kenya, South Korea, Iceland, and the United States challenging government corruption and financial mismanagement with mass demonstrations, citizen investigations, information-sharing, and naming and shaming of corrupt activities.

A Note on antidemocratic movements

Some movements have emerged with more sinister aims—including restoring authoritarian politics after a democratic transition. In Egypt in 2013, for instance, the Tamarod (Rebellion) movement encouraged the Egyptian army to depose democratically elected Mohammed Morsi and remove the Muslim Brotherhood from power, under the pretext that Morsi's government was both too Islamist and too incompetent. Similarly in Thailand in 2014, a popularly backed military coup overthrew democratically elected prime minister Yingluck Shinawatra and installed a military junta in her place. During the Iranian Revolution, a broad-based coalition that unified leftists and Islamists to overthrow Shah Reza Pahlavi was overtaken by well-organized fundamentalist groups led by Ayatollah Khomenei, imposing an authoritarian and fundamentalist religious regime that dramatically restricted individual rights.[25] And since 2016, far-right and neo-Nazi groups in Germany have been relying on the work of nonviolent resistance scholar Gene Sharp to better understand how to build and wield people power to pursue their racist and exclusionary aims.[26]

That such antidemocratic groups are trying to misappropriate these techniques should motivate those of us who are fighting for liberation, justice, equality, and democracy to learn how to use them more effectively.

Where this book is headed

Today, we know much more about civil resistance than we did even a decade ago. Developments in research and the practice of civil resistance itself have made it all the more important—and potentially powerful—to inform people around the world with answers to their urgent questions about how to wage nonviolent struggle effectively and ethically. This book aims to offer those answers whenever possible, while noting current debates and controversies when we just don't have clear answers yet.

In Chapter 1 we dive deeper into the basics of civil resistance—core concepts, which methods count as civil resistance and which methods do not, and how pragmatic uses of civil resistance intersect with moral claims.

Chapter 2 addresses the question of how people build social and political power from below, how civil resistance succeeds, and whether there are conditions under which civil resistance is impossible. Here, the crucial point is that civil resistance campaigns succeed when they become large and diverse enough to reflect a serious challenge to the status quo—and when they begin to create defections from their opponent's side.

Chapter 3 takes on the complicated question of violence from within a movement. Here we review recent research findings that address how fringe violence from within a movement affects the political situation for those pushing for change.

In Chapter 4 we look at myths and realities of civil resistance against brutal opponents. We look at the ways in which civil resistance campaigns have succeeded in spite of episodes of extreme brutality—including against genocidal opponents—and the options available to movements fighting against racist regimes in particular.

Finally, Chapter 5 concludes with a discussion of the long-term effects of civil resistance on different societies—whether successful civil resistance campaigns tend to leave societies better or worse off. We also explore how civil resistance campaigns have changed over the past decade—particularly with the emergence of digital activism—and how movements have persisted in the face of rising authoritarianism, global economic crises, and the global coronavirus pandemic.

Throughout the book I return to a core point: that civil resistance provides immense possibilities for people to organize collectively against injustice, in almost every circumstance. Civil resistance does not always succeed. In fact, nonviolent resistance fails as often as it succeeds. But civil resistance is an increasingly common political approach, succeeding far more often than its detractors would have you believe. In fact, it's hard to find an example of progressive political change that occurred without it.

1

THE BASICS

Power concedes nothing without a demand. It never did and it never will.
—Frederick Douglass

In the Introduction, we defined civil resistance as a form of struggle in which unarmed people coordinate a variety of actions—such as strikes, protests, sit-ins, boycotts, stay-away demonstrations, noncooperation, and lots of other tactics—to build power and force change. Using civil resistance, people show their collective power. Across the millennia, in every part of the world, people have confronted oppression using a wide range of civil resistance approaches and techniques. They have succeeded not because they melted the hearts of their opponents, but because the resisters outnumbered the opposition and therefore changed the political and social balance of power.

This chapter addresses some common misconceptions about civil resistance. They include the ideas that civil resistance requires passively accepting suffering, that civil resistance means being civil and respectful, that protest is the primary form of civil resistance, that civil resistance is only available to people in privileged positions, and that the methods of civil resistance cannot be abused for unjustified or immoral aims.[1] None of these are necessarily true, as you'll see.

How does civil resistance create change?

To understand the logic of civil resistance, you have to first appreciate a particular mental model about how people make change in the world. There are two primary theories of how to make social or political change; depending upon which one you subscribe to, you'll either be more skeptical or optimistic about civil resistance as a way for people to transform society.

Let's start with the skeptics. Many popular myths about political power can obscure or underestimate civil resistance's potential to succeed.[2] This is because a common theory of change, which we might call the *control approach*, focuses on the near-invincibility of entrenched power and implies that only militant and violent action can challenge the system and upset power.[3] The theory underlies justifications for armed insurrection that include that of the Chinese revolutionary Mao Zedong, who famously argued that "power flows from the barrel of a gun"; Algerian revolutionaries against French occupation in 1954–1962, who argued that violence was the only way through which a colonized people could free themselves from an internalized sense of inferiority;[4] some current defenders of the US Constitution's Second Amendment, who argue that the right to own and bear guns is a safeguard against a tyrannical government; eighteenth-century French revolutionaries who believed that the aristocracy could only be truly destroyed in France by executing or terrorizing its remaining members; and Marxist-Leninist groups during the early-twentieth-century Russian Revolution, who argued that violence would be required to seize the means of production from the bourgeois class. Still others see power as the ability to maintain status quo social, political, racial, or economic hierarchies, such as white supremacy. This theory of change accepts militarism as a necessary evil in defending or transforming an unjust society. And its notion of power, which privileges elite politics and the ability to wield overpowering violence, is often taken for granted in the popular imagination. If you subscribe to this theory of change, you will have a tough time believing that civil resistance can create a real or substantive difference in society.

But this theory of change is often wrong. Oppressive systems tend to be much more fragile than they appear. Despite their most earnest efforts, those tyrants who have publicly claimed their invincibility usually admit in private that they are far more vulnerable than their public image projects. Most of the armed revolutions that have succeeded over the past hundred years—from the Russian Revolution to Mao's Chinese Revolution to the Algerian Revolution to that led by the North Vietnamese Liberation Army—were not victorious because they outmatched their opponents militarily. Rather, they succeeded because they had comprehensive strategies that defeated their opponents politically.

Moreover, the control approach cannot explain why so many nonviolent struggles have succeeded over the past two centuries against militarily superior opponents. As we saw in the Introduction, nonviolent revolutions succeeded in overthrowing regimes or creating territorial independence in twice as many cases as violent revolutions did. What's more, the control approach considers those holding power to be essentially a monolithic group. It conflates dictatorships and dictators, forgetting that the latter must be supported by a pyramid of people. It conflates systems and individuals—the people in the pyramid who have their own minds and decisions to make. Theorists of civil resistance argue that there is no such thing as a monolithic regime. Oppressive systems are different from the people operating within them. Dictators are entirely separate from those who must cooperate to hold up the status quo: the militaries, intelligence services, economic and political leaders, and civil workers. Few standard notions of power recognize that governments pay a high political cost if they use violence to restore order. Even if they win through brutalizing their civilian opponents, very few dictators enjoy a stable and prosperous legitimacy after committing atrocities.

So, what theory of change can help us make sense of these historical patterns? A second theory of change—which I refer to as the *legitimacy approach*[5]—starts from an idea of power that focuses on the ability to influence what happens to whom, where, and how. Three fundamental assumptions motivate this approach: (1) power is based on legitimacy rather than coercion; (2) power is never permanent; and (3) no system is monolithic. Let's look at each of these in turn.

First, political power comes from the ability to get other people to cooperate and obey authority voluntarily. They do this when they consider obedience to be in their own interests, or when they see whoever or whatever is wielding that power to be doing so legitimately. Once a population comes to feel that a leader or government doesn't deserve that power and large numbers of people stop voluntarily complying with its directives, that power is very difficult to restore. Leaders or governments that respond by using violence are not demonstrating strength or power. Instead, they are paradoxically demonstrating their weakness, because they have lost the population's voluntary cooperation, obedience, or consent to be governed. Governments that have to use violence to compel cooperation and obedience reveal the fact that citizens wouldn't choose to obey of their own volition. Seen this way, Syrian president Bashar al-Assad's use of death squads, sniper fire, and shelling of entire neighborhoods during the 2011 Syrian uprising did not showcase his power. Instead, it revealed that his legitimacy was hollow and vulnerable—and that he couldn't win back popular cooperation through popular appeals, reforms, concessions, or other ways of responding to the people who had mobilized to confront his regime.

Second, no oppressive system is monolithic. Whether it is a dictatorship, a foreign military occupation, or an unjust economic system, every oppressive system leans on the cooperation and acquiescence of the people involved in what activist and intellectual George Lakey calls its "pillars of support." Those include:

- Security forces, such as the military's various branches; intelligence services; police forces; any regional or local military or policing organizations, like a national guard; semiofficial militias or paramilitaries; and so on.
- Economic elites, such as bankers, wealthy business owners, small business owners, trade associations, lobbyists, and companies.
- Bureaucrats who make sure the government's various functions run, including legislative, executive, and judicial staff; civil servants in diplomatic posts; and public sector workers in sanitation, utilities, postal services, public health services, and other public institutions.
- Independent media and government-run or -influenced media, including TV and radio stations, newspapers, websites, and so on.
- Religious authorities, from top leaders like bishops, imams, or rabbis to those who serve in local congregations.
- Educational institutions, like universities and other academic institutions; student organizations; academic professional associations; and scientific labs for research and development.

- Cultural figures, like television, film, or social media personalities, musicians, athletes, and other celebrities.
- Organized labor, like teachers', nurses', and custodial staff unions; workers' rights groups, like those that advocate on behalf of nonunionized workers; and professional associations, like doctors' or lawyers' associations.
- Civil society organizations, such as civil rights groups, educational foundations, and various advocacy organizations.

Governments rely on civil servants, military and intelligence officials, taxpayers, foreign allies or patrons, and ardent supporters. But governments aren't the only organizations that can't function without daily cooperation from their supporters. Companies rely on their employees, managers, executives, trustees, shareholders, and consumers. Universities rely on custodial staff, security guards, students, administrators, donors, alumni, faculty, staff, and often state legislatures. Broader systems of oppression—like white supremacy, patriarchy, homophobia, xenophobia, transphobia, and ethnic chauvinism—rely on ideological beliefs or justifications, people who perpetuate these ideas, institutions that cooperate with and enshrine these systems into public life, and people who continually cooperate with (and often benefit from) these institutions.

Numerous practitioners and philosophers of resistance have recognized that when people collectively refuse to consent to or obey status quo systems, they can make radical demands of those with institutional power—including scrapping the existing system and replacing it with something else. This is particularly true if they are able to build coalitions and alliances with other groups that expand their bases of power. In other words, it is not only up to tyrants to decide how long they get to maintain the status quo. To a significant degree, it is also up to the people they rely upon to carry out their wishes, as well as the much larger population of people whom they claim to govern and represent.

Masses of people change systems when, through popular collective action, they pull those pillars of support away from the power holder—the government, the university administration, the church—so as to disrupt or collapse an oppressive system. That could lead to:

- Workers refusing to work until safe and fair workplace standards are met.
- Shareholders ousting poor corporate leadership.
- State legislators refusing to carry out the wishes of a corrupt governor.
- A nation's police or security services abandoning a dictator.
- Prominent business owners and bankers pushing politicians for reform.

People power movements win primarily by building enough power from below to separate those in charge from their existing sources of control—or to transform institutions and practices so drastically that existing structures become obsolete. As Frederick Douglass famously said in 1857,

> *Power concedes nothing without a demand. It never did and it never will. Find out just what any people will submit to, and you have found out the exact amount of injustice and wrong which will be imposed upon them; and these will continue till they are resisted with either words or blows, or with both. The limits of tyrants are prescribed by the endurance of those whom they oppress.*

The people who make up these pillars of support—civilian bureaucrats, state media, military and police officers, business owners and bankers, popular public figures, important international allies—aren't necessarily converted to the cause through a genuine change of heart. They often stop cooperating with the status quo because they come to believe that doing so serves their own interests.

In apartheid South Africa, for instance, white business owners' fortunes were fading under the pressure of Black-led[6] boycotts and international sanctions. Few of these white business owners became converts to the African National Congress's (ANC's) vision of ridding the country of racial, political, and economic inequality. But they knew they wouldn't prosper unless they pressured the government to acquiesce to what one trade association member described as "legitimate claims" for racial equality for Black South Africans.

So they put pressure on the ruling party to reform, and they got their opportunity to do so when pro-apartheid leader P. W. Botha suffered a mild stroke and resigned in 1989. National Party leaders appointed reformist Education Minister F. W. de Klerk to lead their party. De Klerk was later elected state president, and, in a speech to Parliament in February 1990, he announced that he would remove the ban on the ANC and release Nelson Mandela from prison after twenty-seven years. These steps led to historic negotiations with the ANC, resulting in a 1992 referendum where a large majority of white South Africans voted to end legal apartheid. Newly able to vote, in 1994, millions of Black South African voters put the ANC in power in a landslide electoral victory. This vignette shows how civil resistance campaigns can put both direct and indirect pressure on economic and political pillars of support, forcing them to accommodate the movement's demands.

The legitimacy approach's third major assumption is that power is never permanent. All power holders must constantly replenish their power: by fulfilling an implicit or explicit social contract, through good performance, or through moral righteousness. They must continually demonstrate their legitimacy both to their own pillars of support and to the broader public. Civil resistance visibly questions the legitimacy of the status quo; large-scale civil resistance reveals that this legitimacy is in crisis.

Here's what's crucial: the legitimacy approach does not assume that the opponent possesses even a baseline level of morality. Power holders may be extremely brutal, arrogant, self-concerned, and petty. In fact, a legitimacy approach to power assumes that there is no such thing as a benevolent dictator; if incumbents think they can kill with impunity, they will.[7] As John Adams wrote to Thomas Jefferson in 1816, "Power always thinks it has a great Soul, and vast Views, beyond the Comprehension of the Weak; and that it is doing God Service, when it is violating all his Laws."[8] But the adversary's lack of morality or empathy does not matter nearly as much as the organized resistance movement's ability to use a broad range of co-ordinated, cleverly devised methods to shake up, overextend, and outmaneuver the opponent while eroding its political, economic, social, and military sources of power.

How do you define nonviolent action?

In some ways, "nonviolent action" is intuitive and obvious: it means taking action without hurting anyone. Civil resistance movements that undertake nonviolent actions do not physically harm or threaten to physically harm any person. People involved in such actions are unarmed; they do not carry weapons, throw Molotov cocktails, and so on.

But the term "nonviolent action" is often misunderstood as passive or submissive. In fact, some people engaged in creative forms of resistance are insulted by the adjective "nonviolent," because their actions are often defiant, disruptive, and confrontational, with a plan of action intended to antagonize the opponent. While civil resistance movements do not hurt others physically, they nevertheless behave in ways that are forceful and coercive, blocking their opponents from achieving their goals or pushing them to act against their wishes. Nonviolent resistance as a strategy involves creating an active conflict with the opponent—one fought with different tools than are used in a violent or militarized approach.

The term "nonviolent action" can also be misunderstood as non-violent *interaction*—an exchange between two groups that is totally free of violence. In fact, those using nonviolent action stick to nonviolent action themselves, but their adversaries often use violence toward them—before, during, and after a confrontation. When people power movements use nonviolent methods like protests, it is often precisely because police or military troops have brutalized them— and police or military sometimes assault people using nonviolent action with tear gas, rubber bullets, live ammunition, beatings with clubs, arrests, imprisonment, torture, and disappearances.[9] When I refer to "nonviolent action," then, I mean nonviolent action by dissidents—regardless of how authorities respond. But there is often a lot of violence involved in civil resistance campaigns, particularly among those that adopt revolutionary goals.

You may have heard the term "nonviolent direct action." That usually implies more confrontational and riskier forms of action than the average symbolic demonstration or vigil might entail. People using direct action have chained themselves to bulldozers, trespassed onto high-security sites and poured blood on office files, glued themselves to the pavement at a busy intersection, or occupied a runway at an airport. Consider these real-life examples:

- During 1999's disruptions of the World Trade Organization's meeting in Seattle, where activists were protesting globalization's effects on poverty, inequality, and the environment, the Ruckus Society used PVC pipes to bind activists' arms together to block traffic.
- In 2013, Sister Megan Rice, who as of this writing is a ninety-year-old peace activist who has been arrested over three dozen times, was convicted of destroying federal property as part of a direct action to protest the global threat of nuclear weapons. In 2012, she and several others associated with the Plowshares movement cut through several fences at the Oak Ridge, Tennessee, Y-12 national security complex to reach the uranium storage bunker. Once there, she and two fellow Catholic peace activists hung banners, prayed, and hammered on the outside wall of the bunker.
- During Donald Trump's inauguration as US president in January 2017, Black Lives Matter activists protested his promised policies by sitting down and forming a human blockade outside the entrance of the National Mall, where the inauguration was taking place.
- Between 2018 and this writing, the group Extinction Rebellion, which demands immediate and aggressive action on climate change, has used a number of direct actions, including flying drones at London Heathrow Airport to ground airplanes, thus keeping them from emitting carbon, and gluing themselves to major thoroughfares in UK cities including London and Edinburgh to stop traffic—again, preventing carbon emissions, however temporarily—and awakening people to the climate threat.

All of these methods are disruptive, often illegal, and often controversial. They inconvenienced and angered other people, from ordinary travelers to political authorities. Those involved risked arrest and physical harm. But in no way did any of these methods physically harm or threaten to harm anyone else.

Nonviolent actions may involve people using their own bodies to dramatize an injustice, protect others from harm, or disrupt the status quo. Such actions can sometimes have unintended consequences. For example, during a wave of protests associated with the Occupy Wall Street movement in 2011, some activists blockaded major roadways. Critics complained that this nonviolent action could unintentionally bring physical harm to others—especially if ambulances, fire trucks, and similar emergency vehicles were stuck in the traffic jam. But a road blockade is a nonviolent method; the possibility of unintended, incidental harm does not make a road blockade a violent activity.

What are common nonviolent actions?

When people think of nonviolent action, protests and mass demonstrations often come to mind. But that's just the beginning. Civil resistance movements have used hundreds, if not thousands, of actions to change their political situations. Some scholars have attempted to catalogue and classify these. For instance, scholar Gene Sharp famously identified "198 methods of nonviolent action" while writing his doctoral dissertation at Oxford University in the 1960s. He grouped these into three categories, as shown in Table 1-1: protest and persuasion, noncooperation, and nonviolent intervention.

Some people may be tempted to see Sharp's list as a "menu" for civil resistance. But actually, Sharp suspected that there were far more than 198 methods. The number he chose to publish in 1973 was arbitrary, and after that he stopped counting. Why? The nonviolent resistance scholar and practitioner Mary Elizabeth King reports, "He told me that he realized that every nonviolent struggle might create its own new nonviolent method."[10] Some technology-savvy scholars have updated Sharp's list to include tactics activated through cellular phones, digital platforms, social media, and even drones. But people involved in movements or researching them haven't had the time to track down and categorize all of the tactical innovations that occur every day around the world.

Table 1-1 Nonviolent Methods and Examples

Protest and Persuasion	Noncooperation			Nonviolent Intervention
	Social Noncooperation	Economic Noncooperation	Political Noncooperation	
Making public statements; mass petitions; leaflets; underground newspapers; mock elections; displays of portraits; protest disrobings; rude gestures; vigils; singing; marches; motorcades; teach-ins; turning one's back; walk-outs; silence	Lysistratic nonaction (sex strike); student strikes; boycott of social events; suspension of sports activities; stay-at-home; sanctuary; protest emigration (*hijrat*)	Consumer boycotts; consumption of forbidden goods; suppliers' and handlers' boycott; lockout; general strike; tax refusal; withdrawal of bank deposits; lightning walkout; reporting in "sick"; economic shutdown; go-slow	Withholding allegiance to authority; speech calling for resistance; election boycott; noncooperation with conscription; civil disobedience	Fast; hunger strike; sit-in; nonviolent obstruction; speak-in; guerrilla theater; alternative institutions; stay-in strike; nonviolent land seizure; defiance of blockade; overloading of administrative systems; seeking imprisonment; dual sovereignty

Source: Sharp 2005; Swarthmore Nonviolent Action Database

Sharp's analyses leave out some kinds of political activity that aren't generally considered techniques of civil resistance: negotiation, dispute resolution, and community organizing. Negotiation and dispute resolution involve ways that a civil resistance campaign can bargain and compromise with its opponents, while also resolving conflicts that arise within a movement. "Community organizing" refers to working with people to encourage them to stand up for their concerns, rights, and interests, to build their power for longer-term transformation, and perhaps to lead or join a movement someday. While these important efforts often complement civil resistance, civil resistance refers to active mobilization and direct confrontation with the opponent.

Table 1-2 Categorizing Nonviolent Actions

	Commission	Omission
Dispersion	Coordinated and dispersed flash mobs, development of worker cooperatives, political boycotts, stay-at-home demonstrations, divestments, embargos, alternative schools and education systems, singing illegal songs, overloading administrative systems, etc.	Coordinated electricity shut-offs, reporting in sick, stay-at-home strikes, etc.
Concentration	Sit-in, nonviolent occupation, march, demonstration, rally, teach-in, reverse strike, seeking imprisonment, turning one's back, etc.	Collective silence, go-slow demonstration, walkouts, etc.

Within civil resistance, Sharp distinguishes between acts of commission—in which unarmed people take an action that the opponent does not want them to—and acts of omission—in which people stop doing something they are expected to do.[11] Following on the work of political scientist Robert Burrowes, political sociologist Kurt Schock also distinguishes between methods of concentration, in which people gather in a particular space, and methods of dispersion, in which people stay away from a particular space (see Table 1-2).[12]

In what order should a movement try these various tactics? That entirely depends on the movement's particular circumstances and context. So far, no one has found a clear and successful formula that works everywhere, every time. However, most experienced activists agree that extensive planning and strategizing are ideal before mobilization begins.

What is the difference between civil resistance and protest?

Protest is one method of civil resistance—and not necessarily the most effective kind. Protest is typically a symbolic action intended to raise public awareness of an issue and demand change. Because protests and demonstrations—especially very large ones—can bring a lot of attention, many people conflate protests with civil resistance. But an effective civil resistance campaign typically involves many nonviolent methods above and beyond protest, like those described in Table 1-1. Few if any civil resistance campaigns have succeeded using protest alone.[13]

What roles do art and music play in civil resistance?

Artists and musicians are often important in civil resistance—both by getting involved directly and by documenting and memorializing what happened during revolutionary times.

For example, street art—which is visual art created in public locations—typically flourishes during civil resistance campaigns. Amateur and professional artists create and display such things as graffiti, tagging, wall and street murals, posters, stickers, street installations, video projections, and sculpture. More recently, movements' artists have created digital street art, like holograms and video projections on the sides of buildings. Street art is different from public art more broadly because it is usually created and displayed without any official sanction, deliberately circumventing and subverting mainstream, legal channels of public expression. Street art often conveys a strong social or political message in a way that comes across as transgressive and rebellious.

As a result, street art can powerfully communicate a movement's claims, its legitimacy, and its opponents' inability to silence dissent. The slogans, symbols, and street performances performed by people living with HIV and AIDS in the 1980s are a case in point. Activists used street banners, popularizing the slogan "Silence = Death." They reappropriated the pink triangle used to designate gay people in Nazi concentration camps, wearing it as a symbol of their struggle against homophobia and government inaction on AIDS and HIV research and treatment. Activists from the associated group ACT UP adopted numerous guerrilla art tactics, including surrounding Republican senator Jesse Helms' home in a giant, inflated 15-foot condom to protest his stigmatization of people with AIDS in September of 1991.

Street art has also featured prominently in antiauthoritarian campaigns. During the 2011 Egyptian Revolution, artists used graffiti to spread slogans calling for President Hosni Mubarak to step down. Some artists moved beyond walls and used their bodies as canvases; one protester in Tahrir Square wrote, "Leave, I miss my wife," across his chest. Many street artists used noms de plume to avoid detection. In situations where being publicly identified is dangerous, street art may be an especially useful way to anonymize resistance. As the pseudonymous British artist Banksy said, "Graffiti is one of the few tools you have if you have almost nothing."

Sometimes, even anonymously painting graffiti or slogans that criticize the regime can be incredibly dangerous. In March 2011 in Deraa, Syria, a group of teenage boys painted "The people want the fall of the regime" on a city wall. They'd been inspired by the recent wave of uprisings in Tunisia, Egypt, and Libya. In response, President Bashar al-Assad's brutal security services arrested and tortured fifteen boys, murdering a thirteen-year-old. The teens' transgressive act—and the government's horrific overreaction to it—is widely considered to be the spark that ignited the Syrian uprising, which led to the country's nine-year-long civil war and earned Deraa's popular designation as the "cradle of the revolution."

Some street artists create work capturing a movement's zeitgeist, during and after a revolution. For instance, during the Cold War, the Soviet Union erected the Berlin Wall between East Germany and West Germany. Street artists covered its miles-long concrete in graffiti. After the wall fell, in perhaps the most famous mural depicting the Cold War era, artist Dmitri Vrubel painted a larger-than-life image of Leonid Brezhnev, the Soviet Union's general secretary, kissing Erich Honecker, the East German Socialist Party's general secretary from 1971 until October 1989. The two men had kissed during the 1979 celebration of the anniversary of the Soviet Union establishing East Germany as the German Democratic Republic in 1949. Vrubel painted the mural on the eastern side of the Berlin Wall in 1990, captioning it in German and in Russian: "My God, help me to survive this deadly love."

In May 2016, artists Dominykas Čečkauskas and Mindaugas Bonanu painted a similar mural in Vilnius, Lithuania—but this time, depicting Russian president Vladimir Putin kissing then–US presidential candidate Donald Trump, captioned, "Make Everything Great Again."

In another iconic piece of street art, Banksy spray-painted and stenciled numerous pieces on the concrete wall that the Israeli government had built between Jerusalem and the West Bank, all of them challenging both the wall and Israel's military occupation of Palestinian territories. His memorable 2003 image, called *Love Is in the Air* (*Flower Thrower*), depicts a masked activist preparing to throw a bouquet of colorful flowers at an unseen opponent. The image aims to replace the Israeli government's common depiction of Palestinian activists as Molotov-cocktail-throwing vandals by picturing dissent as beautifully courageous.

We often see street theater, which is closely related to street art, during civil resistance campaigns as well. For example, in Tahrir Square during the 2011 Egyptian Revolution, protesters would dramatize nonviolently confronting the police, Hosni Mubarak, and other regime authorities. In Serbia during 2000, the Otpor movement—which aimed to remove Milošević from power—held mock funerals depicting the death of democracy in Serbia. In Syria in November 2012, four women staged a rare antiwar protest in the main souk, or open air market, in Damascus; dressed in bridal gowns, they portrayed "Brides of Syria" who objected to the killing. For fifteen minutes they marched through the souk, holding signs demanding that Syrians stop killing one another and singing wedding songs before security forces arrested them. One of the four, Lubna Zaour, told *The New York Times*, "It was a strange sight, brides in a police car."[14] She and her sister were detained, beaten, and then released after two months. Their landlords evicted them, their father lost his business, and their family fled to southern Turkey. Their act of defiance struck a nerve, though; calling for peaceful revolution at a time when government forces are organizing mass detentions and dissidents are beginning to arm themselves for civil war is a dangerous act indeed.

Further, during revolutionary times many people use their creativity to carefully document, record, and publicize various elements of revolutionary processes. As Egyptian muralist Ammar Abo Bakr put it, "What we did in Egypt in recent years was not about presenting art, at least it wasn't to me: We used walls as a newspaper. We learned to do so out of a need: The TV presenter and satirist Bassem Youssef was a doctor, but then he learned to use YouTube. Mosab El-Shamy Rassd was studying medicine, but then he took his camera and took to the streets. Me, I was a fine arts assistant professor. I left the faculty to report on the revolution on the city's walls."[15]

Musicians have written evocative pieces to tell stories about ongoing struggles, often rooting their songs in folk traditions to convey the unity and civic quality of action. Some of the most enduring songs of the classic rock and folk scenes in the United States—by Joan Baez to Bob Dylan to Neil Young—emerged out of protest against US-led wars and imperialism. American activist and political scientist Mary Elizabeth King writes that during the US civil rights movement, songs like "We Shall Overcome" raised courage, declared commitment, united participants, and targeted specific opponents like police chiefs:

> As a contemporary expression of spirituals, freedom songs derived from the black choral tradition that developed from the African and American experiences, matured in the fires of southern slavery. They addressed frustrations, forged bonds of personal loyalty, assuaged fear and dread, and fortified a people under stress. A strong tradition of composing during performance, in response to need, meant that new phrases would be added or a stanza changed to take up a specific issue, such as deciding whether to go to jail the next day. Song leading became an organizing tool.[16]

In the 1960s, soul artists like Nina Simone, Sam Cooke, and Aretha Franklin composed, performed, and popularized music centered in Black liberation. In the late 1970s and early 1980s, rap and hip-hop emerged from neighborhood block parties in the Bronx, where Black artists and dancers mixed influences from soul, R&B, and Caribbean culture to articulate political autonomy and cultural resistance through defiant lyrics and popular beats. Many contemporary Black hip-hop, R&B, and soul artists like Public Enemy, Kendrick Lamar, Beyoncé, and Janelle Monaé continue to popularize music centered in Black liberation in ways that can create a sense of solidarity, urgency, and inspiration among listeners.

Estonia's revolution for independence from the Soviet Union was literally called the Singing Revolution. During the Baltic uprising against Soviet domination in 1987–1991, two million people formed a human chain, joining hands and singing songs based in local traditions, recovering a sense of national unity. In Mali's 1990–1991 uprising against the Traoré dictatorship, a traditional group of what Malians called "songsayers" would travel from village to village to convey news of the ongoing protests. Because large numbers of people were unable to read, oral histories—especially those conveyed by folk music—were a powerful way of communicating the demands of the Alliance for Democracy in Mali (ADEMA) in its struggle against dictatorship.

Live music performances also provide convenient gathering spaces through which movements can recruit and mobilize others. In Serbia on New Year's Eve in 1999, student activists organized a rock concert in Belgrade. That may not sound revolutionary. But it was a rare display of defiance in a one-party state that discouraged rock music because of its rebellious undercurrents. Just months before, Serbian autocrat Slobodan Milošević's militias had massacred Kosovo's Albanians—and in response, NATO had bombed Belgrade. Thousands turned out for the concert, which featured rock musicians and comedians poking fun at Milošević's regime and calling for people to rally behind opposition politicians. As the clock turned to midnight, organizers stilled the festive mood to display pictures and read the names of Serbian soldiers killed during the Balkan Wars—openly rebuking Milošević and his regime for their lack of accountability. Student leader Srdja Popović explained that the purpose of the evening was to tell people, "Go home and think what to do so the next Orthodox New Year we have a reason to celebrate.... This is the year life finally must win in Serbia."[17]

Singing can also reduce fear among protesters, bystanders, or striking workers who fear they're about to be attacked or will face reprisals later. For example, in Lebanon's October Revolution of 2019, among the many songs and chants was a spontaneous rendition of "Baby Shark," sung by demonstrators to comfort a fifteen-month-old baby and his mother who were stuck in traffic because of the massive gathering.

And of course, many artists' creations reflect on and recall revolutions that fell short of their goals. The avant-garde Egyptian artist Laila Soliman, for instance, created and directed plays about the January 25, 2011, uprising that lasted eighteen days in Tahrir Square—showing its feminist revolutionary organizing, its unprecedented coalition crossing social boundaries, and the military regime's incarceration and torture of dissidents afterward. The musical *We Live in Cairo*, commissioned by the Art Repertory Theater in Cambridge, Massachusetts, similarly depicted the dashed hopes of Egypt's young revolutionaries. In this production, playwrights Daniel and Patrick Lazour explore the Tahrir Square street art, showing its slogans, posters, banners, and social media as a canvas, and composing songs about the revolution and counterrevolution.

Of course, music and art can play a role in expressing loyalty and reverence for autocratic leaders as well. Nationalistic music, poetry, and portraiture often feature heavily in stoking sentiments of fealty to ruling elites. Musicologist Nomi Dave, for instance, writes about how musicians and artists in Guinea took pleasure in writing songs of praise for dictator Sékou Touré—even after he died.[18] Much like any technique, then, art and music can play a role in both dissent and loyalty.

But as with journalism, precisely because of the cultural power of telling the truth through music, literature, and visual arts, most authoritarian regimes monitor cultural figures and censor their output. In Iran, for example, Supreme Leader Ali Khamenei has banned independent poetry and books and jailed artists, claiming, "Poetry must be the vanguard of the caravan of the revolution."[19]

Of course, few would expect street art, dissident art, or protest songs to create change on their own. But such art can create a common cache of knowledge and reinforce transgressive narratives, complementing and emboldening the work of other activists. As American leftist historian Howard Zinn is often quoted as saying, "They have the guns, we have the poets. Therefore, we will win."

What is the role of humor in civil resistance?

One way to show that an adversary can't control all of the people all of the time is to joke about him. In her book *Humor and Nonviolent Struggle in Serbia*, political scientist Janjira Sombatpoonsiri argues that humor can serve very specific functions in the waging of nonviolent conflict.[20]

First, humor—especially satire and parody—can directly challenge regimes' propaganda by undermining its original purpose and creating levity and clarity about the truth. Czech thinker, activist, and eventually president Václav Havel's foundational insight about building power from below is the necessity of "living in the truth"—that is, refusing to capitulate to the opponent's self-serving and false narrative of events.[21]

Second, humor can bring levity, cheerfulness, and a carnival-esque mood to an otherwise antagonistic, grim, or grave situation. This shift in feeling can be especially important when the regime has started to use force against dissenters. Festive events can attract large numbers of people seeking refuge from monotony, hopeless-ness, and betrayal. During a protest against Syrian dictator Bashar al-Assad in September 2011, for example, unarmed activists brought fireworks and video cameras to confront security forces armed with tanks and mortars. The videos captured the absurd disjunction be-tween that display of military might being mocked by protesters shooting fireworks into the sky—and powerfully showed the Syrian government's disproportionate response to an unarmed civilian uprising.

Third, humorous actions can often allow people to imagine new ways to challenge the status quo. In fact, humor is so threatening that it can be deadly. In totalitarian systems, telling a joke that criticizes those in power can be a capital offense. That's because totalitari-anism is based on completely controlling the social and historical narrative, what's considered "the truth," and the flow of informa-tion more broadly. In Stalin's Soviet Union, hundreds of people were convicted of telling jokes that defied the regime and were sentenced to gulags or death. Between 1942 and 1944 the People's Court of Berlin issued 4,933 death sentences for people telling "defeatist jokes" against the Nazi Party. In 1944, one Berlin munitions worker named Marianne Elise K. was executed for undermining the war effort "through spiteful remarks." Her crime? Telling this joke to her fellow munitions factory workers:

Hitler and Göring are standing on top of Berlin's radio tower. Hitler says he wants to do something to cheer up the people of Berlin. "Why don't you just jump?" suggests Göring.[22]

A coworker who overheard the joke reported it to local authorities, leading to Marianne Elise's execution.

Despite these attempts at total control, jokes satirizing Nazi officials and Stalin's regime were common during those authoritarian periods. They were typically whispered in barrooms among trusted friends and confidantes as a way to blow off steam, and they were not necessarily intended as active resistance. But the ubiquity of criticism and satire even under totalitarian regimes shows that no system can achieve complete control over all of the people all of the time. And once many people start telling jokes, they might begin to believe that the emperor has no clothes. That makes humor especially transgressive and subversive in oppressive systems. As the Iraqi writer Khalid Kishtainy writes,

> *Humor is more required in a nation's darkest hours, for it is at such times that people begin to lose faith in themselves, submit to despair, and descend into melancholy and depression. Life appears to be meaningless, and the homeland feels like a spider's web. People lose contact with fellow citizens and eventually come to accept their solitude. The will to stand together and resist is thus destroyed. Humor is the best remedy for such ills. Laughter lifts one from melancholy and lethargy; a political joke told by another reconnects citizen with citizen. Both are no longer alone. There are others who have shared my thoughts; we have shared suffering and hopes. Laughter is a collective fraternity. One doesn't laugh alone.*[23]

This is why, Kishtainy argues, the development and widespread use of political humor and satirical literature are essential to any successful civil resistance strategy.[24]

What are "parallel institutions"?

"Parallel institutions" are unofficial social, cultural, economic, and governance systems and practices that circumvent—and perhaps ultimately supplant—the regime's structures. They succeed when they can meet community needs that the existing system does not. They're "parallel" because they're working alongside but separate from existing oppressive institutions. Movements develop such institutions—and build legitimacy and authority—before they have fully "won."

We can find many examples throughout history. For instance, in the introduction, we discussed how important such institutions

were in freeing the thirteen American colonies from British imperial rule. During the twentieth century, many self-determination
and independence movements succeeded in part by building such
parallel institutions.

The Irish independence movement is an instructive case. The
movement began in the 1870s, during which Irish nationalists
demanded autonomy from Great Britain. Arthur Griffiths was
the chief architect of Sinn Fein (meaning "Ourselves"), which was
established in 1905 as a political group committed to Irish self-
government. Griffiths believed that total self-reliance would create
true independence. In 1918, as thousands of British soldiers were
dying in World War I, Sinn Fein helped to organize a massive civil
disobedience campaign in which two million Irishmen refused military conscription. Griffiths then used British elections in 1918 to run
Sinn Fein candidates, who swept the elections in all Irish areas except for Unionist strongholds. The newly elected Sinn Fein ministers
refused to sit in the British Parliament, instead meeting at Mansion
House in Dublin and declaring themselves the Dáil Éireann, an
independent Assembly of Ireland, which still exists today. This
shadow government, although labeled a terrorist organization
by the British government, established authority in Irish towns,
created new courts, encouraged local companies to purchase only
Irish-made products and not import from Britain, refused to pay
British taxes, and closed British-backed workhouses. Nevertheless,
the conflict escalated, culminating in the Irish War of Independence
between 1919 and 1922, after which most of Ireland seceded from
the United Kingdom and formed the Irish Free State. But while the
bloody events of the Irish War of Independence are often given as
the only narrative for Irish independence, historian David Carrol
Cochran writes that the movement ultimately succeeded because it
had paved the way by creating alternative institutions and entirely
severing the Irish from any political and economic cooperation with
Britain. As Cochran writes, "The historical evidence is clear that the
Dáil's campaign of noncooperation and parallel government did just
as much or more to make Ireland ungovernable and force the British
into negotiations."[25]

In fact, the Dáil reportedly inspired India's Jawaharlal Nehru and
Mohandas Gandhi to similarly break free from British colonial domination by developing parallel institutions. They were impressed